Hell, and God, and Nuns with Rulers

John Collings

First printing

This is a work of fiction. Names, characters, businesses, places, events and incidents are either the products of the author's imagination or used in a fictitious manner. Any resemblance to actual persons, living or dead, or actual events is purely coincidental.

ISBN: 978-1-61296-520-8

PUBLISHED BY BLACK ROSE WRITING

www.blackrosewriting.com

Printed in the United States of America

Suggested retail price $16.95

Hell, and God, and Nuns with Rulers is printed in Book Antiqua

Dedicated to Christine Collings who has put up with me locking myself in a room every night so I can write.

Hell, and God, and Nuns with Rulers

Part One

Hell

Chapter One

Facebook drama. Teachers' notes. Billboard T-shirt fashions. Cool car envy. Counselor sponsored interventions. Minimum wage wallet. Clearasil lies. Home busywork assignments. Lunchroom indigestion. Unsatisfied hormonal dating scene. And worst of all, ignorant parents.

It's hard enough living as a teenager nowadays without all the crazy pressure we receive from parents. Someone needs to create a rule where parents cannot talk or interfere with their children's business between the years of thirteen and twenty. Parents have a tendency to just mess up our lives even more. They don't understand the pressures a teenager goes through. Instead of giving us a constant supply of advice, they should just give their sons and daughters a bank account to provide them with enough money to eat, hang out with their friends, and buy the occasional song on iTunes. This way we would stay out of trouble. They don't need to know about our dietary habits, important social connections, or the makeup of our day. In reality, they don't need to know *anything* about us, and we don't need to listen to their silly conversations about how they've lived through the teenage years, they understand this time of our lives, and "why can't you just let us help you?"

I have never heard anything more idiotic. They haven't been through what a modern teenager has been through. They can't sit there with a straight face and say that they've experienced anything a typical teenager experiences in this day and age. Their idea of technology was a pair of pants that had so many zippers some didn't even open up to a pocket. The hardest choice they had to make was whether to belong to the new Pepsi generation or the Classic Coca-Cola generation. Bullies back in those "good old days" lugged their big, grotesque bodies down the halls of school and probably belonged to the football team. How could these people understand the kind of pressures a modern teenager experiences? They can't. They should just keep out of it.

They can't understand the humiliation of showing up at school with a flip phone, while other classmates have parents who stood in line for a whole weekend so their sons or daughters could have the latest iPhone. How can they understand that the only way to fit in with a group at school is to either choose to drink over the weekend or smoke pot in the bathroom during lunch? How can they explain how to stand up to modern day bullies when those bullies are ninety-pound weaklings hiding behind Facebook accounts? They barely understand the world they live in as an adult, and they expect to give us advice about how to live as a teenager. They imagine that teenagers live in a world with a golden sunset sky. They don't understand that a storm can move in and cast a hazy shadow over the teenage world — the world *I* now live in. They remember so well their own sunny teenage days, while I sit here getting soaked with a constant drizzle. Society pressures me like crazy. I have to deal with the responsibilities of an after-school job. I have the raging hormones of a teenager looking for a meaningful high school relationship. And I have to maintain my grades so I can earn a GPA worthy enough to get me out of this hellhole I live in right now.

Add to this a horror that could only come from living in my family. After my seventeenth birthday, my parents wanted me to receive the holy sacrament of confirmation in the Catholic Church. Their catechism refers to this holy sacrament as the "baptism for adults." Let me explain what that means. A baptism in the Catholic Church typically occurs when a child is a few months old. It is supposed to wipe away original sin, so that when we die, we can live in the glory of God. Nobody can possibly understand what baptism means when they are a drooling baby, and that baby can't have any possible connection with God. Unless the baby remembers being thrown out of Heaven and onto Earth, he or she doesn't even know who God is. They care more about the dump in their diaper. The idea is to baptize infants in order to protect the innocence of children. According to the holy teachings of the church, we are all born with original sin. If we die before this sin is erased, we will end up in Hell. This is a cruel joke God must like to play on the uninitiated.

I think of it this way: God sits up on his throne in Heaven and tells the next soul in line, "Bob," to hop into the body of a newborn baby. The soul says, *"Whatever you say, God."* Bob jumps through the celestial stratosphere and into that newborn. God looks down at Bob as a baby and says, *"Oh by the way, did I forget to tell you that because of a malfunctioning liver, this kid will die in fifteen minutes."* Bob looks up to Heaven, realizes how screwed he is, and gurgles since as a baby, he doesn't yet know how to speak. Of course the omniscient God knows what Bob tried to say and tells Bob, *"Don't worry, you can come back up to Heaven as soon as you clear up that original sin thing."* Bob responds by having explosive diarrhea. *"Well, you need to get baptized in order to rid yourself of original sin,"* God explains. Bob screams like a newborn. God looks down at Bob, shakes his head, and says, *"You shouldn't have been born in a general hospital now, should you?"* Five minutes later Bob dies. He opens his eyes to see Lucifer. The Devil says, *"Hi, Bob, I've been waiting for you."*

Essentially, this is the reason we get baptized so young — to avoid the pains of Hell. But when we grow up and become conscious of our own decisions, we confirm our faith with the Catholic Church in the holy sacrament of confirmation. In other words, we show God that we understand all of his teachings and accept his love into our hearts. It allows us to make a conscious choice to profess our faith as we understand it in the adult world. For this reason, my parents forced me to be confirmed in the Catholic faith.

Chapter Two

Tristan Adamson

Sundays Suck

Every child in America would claim that Sunday is one of the best days of the week, but they would be lying. If you really look at it, Sunday is the worst day of the week, and the older you get, the worse it becomes.

First of all, they chose this day as your last day of freedom which would depress any logical thinker. Compare it to a death march to your execution. Think about it. On that day, when you make your final journey, the people who perform that last rite want to be sure they have a guilt-free conscience before they flip the switch, inject the poison, or kick out the chair from underneath said member on death row. So in order for executioners to sleep with peace of mind, they give the condemned a final request. They supply the dying man with his choice of a big meal. They walk him outside for one last final breath of fresh air. They give him all the dirty magazines and literature he could possibly want, and allow him to have any form of entertainment that comes to his whimsy. Except he can't enjoy it because in the back of his mind, he knows he is going to die. This is just like living on a Sunday during the school year. You get the freedom to do all the fun stuff you want, but you can't enjoy it because you know you have to go back to school the next day.

Most teenagers would rather have a sentence of death.

The Catholic Church also obligates you to hold Sundays in holy esteem. Just like the condemned man, the Church reminds us of our mortality and that our fate lies in the hands of an angry God. The man on death row must put on his best prison blues, and listen to a priest preach about Heaven and Hell. This is actually cruel and unusual punishment, since it only serves to remind the guilty man of the place his soul will rest.

Teenagers view Mass in a similar light. We must sit on a hard bench in uncomfortably scratchy clothes just to listen to some preacher remind us of our sins. He forces us to recall the impure thoughts we had about people in class. We have to think about all the times we cussed during the week. We have to think about the ways we don't obey our mother and father, the ways we treat our fellow teenagers, or the crazy thoughts that run through our head, of which our Lord and savior definitely doesn't approve. How do I know He doesn't approve of them? Because my priest reminds me every week. This makes Sunday cruel on two accounts. First, it sucks all of the fun out of anything enjoyable, and second, it treats us as poorly as convicted serial killers and rapists.

The third reason Sunday sucks happens on your sixteenth birthday. On this day, your mom and dad will sit you down in a room and tell you of the importance of learning some responsibility. They'll claim that picking up a trade is the perfect way to learn this. They want you to find a job that won't interfere with your schoolwork, so they'll let you work a couple of days a week, but they want most of your scheduled shifts to fall on the weekend. If you want to have any semblance of a social life, you will make sure you get scheduled for work on Sundays. Which means you can't even have fun on Sundays anymore. You must now drudge off to work and bang away on some silly monotonous job. Convicts on death row aren't treated this cruelly. They get Sundays off from any labor. They don't have to make license plates or wash all of the prisoners' clothes. They especially don't have to flip burgers for a bunch of people coming from church and taking their family to some cheesy fast-food restaurant. In this way, condemned men on death row have it better than teenagers on Sunday. They don't have to work.

So, for the obvious reasons of being forced to attend church, work, and trying to enjoy our last moments of freedom, nobody could pick a worse day of the week. Because schools love all the immense torture they dole out, they won't recognize the pain Sunday's cause. They should give everybody a three-day weekend, every weekend. This makes Monday the crappiest day of the week, as every American already knows.

. . .

I got a *D* on this essay, and my teacher, Mrs. Baker, said she was being kind by giving me such a high grade.

She sat me down in a chair next to her desk to talk to me about my writing and what I could do to improve it. She tried to explain this to me in a whispered voice so I wouldn't be embarrassed by what the other students could possibly hear. The other kids pretended to work on their homework assignments, reading the first act of *Macbeth*, but I could see them listening to my humiliation.

Mrs. Baker told me that even though she could see the unique aspect of the metaphor, I really shouldn't compare myself to a person on death row. She told me that I shouldn't write euphemisms like this. I wanted to ask her what a euphemism or a metaphor was, but was scared that she would tell me what it was. She also told me that words like "crappiest" and "sucks" should no longer exist in my vocabulary, especially for something as formal as this. What she told me next didn't make any sense. She told me that despite all of this, she really loved my "voice," and it was the strength of my writing. She told me that this was the area I should build upon. I don't see how I can have a wonderful voice and still

13

not use the words that gave me that wonderful voice. I don't think Mrs. Baker really knows anything about writing.

She then went on to complain about the five-paragraph essay. She told me that at this stage in my writing I shouldn't write in a formulaic style. Middle school students write that way. I shouldn't worry about five paragraphs, but instead I should start worrying about presenting a good argument. I really didn't understand what that meant, but I nodded my head in agreement to speed up our little chat.

The last thing she told me was that I needed to stick to the prompt, and not write about something completely different. She once again reminded me that the prompt was to write about the best day of the week and why I thought that way, not to write about the worst day of the week. She thought that even though I did a good job covering this subject (another lie because she just told me I *didn't* do a good job covering this subject), I still needed to stick to the appropriate prompt in order to get a good grade on the paper.

Then she handed back my paper, told me to take my seat and get to work on my assignment. She then asked Stephen Bluestein to come up for his conference. I pretended to do my homework while Mrs. Baker gave Stephen a whispered glowing review of his essay on Saturday, the best day of the week.

I hate Mrs. Baker.

Chapter Three

Sundays got even worse with the start of my confirmation class. First I had to get up early in the morning to make sure I made it to the seven o'clock Mass so I didn't have to rearrange my busy schedule. Then I had to run home, change into my greasy Burger House uniform so I could make it to work by ten and prepare for the busy Sunday lunch rush.

I considered these moments between Mass and work as the worst that Sunday had to offer, because my dad sat downstairs with the morning newspaper spread out before him. He drank a cup of coffee while waiting for my mom to wake up so she could make him breakfast of two eggs, over easy, French toast, and a side of bacon. I, on the other hand, partook of a bowl of cold cereal because my mom never woke up early enough to prepare the same kind of breakfast for me. My dad relished this time of the week because he and I could have a one on one talk. I dreaded those moments.

My dad owns a large investment broker company. They do something with the stock market that I can't for the life of me figure out. My dad tells me that I will learn about that in college. He wants me to follow in his footsteps. I still haven't decided if I like the idea. He also wants me to grow up as a good Catholic. Once again, I'm not quite sure if this is the path for me. In fact, the more I learn about both of these organizations, neither of them excites me. But because I've just turned seventeen, my father often reminds me that if I live under his roof, I will have to live by his rules.

The conversations we have these mornings usually revolve around one of three subjects, which never interest me. I would welcome subjects such as new movies, the changing season, or even the Broncos. But no, it always has to do with the importance of building up a good work ethic, raising my grades at school, or the value of living by the precepts of the Catholic Church. I found that if I just nodded in agreement I could drown out whatever soapbox he stood on any given Sunday morning.

On the day of my first confirmation class, I could see the eagerness in my dad to talk to me because he had already put the paper down and sipped greedily at his coffee. He waited for me to finish making my delicious bowl of cereal so he could have the desired conversation. I could feel an ugly one coming on so I slowly put together my breakfast in the hope that Dad would get bored and forget about the lecture. I had a hard time putting it together slowly while trying to make it look natural. I eventually gave up, sat at the breakfast table, and got ready to listen to that week's lecture.

"So, Tristan, you start your confirmation class today, don't you?" Only a CEO would go straight to the subject he wanted to talk about.

"You got that right," I said as I shoveled a spoonful of soggy Frosted Flakes into my mouth.

"Are you excited about it?"

I tried to chew faster because I knew the faster I ate my breakfast, the quicker I could get this conversation over with. "I guess. It does make my Sundays even busier."

I could see the word *wrong* in bright red letters etch itself across his brow. I should've known better, but sleep still swam through my brain. It didn't help that the few moments I had among the living on Sunday were spent fighting against Father Brett as he delivered his listless sermon at seven in the morning.

My father's eyes narrowed. "Tristan, it shouldn't concern a young man how he spends his time when he uses that time to improve his self-worth."

"And going to a confirmation class once a week will do that for me?" I must've been in an ornery mood, because I didn't need to pick this fight with my father.

"Of course this will do that for you. Tristan, this is a moment in your faith when you should confirm your commitment to God." I could see the outcome of this conversation, so I started to shovel my breakfast into my mouth quicker. I wonder if my father recognized this ploy. "A commitment to God is an important thing in life. It shows people what you care about and it lets them know where you stand on certain issues in society. By making this pledge, your social standing will rise and people in business will respect you more. It allows them to see that your commitment is a strong one, and they will believe that you share this strong commitment with them as well. Not only will your soul benefit, but your pocketbook will as well. This could be one of the most important decisions you make in your life."

Ironically enough, I didn't know it was my decision.

I knew I needed to placate my father or this conversation would turn into a yelling match, something I definitely didn't want to get into because it would wake up my mom and put me in a bad mood before I went to work. I had a hard enough time putting myself in a good mood to go there with an argument bubbling over in my mind as I drove to Burger House, which would ensure a "craptacular" day at work.

I looked over at my father. "I see your point. My nerves are just getting the better of me. It always freaks me out going into a new situation. In my mind, it's some big unknown and I really don't know what they'll teach me there, so I have some reservations about it."

This made my dad smile. I knew how to manipulate him in certain situations — just give him what he wanted. He put down his cup of coffee and patted my hand. "I can see why you would have some concerns, but I think as soon as you start these classes you'll find them very rewarding."

"You're probably right," I said as I gathered up my cereal bowl and ran it to the sink. I looked back at my dad. "I'll see you later tonight to tell you how it went, but right now I have to get to work."

He took another sip of coffee while picking up the paper again. "Get going, Tristan, and have a good day, son."

. . .

It will always amaze me how many people eat at the Burger House on Sundays. It usually starts around eleven o'clock with just a trickle of people. But within fifteen minutes, people pack the lobby wanting their share of juicy goodness held within each of our "one hundred percent" beef patties.

I don't really believe that there is any juicy goodness in our burgers; I just like to quote the commercials I see on television. If you've ever had one of our burgers you know how little juicy goodness they actually have. It just sustains you between bigger meals. Kids have it served with a little toy in order to condition them into thinking the Burger House is the most wonderful place in the whole world. I bet they have each child in America salivating like some bizarre Pavlovian dog every time they hear the words *Burger House*. But I really don't want to complain about the politics of some greasy hamburger joint. I really can't because they do employ me and besides making a little extra money, they get me away from my father every Sunday. I can take the fact that I smell like grease when I get home at night if it means spending just a little less time with my family.

I don't even care about the mindlessness of the job. They don't want me anywhere near any customer, which makes me happy. This means that I do not have to work the drive thru or the front counter. They don't even want me to work the drink station, a job so mindless that Burger House constantly has to find a new employee to handle this responsibility. Most people can't stand it longer than one or two days. The record for getting tired of pushing the small, medium or large drink button before the person quits stands at fifteen minutes and twenty-six seconds. The longest somebody stood at that position is two months. I think they diagnosed that guy with some neurological disorder. Luckily, they throw me in the kitchen where I can prepare the juicy goodness.

Of course working back in the kitchen has some drawbacks. The potential for burns is very high. During the first couple of weeks working there I found new and interesting ways to burn myself. Grease can always splatter as you flip the burgers. The spatula can be really hot after you slide it from the grill, a vast plain of sizzling hot stainless steel. You can trap a hand into the bun toaster, and if that wasn't enough, eight vats filled with boiling grease attempt to deep-fry the stray phalange. Potential burns wait for you in a veritable minefield around every corner, and whatever doesn't kill you turns your skin into a pepperoni pizza pie of pimples. So between the smell of working in a fast-food joint, the occasional burn showing up on weird locations on my body, and the high school embarrassment of being known as *Zit-face*, my love life floated somewhere in the bottom of the crapper.

I still get the occasional make-out session every once in a while. I got it on the other night at a party. The heavy petting was going pretty well, but I got nervous halfway through and left the session to find some fresh air. It screwed me up so much that I didn't even get a name or digits. My "dumbassity" shined like the morning sun with that one.

I didn't really have time to think about my mistake that Sunday, though, because of the after-church rush we were experiencing. Like I said, the first few stragglers come in around eleven. Those people don't go to church and just want something to help them overcome the hangover from drinking the night before. They don't know the danger they've placed themselves in because fifteen minutes later, church gets out. First, you get the smart ones who sneak out right after Communion and don't wait around for the final blessing. But then you get the accumulation of humanity that pours out of church doors, believing that they've done their good deed for the week. This condones their lives of debauchery and sin. What better place to maintain this tradition than Burger House? They get to feed their hunger for American food, and my employer has given me the responsibility of making sure the burgers come out quickly so we can get as many people through the line as possible.

The owners of this particular Burger House were smart enough to live by the number one business principle — location, location, location. They built their business right down the street from the Catholic church, a half mile away from the Presbyterian church, and they also happen to be the closest fast-food joint from the Mormon Temple. And what better place than the Catholic church to get a whole bunch of huge, hungry families than the Mormon Temple. There are two Baptist ministries within shouting distance from the building. This perfect location keeps the Burger House busy all the way through lunch every Sunday. I wonder if the owners of the restaurant visit each of these churches every Sunday to be sure the people there remember to pay their tithe to the American economy after they pay their tithe for their soul. If so, it is probably the smartest thing they can do, since they make most of their money on Sunday. Just as most retail businesses make enough money on Black Friday to sustain them throughout the year, this Burger House makes enough money on Sundays to sustain itself throughout the rest of the week.

I work in the kitchen, usually with my best friend, Tessa, as we attempt to keep all of these people happy. She works the grease vats to make all the French fries, as well as the occasional chicken sandwich or chicken strips. I work the grill to keep a healthy supply of juicy goodness sliding down our patrons' throats. We work together, making sure to toast the buns and fill them with the various condiments.

Rarely do we have time to look up from our work, but when we do look out into the lobby, it's fun to see our progress with the rush. It so happened that on the Sunday of my first confirmation class, I looked up halfway through the lunch rush to see the sight that made my heart jump. In the middle of wrapping a dozen burgers, I stopped.

Tessa saw my hesitation and asked me, "What's up, Tristan?"

"It's *Him*," was all I could say.

Chapter Four

Tessa looked at me weird like some bizarre foreign language poured out of my mouth. I had a hard time believing she hadn't listened to me as I had told her about the different form of juicy goodness I had the night before. I looked at her again and said, "You know, Him — the one from the party I told you about."

She looked over at Him, and then she looked back at me while still trying to ponder my words. She looked back at Him again. I could see the tiny wheel in her head spin before the lightbulb went on. "You mean the guy from the party the other night?"

She apparently didn't know how to control the volume of her voice, because I had to throw an unwrapped burger at her to remind her to keep it down. It slapped against the wall, and the juicy goodness slowly slid down the tile. She quickly got the hint and scanned the group of customers seeing if she could pick *Him* out. "Which one is he?"

My heart raced as I tried to look in his direction while making it look like I could care less that He stood in the lobby. I always wished I could do this better because as soon as I tried to be casual about it, He must have felt my eyes all over him. He looked over in my direction. His big, dark brown eyes fixed on mine and our eternal stares locked with each other. His look penetrated through the stifled air of the lobby and into the grease-saturated air of the kitchen. A worried, confused look etched itself across his brow, but soon recognition hit him. He knew where he had seen me before. He knew our connection. His eyes got softer, and a smirk grew upon his full lips.

Tessa decided to use this exact moment to break the spell He had me under. "I figured it out. Is it the guy in the back staring at us?"

A wave of confusion and embarrassment rushed over me. My thoughts returned to that night. I thought about all the things this world has taught me and how the emergence of this one person questioned everything I had once held as true and safe. How could one person have that much control over another, especially when I didn't even know his name? He looked just like any other teenager. He wore his hair in a mop that barely covered his eyes. He looked as if he'd arranged it without any thought, even though every teenager knew he spent half of each morning making it look just right. He dressed a little better than most teenagers, but that shouldn't have made him stand out the way he did. He wore a dark suit and a slim black tie that classed him up a bit more than the rest of the church crowd. He flashed the smile that haunted my dreams since that night. I couldn't erase it from my memory, no matter how much I tried, and once again it stared at me from across a crowded room.

I immediately felt self-conscious. I knew my mouth hung open in disbelief. A Burger House baseball cap hid my unkempt hair, and I wore a red work shirt with as many grease stains on it as a heart attack patient's colon. It probably didn't help that I stood there holding on to a cooked hamburger ready for mass consumption. The lock His brown eyes had with my light blue ones made my heart race and jumbled up my thoughts. I could no longer do the mindless job that was required of me.

Tessa whispered loud enough for the whole restaurant to hear, "I think he's staring at you, Tristan. What are you going to do?"

We all hope that when presented with moments like these we handle them with grace, but my actions did not make me look bold and distinguished in front of the one staring me down. I let out a barely audible yelp. The burger I held flew out of my hand. Ketchup, mustard, and tiny dehydrated onions escaped from the bun and flew into the air. The pickle exploded from the juicy goodness and lodged itself into the ceiling above my head. I squeezed my eyes shut to break His lock with mine and ducked behind the line. When I felt safe, I looked up at Tessa.

She looked down at me and just shook her head, "Smooth, Tristan, that's going to play well later on."

"What's He doing?"

"Standing there laughing with the rest of the crowd out in the lobby."

I needed a bigger escape from the situation. My boss, Dan, would have no intention of letting me hide behind the line during the busiest time of the week, but I couldn't face the crowd out there. Especially, Him. Luckily, I had practiced the art of throwing up on cue. It had helped me get out of many tests during my years of school. I could work any trouble in my tummy into a full-on pea soup puke attack. With all of my nerves firing off from the moment I had just experienced, I didn't need too much motivation to make my stomach tumble the way it would if I were riding on a rollercoaster with an expired warranty. I rushed from my hiding spot and ran to the dry storage room in the back of the restaurant. Dan was there doing the inventory for the week and avoiding the crowd gathered in the lobby. I ran over to a large trash can in the corner which he used to discard anything that had expired, and proceeded to throw up into it.

Dan looked over at me and asked, "Is everything okay, Tristan?"

I looked up at him and said, "I don't feel so well."

■ ■ ■

I had the rest of the day off. I snuck through the back door so I wouldn't have to face Him as I left. Dan went to the office to find another employee to take my place, and I got a worried look from Tessa. Luckily for me, she couldn't come back and ask me what was up because the rush was still on. She couldn't possibly pull herself away from it. If she did, the whole kitchen would have collapsed, and like a domino effect, the whole restaurant would have gone down. One bad day at any restaurant could spiral down through the weeks and eventually shut down the whole place.

First, one family who couldn't get their juicy goodness in a timely manner goes off about how they will never show their faces in that despicable place again. Then other families will ask why, and the first family will tell how they had received terrible service. The word would quickly spread, and fewer and fewer people would show up to eat. The employees would start to get a bit more lax about how they handled themselves. They'd move slower, they'd make crude jokes with each other, they'd ignore the few customers that did come into the restaurant. This would just add to the problems the restaurant already had. Now because of one bad day, more reports of the same kind of service would start to spread like hot grease on a pile of snow. This gives credence to the complaints because of the truth behind them. On top of that, people would start complaining about the "fucksadaisical" attitude the employees have. They won't take their children there due to the little ones' exposure to such a strange environment. Soon, no families will come at all. In fact, very few people will come. Only crackheads and midnight hookers will show up at the restaurant, and they don't eat. They pedal their wares.

The bored employees at the restaurant will start to participate in crack and casual sex. They'll end up either spending their time on a street corner wacked out of their brains on some silly drug, or dying from syphilis. They will get help for these terrible diseases but the restaurant at that time will have closed down, and the employees will no longer have insurance. In the end, Tessa will have ruined the lives of the other employees, all because she left the line to talk to me about the guy who showed up at our restaurant unannounced.

Tessa would never let this happen. She kept to her responsibilities as I quietly slipped out the back door. Of course, I couldn't go home without having to hear another lecture from my dad. Also, it would require me to come up with a pretty good lie, or I'd have to explain exactly what had happened at the party the week before. As far as my dad knew, no party ever existed. He thought Tessa and I went off to see the newest zombie flick. I wasn't about to tell him I had spent time dealing in drinking and debauchery. It was easier for me to just go someplace where I could hang out until it was time to go home.

I knew the perfect spot — Red Rocks Amphitheater. It was October, and even though the days started cooling off, we still had enough nice weather to spend time outside. Of course concert promoters still freaked out that some crazy snowstorm would hit the Denver area, so they would stop scheduling concerts at Colorado's most famous venue by this time of the year. Most people would think this also meant that no one could get into the setting, but during the day the park left the venue open for people to enter. Usually this meant that I had the place to myself and nobody would bother me. Occasionally, a runner would come out to do some stairs or a couple would find a quiet corner for making out. But for the most part, you could find yourself alone with your thoughts, so I would go there often.

Weather could not destroy the perfection of this place. At the time, the cool, brisk air helped to clear my head from all the confusion I had just experienced. I could look out over the plains that ran from the mighty Rocky Mountains. The view was perfect for watching all the hustle and bustle of the city of Denver. On this specific day, nobody disturbed the place but me. I could hear the echoes from past concerts reverberating through the silence. I could collect my thoughts and think about my next move.

My thoughts kept returning to Him.

. . .

I had met Him at the party. Well, I don't know if we "met" exactly, because I still didn't even know his name. It was one of those weird parties hosted by a guy who went to the local Catholic high school. This meant that he had friends who also went to that school as well as friends who went to the local public high school in his neighborhood. His friends from the Catholic high school had friends from the local public high schools in *their* neighborhoods, and they would bring them, too. These people had other friends and cousins and brothers and sisters who also showed up. Because it was a high school party hosted by one of the wealthier high school students, everybody soon knew about it and the three kegs ready for consumption.

The party previewed what college would be like, but at the same time it brought a lot of different cliques who didn't know each other together in one place. This could possibly lead to two things — a lot of fights between rival high schools, or an over-explosion of hormones brought together in one place without any adult supervision. While standing in line to refill my cup with beer, I saw Him for the first time.

He stood across the room finishing off the beer he had in his hand. He was engaged in a conversation with somebody who apparently also went to the same school as he did. His hair kept getting in his face and he had to keep brushing it aside. His athletic build made me wonder if he played any sports. He could have easily played wide receiver for the football team or a forward for the basketball team. I kept hoping He was neither of these but rather someone who cared about the more important things in life. I knew I would never find out because a guy like that would never mingle with a guy like me.

I finally made it to the tap of the keg to get a refill on my beer. I tried to get this guy out of my head, but for some reason I had to keep looking back at him. He must have felt me staring, because he turned his head to look at me, and gave me my first full dose of those deep, dark-brown eyes. They burned right into my soul and flustered me as I filled up my cup.

Beer started flowing out of the cup onto the leg of my jeans. It woke me up from his trance, and I quickly diverted my eyes. I muddled my way into the crowd to avoid any other interaction with this guy from across the room. But apparently, however much I tried I should have known He was the kind of guy I couldn't avoid, because he kept showing up.

He even showed up at work during my shift to fluster me even more. I just wish I knew his name so I could stop calling him *Him*.

Chapter Five

When it was time, I stopped looking at the October clouds as they rolled over the plains of Colorado, and I left my secure spot at Red Rocks. An autumnal breeze blew through the crags and crannies of the foothills as I made my way back to the car. When I first arrived at my sanctuary, the wind made me wish I had brought my jacket. But I was more worried about the overwhelming wave of nausea plaguing me ever since He had shown up at work, and I had left it in the backseat of my car. I knew I needed to leave these thoughts behind me and make it to my confirmation class or I would never hear the end of it from my father.

I drove down the hill toward our church. It had grown into a part of my life. In fact, I had probably spent more time in that church than any other building besides my own house. My parents forced me to spend the first eight years of my education learning the principles and the doctrines of Catholic society. Nuns, priests, English, and science teachers alike had pushed these Catholic ideals on me. In fact, if a class didn't have a Catholic spin to its teachings, then they couldn't have taught it at my school. I even remember how these principles were once applied to a game of Red Rover during gym class. If we caught a person and didn't let them break through our line, then we would all applaud the fact that we saved another good Catholic.

I spent eight hours a day, five days a week, thirty-six weeks out of every year for eight years in this building. Add in an hour every Sunday for Mass and all of the extracurricular activities I took part in, and that's an inordinate amount of time spent in this building. I knew every little hidden corner of the school. I knew where you could hide if a nun was looking for you with her ruler. I could find a book in the library by touch alone. I could even probably point out the wear in the carpet from the students lined up and guided to their next location.

I even knew about the youth center in the back of the building. Administration hardly ever opened up the youth center because they had filled it with numerous types of entertainment — pool, ping-pong, and air hockey tables. During my middle school years, we could go there on Friday nights to spend time with other Catholics as we enjoyed the frivolous activities this room had to offer. The people that ran this part of the church would organize dances and have various tournaments to keep us off the streets and in the hands of God. My confirmation class also took place in this room.

I drove to the back parking lot that was used only for those Friday nights when parents came to either drop off or pick up their kids from the youth celebrations. It felt weird being back here without anybody to guide me to the door. I parked the car and made sure I put on my coat so the rest of the people attending class wouldn't know I worked at the Burger House. It probably even helped with the greasy smell permeating my clothes. I grabbed a pencil and made my way slowly toward the door.

I showed up a little late because I knew I could sneak in and still get the credit needed to please my parents. I could always talk to the person in charge of the program afterward and claim that work had detained me. They couldn't complain because my parents had already paid for the class.

The fact that a couple of other stragglers showed up just as late comforted me. They left their cars in the dark parking lot and made their way to the youth center. I could barely discern their faces as I walked into the familiar room. The church had pushed the various games into the corners of the room and placed rows of folding chairs in their place. Father Brett stood in front of a group of teenagers. He held a clipboard in his hand as he went through roll on the sheet.

"Theresa Thompson?"

"Here."

"David Underwood?"

"Yo."

"Samantha Zook."

"Yes."

He then looked at me as I took my seat in the back row. "And who might you be?"

"Tristan Adamson."

The man in the front of the room searched the clipboard for my name, "Ah, yeah there you are." He then looked over my head toward the back door. He directed his attention to another straggler who had walked in behind me. "And what is your name?"

"Thomas Edwards."

Just like everybody else in the crowd, I turned around to see what this Thomas Edwards person looked like. Much to my surprise, I found myself looking into the face of Him. I had finally gotten my wish. I no longer needed to call Thomas Edwards *Him*.

. . .

I quickly turned back, hoping that Thomas Edwards hadn't seen me, but I think with everybody looking at him except me, I looked that much more obvious. No one else sat in the back row. Everybody dressed up in nice clothes, not necessarily in their Sunday best, but not some scrubby, well-worn jacket hiding a greasy uniform from a burger joint. The smell of my clothes probably attracted Thomas Edwards to my direction even more. Add to it the fact that we had some recent history, and he was apparently on the lookout for me, so I stood out like a sore thumb.

I started to wish I had gotten there a little earlier, because then I could have hidden somewhere in the middle of the seats. I wouldn't be stuck in the back row with a whole bunch of seats open for Thomas Edwards to choose from. Luckily for me, he sat in a chair on the corner of the row. I started to breathe a little easier and kept my focus on our teacher's lecture. I could hear Father Brett babbling on about the work we had to do in order for the Catholic Church to acknowledge our confirmation, but my thoughts kept racing down the row to the person sitting there. I knew if I looked that way, it would be all over. I tried to keep my attention directed forward, but I just couldn't resist. I needed to know about this person that sat at the end of my row. The thought tickled the back of my imagination and wouldn't let go. I needed to satisfy this urge so I took a peek down the aisle toward Thomas Edwards.

I didn't get what I hoped for. He smiled and gave me a little wave. My attention went directly back to the priest. That one little gesture strengthened my resolve for the rest of the one hour class. I no longer needed to feed the urge to look over in Thomas Edwards' direction. Instead, I paid close attention to Father Brett's lesson.

The whole discussion of the night focused on the subject of faith.

He started off by stating the obvious, *"Faith is belief in something you cannot see."* Duh? Like I needed someone to tell me this. I have heard statements like this ever since the first grade. Nuns with rulers beat it into our heads that we must take that leap and believe in the Lord. It made me chuckle to hear what the teacher said next.

"We have a choice to believe in that faith or not believe."

I never had a choice. I looked around the room. I saw a couple of girls I knew since first grade texting somebody lucky enough not to be in the confirmation class. I saw a couple boys' eyes start to glaze over and fall into a sleep that made it seem like they were actually paying attention. Of course a couple of kids sitting up front took studious notes, but these kids had to get an *A* in whatever class they enrolled. I don't think there was one person in the classroom who wanted to be there of their own accord. Their parents forced them to make that leap of faith. They had no choice unless they wanted to disappoint their parents. The parents made them feel guilty if they didn't believe. I knew that was the reason for my attendance.

I wondered whether Thomas Edwards's parents were the same way. I threw another peak in his direction. He was busy taking notes and paying attention to the teacher.

Chapter Six

Tristan Adamson

Hell, and God, and Nuns with Rulers

Some people would say that Jewish parents have cornered the market on guilt. This noble race knows better than any other type of parent how to make their children feel uncomfortable at any given moment. They can use the fires of Hell and the pains of their past to make their children feel bad when they complain about the scratchy pants they received for Hanukkah. Even though they might have pretty effective skills when dishing out guilt, the Catholics have made strong inroads with this ability. In fact, the parents of Catholic children have made so much progress in this area of expertise that they now hold the title for the best guilt trippers on the planet.

Just like the Jewish people, the Catholic parents have the fear of Hell on their side and they know how to use it. They instill it in their children at a very early age. From the moment their child can enjoy stories, these parents pull out their big old picture book of Bible stories. These books tell wonderful stories about animals going into an ark two by two, or how three wise men showed up at the birth of some random kid to give him gifts of precious metals and smelly stuff. But other stories involve what a young person's life will be like if they are condemned to Hell. Red painted men with horns and long tails walk around with pitchforks forcing people to take leaps into big old pits of fire. Parents force their children to look at pictures of the anguished faces of people burning for all eternity while Lucifer dances behind with glee. Catholic parents will point at these pictures and tell their children, "Look what happens if you don't brush your teeth at night." On a side note, Catholics generally have very happy dentists.

If Catholic parents can't scare their kids by using the devil, they can always use God. We should all fear God; at least this is what they tell children at a very early age. God will not be undone by a mere human. If He thinks someone is showing Him up in any manner, He will use His might and power to smite that person. Many Bible stories confirm this. Children's Bibles even furnish pictures to better illustrate these messages. God threw Adam and Eve out of Eden. After Noah got on the ark, God flooded the earth. The picture in the Bible depicted men drowning as Noah sails by with a smile on his face and a cute cat in the crook of his arm. Imagine being five years old and seeing a picture of a man wearing a toga and wielding a sharp knife to stab his son, or the picture of the Hell on Earth that God created while he destroyed Sodom. These frightening pictures, combined with terrifying stories, can even help Catholic parents' guilt their children into being potty-trained.

Finally, Catholic parents having something that would make the Holocaust look tame. They have nuns with rulers. There is nothing scarier on this God-given Earth than a nun with a ruler. Just one of these formidable beasts will stare down an army of highly trained super ninjas. With one crack of that ruler, it will cause those ninjas to wet their pants (they don't have many Catholics in Japan) and run away like Shaggy and Scooby Doo being chased by some imaginary ghost. The only problem with being a Catholic child is that when faced with this dilemma, they can neither pee their pants (see earlier argument) nor run away. They must face the nun and whatever terror she may inflict upon the knuckles of said victim.

Many Catholic boys and girls wake up with their knuckles aching, and they don't even know why.

So it is obvious that even though all parents know how to use guilt trips to their advantage, no parent knows how to use them better than Catholic parents. They have many more tools at their disposal, such as: Hell, and God, and nuns with rulers. Just feel lucky you don't have Catholics for parents.

. . .

This time Mrs. Baker went backward down the list as she talked to each student about their essays. I followed Stephen Bluestein. She started off by pointing out her pride at the fact that I could use a semicolon correctly. I guess this would mean a lot to me if I knew what a semicolon was. She then went on to explain her dissatisfaction with the fact that I couldn't stick to the prompt. My voice and subject matter interested her but she couldn't understand how it had anything to do with the relationship between Macbeth and Lady Macbeth. She would even accept my consistently writing the five-paragraph essay if only I could stay on topic. Maybe I could stay on topic if I actually sat down and read *Macbeth*, but I just can't get into Shakespeare.

She handed back my paper with a big red letter *F* on it. She went on to explain that she might've found it in her heart to give me a *D* if I hadn't dismissed the Holocaust as being less terrifying than a nun with a ruler. Apparently, they never taught a theology class at the public high school she attended. She is definitely not making any brownie points. I can't move her to the list of teachers that I like. But considering the fact that only my first grade teacher, Mrs. Flarrety, has made the list, I doubt Mrs. Baker would really care.

Chapter Seven

I snuck out of the confirmation class before I ran into Thomas Edwards. This way he couldn't talk about what had happened on Friday night. Father Brett, I found out later, had caught Thomas before he could corner me because Thomas still needed to pay for the class. While Thomas tried to work out the logistics of this problem, I snuck out the door and rushed to my car. No other person beat me out of the parking lot that evening. Everybody else was busy reminiscing about the times they spent in middle school and how much they'd grown over the last couple of years.

I spent most of my grade school years hiding in the shadows. My fellow students at the confirmation class probably didn't even remember me from those blurry years. Even if they did, my name only rang a bell when they heard it mentioned during roll call. Nothing much has changed, and I didn't want to participate in those inane conversations. I definitely didn't want to get cornered by Thomas Edwards. He would be the only person in the room who would want to talk about our past, even though I had only known him for a short period of time. Instead, I opted for the quick getaway.

The fact that I snuck out early didn't really help solve my problem. In fact it just made things more awkward. Some time or another, I would have to have a confrontation with Thomas Edwards. I couldn't avoid it. This person knew where I worked and attended the same confirmation class. I couldn't go up to my parents and tell them I no longer wanted to go to the confirmation class. Like I said earlier, even though the church told us confirmation was a conscious choice of freewill, someone else really made the decision for me. My parents would flip out if I told them I wanted to drop out of the class. They would start using the power of Hell, and God, and nuns with rulers to force me to make the decision they wanted me to make.

This could even open a door, and I would have to tell them some of the things I wasn't comfortable sharing. A simple guilt trip discussion could potentially turn into something more dangerous in the long run.

I could just stop going to the confirmation class, but that wasn't a good idea either. My mom had already taken me shopping for a new sports coat. We even had a tailor measure me so the coat would fit perfectly. I would wear this coat as I stood in front of the archbishop of Denver while I confirmed to everyone in attendance that I was committed to God. If I stopped going to class, Father Brett would embarrass me by saying that I had not finished the class and I couldn't be confirmed in the Catholic faith. That would be a lot of money wasted on the class and the new sports coat. My mom would freak and my dad would never forgive me.

I knew that I had at least a week to figure it out. The schedule at work only had me on for Monday. Since I got sick on Sunday, I could use that to my advantage and call in sick again. I could fool my parents by going to work and then spending the evening up at Red Rocks. In fact, with all the crazy things happening, I was looking forward to another night of peace and quiet. Even if Thomas showed up at my work every day that week, he wouldn't find me. The only other thing he knew about me was my enrollment in the confirmation class. The confrontation would surely take place on the next Sunday, and I needed to prepare for it. I could think of only one person who could help me out.

I called my best friend, Tessa, to see what I should do.

. . .

I met Tessa at Red Rocks on Monday. The coolness of autumn had started to creep in. Clouds hung in the sky, obscuring my view of Denver, and made it a little difficult for Tessa to find me even though I sat in the middle of the auditorium. I knew from past experience I could hide in plain sight if I limited my movements. The little amount of humidity in the air didn't chill me, but I wrapped myself tighter in my jacket to hide from other dangers.

Tessa hiked up the steep steps looking all around for something out of place in the big structure. I could see her breath as she panted against the elevation. Each little puff from her lungs hung in the atmosphere before it dissipated into the cool October air. I know I should have made some kind of motion to make it easier for her to detect me, but I enjoyed the last few moments of solitude before I had to have a conversation with her. I let her continue to look for the haystack in the middle of the big open field. She eventually did find me and huffed her way to where I sat. She plopped down next to me and leaned back to rest upon the wooden bleacher seat behind her. Her hand went into her coat pocket and pulled out a crumpled pack of Marlboro Lights. She tapped out a cigarette as she said through shallow breaths, "Being in this place always makes me want to smoke."

"Being anyplace where you can smoke makes you want to smoke," I replied.

Tessa already had a smoke dangling from her mouth as she said, "Well, ever since the cool group decided that it was no longer cool to smoke, it became more important than ever to pick up the habit. Now, anytime I get the opportunity, I love to blow smoke in their faces." She pulled out a white Bic lighter and sparked up the tip of her cigarette.

"Cute. I wonder why you can't ever keep a boyfriend," I said sarcastically.

She inhaled deeply on her first drag and leaned back again to enjoy the view. "I'm okay with that because when I find the right one, he won't care what I put in my body. He'll have the same attitude I do."

"Until then you'll keep bouncing around from loser to loser."

"Don't blame me if I don't have any standards, unlike you with your standards." Tessa flashed me a skeptical look. "I have never met anybody that set their standards as high as you."

I turned around to face her. I sat Indian-style and looked up toward the two monstrous rocks that enclosed the auditorium. "My problem doesn't come from my standards. The problem lies more with my parents' standards."

"Your dad's standards," she corrected me.

"We both know that my mom takes on whatever standards my dad deems appropriate, whether she believes in them or not."

"You make a good point," she said as she took another drag. "By the way, nice show you put on yesterday. I'm still a little pissed off at you for abandoning me on a Sunday."

"Dan doesn't suspect me, does he?"

"Of course not, but he asked me if I could cover your shift tonight. I told him I couldn't because I had this huge project due at school. You just better never do that to me again. You hear me?"

"Sorry, but I needed to get out of there."

"Yeah, I could tell." Tessa started to experiment with smoke rings while saying, "Does that guy really make you so nervous that you need to run out of the building instead of looking at him?"

"You mean Thomas Edwards?"

"Who?"

"Thomas Edwards, the guy that showed up at the Burger House last night."

The experimentation with the smoke rings stopped and she sat up. "I thought you didn't know his name?"

"I didn't know his name until I went to my confirmation class last night. Guess what? He's in my class."

Tessa gave me a shove that almost made me fall into the aisle behind me. "Get out of here! That is crazy. It's like fate... or this guy is stalking you."

"I really doubt that Thomas Edwards is stalking me. It's just some crazy coincidence."

Tessa didn't seem to care about my explanation. "Thomas Edwards. Nice name. It just rolls off the tongue."

I needed to get her attention back to the more important problem at hand. "Tessa, I really need your help. I don't know what to do."

"What do you mean you don't know what to do?"

"He sat right next to me in my confirmation class. I can't avoid that class without getting into trouble with my parents, and now I can't avoid *him* because at some point he will want to talk to me. What should I do?"

Tessa looked at me incredulously. "What else can you do, Tristan? Talk to him."

. . .

People give advice freely when they have no involvement in the situation. Tessa had no idea what her advice meant for me. She had never experienced my situation; she didn't know what happened. Well, she *did* know what happened because I told her what happened. Even though I explained all of the conflicting emotions going through me at the time, she still didn't really know what happened because she hadn't experienced it the way I had. A person can read about something, listen to people talk about it, or watch it on television, but unless they go through it themselves, they can't fully understand what it means to have that experience. I don't even know why I asked Tessa for advice, because she wouldn't tell me the things I wanted to hear. I'm not quite sure what I wanted to hear, but I know for a fact I didn't want to hear, *"Talk to him."* I could get better advice from a paraplegic gorilla.

All of this worrying about Thomas made me think more about the night I met him. After I caught him staring me down at the party, I left the keg and hopefully his eye contact for the rest of the evening. But a huge beer puddle stained my pant leg not that this should really bother me at a high school party. Every party has drunk teenagers running around, doing foolish things all of the time. I once saw a kid puke in a potted plant and then pass out on top of it. I've seen the semi-sober attack the ones passed out with permanent marker, and people wake up with words, mustaches and penises drawn all over them. Naked strangers wake up with other naked strangers in strange bedrooms. And each time one of these events happens, it spreads to the whole student body even before the party has ended.

Parents think they understand what's going on in their child's life, but they don't. They can't relate to today's modern technology. Parents will scoff at the fact that every student in the school will know about an event within fifteen minutes of it happening. They come from an era where they gossiped using handwritten notes. Nowadays, half of us don't even know what a pen looks like. We accomplish everything with these fancy devices we carry around in our pockets. We call them "smart" phones. We don't call them smart phones because they're super smart devices, but because you need the smarts to operate one — something our parents do not possess enough of. These devices come with cameras to take all of the embarrassing pictures as soon as an embarrassing situation presents itself. The photographers download the pictures onto Facebook with comments detailing exactly what happened. Then they send out text alerts for people to view the embarrassing situation. And since no teenager ever turns off their phone, the whole student body views the embarrassing moment, laughs about it, and shares it with anybody they're associating with at the time.

This can destroy a fragile teenager's existence. Forget about the penis drawn on your forehead, because from now on everyone will call you "Dickhead." You can never escape the embarrassment. It will follow you to your grave, maybe even longer. They'll be lowering you into the ground, and they'll engrave the tombstone with, *"Here lies Timothy Rickston, affectionately known as 'Dickhead' by all his friends."* Even in death, you can't escape this fate.

I found myself in a similar situation at that party when Thomas stared me down. The beer stain I had on my pant leg could easily look like a pee stain. From then on, my peers would fondly refer to me as Admiral Pissedon or Captain Depends. I needed to solve this problem before it got out of hand.

I went to find a bathroom where I could dry off before somebody could snap an embarrassing picture. I discreetly hid the indiscretion with my beer cup as I wandered down a dark stairwell. I hoped it led to a basement and hopefully a bathroom with a hair dryer. I turned around and scanned the party to make sure nobody saw me sneak downstairs. It looked like everybody was too busy enjoying the overall groove of the moment to notice I had disappeared. I quickly ducked down the stairs and into the basement.

It smelled musty down there as cool air swirled around me. I started to think I had made a mistake. I knew the owners hadn't carpeted the floor, because I could hear the clack of concrete as my shoes hit it. I almost turned to leave when I felt a light cord hit me in the face. I reached out and grabbed it. A single light bulb above my head lit up. I stood in the middle of a small concrete room. There were no doors here — just a sink, a washer, a dryer and some laundry detergent. It wasn't a bathroom, but it could still work for my purposes.

It was then I heard a noise behind me that I dreaded the most, a stranger saying, "Hello there."

Chapter Eight

My mom called it a phase. My teachers called it hormones. My dad called it a complete and utter disrespect for authority. Whatever you called it, it just meant I was not myself.

It started at school the next day. I couldn't pay attention in any of my classes. Usually I didn't have a problem with this because I would just stare out into oblivion and nod my head every once in a while. Most teachers find this adequate and believe that I actually pay attention to whatever they're talking about. I find it easy to do when you don't have anything on your mind, because it gives teachers the empty sponge they always refer to when they talk about educating their students. It doesn't work as well, though, when something else lingers on your mind.

It made me restless at school. I couldn't stop thinking about next Sunday night. What could I do about Thomas Edwards? I absolutely couldn't avoid talking to him. How could I handle this inevitable confrontation? I couldn't see any possible way of avoiding the situation. These thoughts just constantly ran through my mind, and I no longer could achieve the zombie stare, because too many other things bounced around in my brain.

I guess this didn't translate well in my seat, because I squirmed around while the teachers gave their lectures. If the people sitting around me weren't distracted by that, my crazy little mumblings got their attention. I would sigh to myself and say little things under my breath. I knew what I said, but nobody else could understand it. One student, Sarah Theissen, thought I was on some kind of drug. Needless to say, the teachers sent me to the office in a couple of different classes because I wouldn't, or more exactly, *couldn't* comply with their requests to stop distracting everybody else.

The principal just assumed my squirreliness came from the fact that I had gotten into trouble. When he couldn't find anything wrong with me, he sent me back to class. I enjoyed the little distraction, but it still didn't solve my problem with Thomas Edwards.

At home, things weren't much better. I always felt the eyes of my parents on me. They could bore down into my soul, and I started to believe they saw every little secret I kept hidden there. They knew what happened at the party. They knew what I did there. And they knew about Thomas Edwards.

Of course my rational mind told me that there was no possible way they could know, but then images of Hell, and God, and nuns with rulers would enter my head. My irrational mind would take over.

My mom would walk into the room and say, "Hi."

I would scream, nearly jumping out of my skin.

My dad would ask me questions about work, school, or confirmation class, and I would quickly respond with another question.

I wouldn't pay attention to what I needed to do while completing my chores. Dishes would end up in the refrigerator while milk found its way into the cabinet. Sinks would overflow in the bathroom. I would knock over the yard tools in the garage because I wouldn't look where I was going. My clumsiness became a huge problem, and someone was going to get hurt. My parents couldn't ignore my behavior.

By Saturday, my dad took me aside and asked me if I was on drugs. I assured him I was not, and I was just a little "off" that week. As much as he wanted to believe that, my behavior still made him a little skeptical. After that conversation I looked forward to Sunday night because no matter what happened, I wouldn't have it hanging over my head anymore. Whether things went my way or not, at least I'd have it out of the way and I would no longer need to worry about it.

. . .

My clumsiness also followed me to work. I know I had taken a day off during the week and considering I didn't have many expenses, missing work didn't hurt me that much financially. But I couldn't take many more days off because my parents did expect me to pay for my own gas and any extracurricular activities I wanted to participate in. In other words, I needed to get back to work.

It still made me nervous to go back. Thomas Edwards didn't know *when* I worked, but he definitely knew *where* I worked. I could see him staked out in the parking lot of the Burger House. He would eat tacos and drink soda from the Mr. Taco down the street. A pair of binoculars would dangle around his neck, and he would periodically check through them to see if the situation within the restaurant changed. When he saw me finally enter the restaurant, he would roll down his window, throw out his large soft drink, put on his mirrored sunglasses (even though it was nighttime), push a fedora onto his lush hair, and get out of his car. His dark shoes would dance around the puddles in the parking lot, and his hands would bury themselves into the pockets of his overcoat.

As he walked into the building, nobody would notice anything out of the ordinary. This stranger would walk up to the counter. Sheryl, who always worked the counter, would look up at Thomas Edwards and roll her eyes at him. "Welcome to Burger House. May I take your order?"

Thomas Edwards would lean in and whisper. "I would like a number twelve."

Sheryl would straighten up her posture. She would look around

46

to see if anybody was looking at either of them. When she satisfied her paranoia, she would motion for Thomas Edwards to follow her. He would walk behind the counter and follow Sheryl back into the kitchen. When I was in plain view, she would gesture in my direction, "Your number twelve, sir."

I would turn to see what was going on. Thomas Edwards would stand there staring me down. He would point at me and say, "Tristan, we need to talk."

Okay, I might have over exaggerated a bit, but one of many scenarios like this still played through my mind. I had envisioned versions of this story playing out in *Lord of the Rings*, or *Star Trek* fashion. I even once envisioned it as a bizarre episode of a Nicholas Sparks novel in which everybody except Sheryl and Dan dies in the end. I worried and worried so much about this at work that it became an obsession for me. I had a hard time concentrating on what I needed to do. Buns would get burned. Burgers would fly off my spatula. One time I even sent out a set of Supreme Burgers without any condiments on them.

Dan started to get upset with me. First, I had ditched work on one of the busiest days of the week, called in sick the other day, and now I performed my job at a sub-par level. He even threatened to switch me to the drink station if I couldn't pull myself together. After that, I quit envisioning my confrontation taking place at work, and concentrated more on what I needed to get done.

The funny thing was, even if he did show up, I couldn't do anything about it. Dan wouldn't have let me leave my post to work out something with a practical stranger. Thomas Edwards could have stood in the lobby all night and stared me down until I was done with my shift, but who would be the creeper then? My little cocoon in the back room protected me. I started to not care if some strange detective, James Bond, or Luke Skywalker came looking for me. I had a job to do, and I didn't need these stupid little distractions.

These thoughts actually helped me get through the rest of the week. I should've gone to work earlier, than I would have started feeling better about myself. I still knew that something on Sunday would happen, and work helped me feel like I could tackle that problem, too. Actually, my confidence was not much bigger than that of a mouse caught in a corner facing a hungry cat. If Thomas Edwards walked through the door of the Burger House and I saw him, I would've instantly jumped back into panic mode. Random food would have gone flying through the air again, and the fear I lived under all week would instantly return.

Thomas Edwards never showed up at my work though. I worried about nothing. I made my life a living hell thinking that every time I walked around a corner this individual would confront me. I was worrying myself sick for no reason at all. I think I might've even developed an ulcer during the week because I had a hard time digesting spicy food. Maybe I made a bigger deal out of this than I should have. Maybe Thomas Edwards didn't want to have anything to do with me. Maybe he had gotten my message loud and clear, and he just needed to stay away from me, if he knew what was good for him. He could've come into my work. He could have talked to Tessa and found out where I went to school. He could have followed my car home and rang my doorbell to have a little talk while my parents looked at us in the background. But he didn't do anything. My luck might've been so great that he dropped out of the confirmation class. Maybe Thomas couldn't come up with the money Father Brett needed for class. If he couldn't come up with the money, Father Brett wouldn't let him attend the class. Maybe he convinced his parents that he didn't need to get confirmed at this moment in his life. Maybe he convinced them that the classes weren't exactly what he was looking for, and he could find something better in a different church. Maybe I just concocted my problem with Thomas Edwards in my head and I would never run into him again. I just happened to experience a couple of bizarre coincidences. I started to believe I would never have to worry about Thomas Edwards ever again.

Chapter Nine

I had the perfect plan for class. I would make sure I was the first one to class, so I could pick a place in the first three rows, right in the middle. I could avoid Thomas Edwards from this perfect spot. People would start to filter in, and just like last time, they would take seats in the front part of the room. They would start by filling in the sides and then the middle. People would surround me. By the time Thomas Edwards showed up, he would have to sit anywhere but next to me. He would have to sit in the back with all the other losers.

I even came up with an exit strategy. I had thought of this as the essential part of the plan because he could still follow me out to the parking lot. Out there, he could corner me and have the confrontation I knew he wanted to have. I needed to think of a way to avoid this. First, I needed to make a quick friend. Now I know I can't claim this as one of my strengths in life, but if pushed into a corner I knew enough to be social. People from my grade school had enrolled in the class and I could latch onto them. This would give me the perfect setup for the next part of my plan.

After Father Brett finished lecturing to us about Heaven and Hell and dismissed us for those last fleeting moments of Sunday freedom, I would have to latch on to the "insta-friend" I had made. I would talk to this person with renewed interest as we made our way slowly to the door. I would avoid eye contact with Thomas

Edwards and as soon as I made it out the door, he would have no chance of cornering me. If I could keep this up for the ten weeks of the class, I would never have to confront him. If my luck held up, Thomas Edwards would grow weary of ever trying to make contact with me and just move on with life. No one could come up with a more perfect plan. I couldn't see any problems with it.

I made it to class early and my ambition instantly rewarded me with more luck than I ever thought possible. Only one other person had shown up. She had already found a seat in the second row, right in the center. She had her books and pencils on the chair next to her. She obviously wanted some human contact, because she kept looking down at her cell phone while she waited for somebody to respond to a text.

I made my way to her aisle pretending to look for the perfect spot. I tried to make eye contact with this girl, so I could easily start up a conversation with her. She looked up from her cell phone in my direction. Lucky for me, the girl, Lauren Mueller, had graduated from my middle school the same year I did. I only got along with her and a couple of other people at the school, partly because we both liked to listen to Led Zeppelin, Queen, Elton John, and other classic rock artists. I knew I could easily start up a conversation with her. She looked at me a little weird as if trying to figure out where she knew me from. My opportunity to pounce had arrived.

"Lauren? Lauren Mueller?"

The quizzical look grew on her face. "Yes? Do I know you?"

I stood there with a hurt look on my face. "Lauren?" I slid into the aisle and took a seat next to her book and pencils. "We went to middle school together. Tristan. Tristan Adamson."

The light clicked on. Her face went from worried concern over a possible serial killer, to recognition of a childhood friend. "Tristan! Oh my God. It's so good to see you."

"I know. I haven't seen you in forever." Things couldn't have gone much better than this.

"What've you been up to?"

"Well, my parents decided that I didn't need to go the Catholic route through high school, so they sent me off to Arapahoe. You?"

"Unfortunately, my parents decided I needed to keep up with the Catholic values. They also want to keep me away from boys."

My face cringed at hearing it. "Ouch, they didn't send you to the Academy?"

"They sure did. School uniforms and everything."

"Sorry."

"It's okay." She looked down at her cell phone again. Evidently, the lack of response started to distress her a little.

I motioned to the cell phone. "Somebody not getting back to you?"

"Yeah." She put the phone on her lap and looked back at the door. "I'm waiting for my cousin. He just moved here from Oregon and doesn't know a lot of people in town. His parents wanted him to get confirmed and thought maybe he could meet some new people in the process. His dad told me he'd get here a little early so I could introduce him to some friends, but he's running late."

"That sucks. Why didn't you introduce him to your friends last week?"

"Because I had a cold last week and couldn't make the class. Oh wait, there he is." I turned to the door to see her cousin. "Thomas, you made it."

. . .

They had me cornered like a beaver in a trap. I looked around for some sort of escape plan, but none presented itself. The room was completely devoid of any other human contact. Lauren and I sat in the direct center of the room. I felt as if I stood in the large red dot of a bull's-eye, and Thomas Edwards was the arrow.

"Thomas, I've saved a seat for you." I looked down at the seat next to me as my mind screamed, *Chew your leg off! Run away! Damn it all to Hell!* Lauren pulled away her book and pencil, leaving that metal folding chair empty.

I looked back at Thomas Edwards. He walked over to where that stupid girl motioned for him to come. She even had the gall to smear salt into my wound. Gently, she placed a hand on my arm. I could feel her smile on my back as she said, "You should get to know my cousin. He's actually a lot like you."

Everything slowed down. His hair bounced with his stride. It flashed those brown eyes between each bounce. A smirk etched itself across his face as he came to recognize the person sitting next to his cousin. I saw Lauren gently pat the seat next to me again. Thomas raised a hand next to his eyebrow and flashed his index finger to indicate hello to both Lauren and me. My heart thudded in my chest. It attempted to escape from the inevitable humiliation of this experience. I almost wished it would explode from my chest because it would mean the certain death I had hoped for. Unfortunately, I would have to live through the next few moments.

Thomas Edwards walked slowly down the aisle and Lauren got up to greet him. He stopped right in front of my seat. Lauren leaned in to give him a hug. They kissed each other on their left cheeks. They released each other from their embrace and I waited for the true terror to begin. My mind raced with ways for me to avoid this situation. It meant either puking again, or racing to the bathroom. I debated between the two choices when Lauren said, "Thomas, I'd like you to meet an old friend of mine from grade school, Tristan."

I knew I should have dashed for the bathroom where I could've puked, but instead I lost complete control of my body. I felt like that little kid who died and said he went to Heaven. My out-of-body persona could see myself as some puppet persona doing all different kinds of things, but I had no control over them.

I could see myself stand up from my seat. My hand extended out in a gesture of new friendship. A smile grew. My eyes softened for the first time in weeks. My reaction took Thomas a little by surprise. The confidence in his eyes retreated a little, but he still took my hand to shake it.

"Very nice to meet you, Thomas," I heard myself saying.

My out-of-body persona screamed at my puppet persona, *You idiot, this boy will destroy you. Run away while you still have a chance!*

My puppet persona wouldn't listen to my out-of-body persona's pleas. Instead, it listened to Thomas telling my puppet persona how glad he was to meet me. I saw my smile grow even more inviting. All the plans I had labored over started to unravel and I could do nothing to stop them. Everything I had been avoiding started to come true.

Lauren smiled because the two of us seemed to be getting on so nicely. She looked over in my direction and said, "Thomas just moved here, and he doesn't know a lot of people. It kind of stinks because he had to leave all of his old friends back in Oregon, and it's really hard to make new ones in a new place."

Thomas laughed sheepishly and said, "Lauren, you make me sound like such a loser."

I saw myself wave off such an absurd notion and said, "Don't make me laugh. It has to be hard moving to a new town. It's really hard meeting new people. Maybe we could hang out sometime. I could show you around town."

Thomas smiled, "I'd like that."

My out-of-body persona shrieked, *Noooooooooooooo!* but my puppet persona wouldn't listen.

. . .

Small chitchat ensued as more students filtered in. The second the clock ticked to six, Father Brett entered. He once again droned on about the important things we needed to know for the completion of our faith. This week we talked about God. It made me smile that he decided to tackle a small subject, and I tuned out when he said, "*Our minds cannot truly comprehend God's infinite and eternal characteristics.*"

I wanted to raise my hand right then and ask, "Then why are we taking a class to comprehend God's infinite and eternal characteristics?" But I refrained from doing something so rash. Plus, my mind was reeling from the situation I found myself in, now that Lauren scheduled me to take Thomas Edwards out to show him around town. How had I gone from the perfect plan of avoiding Thomas Edwards to becoming his personal chauffer? I knew exactly how to answer that question — Lauren Mueller. She had caused so much suffering and pain in my life. I spent half of class trying to think of ways to get out of taking Thomas Edwards out, but halfway through this class, Father Brett said something that brought me back to his lecture.

"God can make good come out of every event in life."

That irked me even more. I got more pissed the longer I sat in class. Here I thought religion actually comforted and helped you make sense out of the difficult moments in life. Now this priest I barely knew was giving me some existenshital mumbo jumbo about how bad things can actually be good. I'd have a better time understanding the infinite and eternal characteristics of God. This crap just wasn't fair.

Father Brett continued to lecture, *"A cross is never fair."*

What? Could he hear my thoughts? Did he know what I was thinking? Was he God? Forgive me for that last one, God. I probably stepped over the line a little there. I needed answers to these questions running through my brain, but more specifically, I needed answers to the ultimate question: What should I do about Thomas Edwards?

Father Brett continued to spout out his infinite and eternal wisdom, *"These unfair situations define us. They can become our finest hour and our greatest accomplishment while on Earth."*

How could walking around downtown Denver ever become my finest hour and my greatest accomplishment while on Earth? I started to get even more depressed because I started to think that God didn't have any greater plan for me than being an unwilling tour guide.

Father Brett summed up the lesson with a quote from Aldous

Huxley, *"It's not what happens to you that is important, but rather it's what you do about it that matters."*

I almost listened to this final thought until I remembered that it came from the nutcase who wrote that book about all of us being bred in test tubes. That book probably had an important message to it, but I lost interest after the first chapter. I looked over at Thomas Edwards sitting next to me and came to the conclusion that confirmation class was becoming the worst thing that ever happened to me.

. . .

I spent the end of class living up to the farce. I smiled politely at Thomas and confirmed with Lauren when we would meet at the Sixteenth Street Mall. We would wander around downtown and get all chummy with each other. My stomach would churn the whole time. Lauren would wander around completely clueless, and Thomas would get exactly what he wanted — more moments of what he lost from the party.

I did have one thing going for me though. At least he couldn't talk directly to me about what had happened. All night long, he played this same little game of pretending we had never made each other's acquaintance. I could keep up the charade, and he would have to play along, too. Lauren would think she had planned the perfect evening. I just wanted to scream at her, but I knew that would break down the pretense Thomas and I had put up for her benefit.

I could use this to my advantage. Lauren would be with us the whole time, and he would never have the opportunity to confront me about the incident. This would only happen as long as I continued to play up to this farce. He could count on me not to destroy that fragile deception because if I did break down and exclaimed I knew Thomas then I would have had to explain how. If I had to explain how, then I would be required to tell all the gory details of that evening. I was okay with this, and by the way Thomas acted, I think he was on the same page. In a weird, bizarre way, my mortal enemy also became my greatest collaborator.

I just confused myself even more with thoughts like this.

Anyway, we had set up a time and a place where we would meet each other the next Friday night. I said my goodbyes to get out of that personal Hell as fast as I could. At that moment, Lauren said something that would haunt me all the way home, "I think I see a friendship blossoming."

Why would she say something like that? I had planned to hang out with her and Thomas one night and then never again. I had no intention of seeing him again once I did my "duty" and showed him around. What did she expect? Did she want us to call each other every night to talk about how our days had gone? Were we supposed to hang out every weekend looking for exciting things to do during the most unexciting time of the year? Were we supposed to cut little gashes in the palms of our hands and mix our blood together so we could claim each other as blood brothers for eternity? I hadn't committed to this. Thomas probably didn't feel this way either. I mean, what were we? Were we so desperate that we needed some high school girl to hook us up in this eternal friendship? I had friends at school. Okay, maybe not, but at least I had a good friend in Tessa. Thomas was also capable of making friends. He went to some school where he could make friends with plenty of guys, so why would he need his cousin to help him out? This was totally and completely embarrassing, and I needed Tessa to help me figure it out.

I scheduled another session with her at Red Rocks. We could work out this problem together. I needed to make sure I made it to my next Monday night shift, so I scheduled our rap session for Tuesday night. I just told my father I had to get some work done at the library. It worked rather well because he had just gotten my progress report. My grades caused a lot of friction in my house, especially my grade in English. He demanded that I bring them up. I knew that I could do this, but I needed to take care of some of my bigger problems before I tackled that one.

Chapter Ten

Tristan Adamson
Literature and Composition
Mrs. Baker

Individuality

As every adult can tell you, teenagers know everything. They know what our society will find exciting even before society knows. Teenagers set the latest trends in life, and let's face it, there is nothing more important. People won't treat you with respect if you hide behind a business suit or tie. I still don't know why some people consider this fashion the most powerful in the world. We should consider the most powerful ones to be those who display their individuality through their dress. Just look at the students of any high school in America, and you'll be able to determine who are the most powerful by the way they dress. They set the trends, and show off their individualism.

A girl will express her individuality by pushing the limits of the dress code to the extreme in order to exude sex. She will figure exactly how short her skirt can be without getting in trouble for it. In fact, these girls are constantly stopped by teachers and administration who will ask the girls to stand with their arms straight down to see if the skirt length meets with the school's dress code policy. The girls know they can use this to their advantage. They will make a big deal about the faculty mistreating them. They will stomp their feet; they will challenge the authority; they will make sure that every student in the hallway at the time will notice. Once they have the perfect audience, they dangle their arms to their sides and show the administrators that they know how to follow the dress code.

The best way for a teenage girl to show off her individuality is for her to join the cheerleading team. Schools allow this so they can sponsor the cool without these individuals having to break the rules. Have you seen how short they make those skirts? The faculty should stop every one of those cheerleaders for wearing too short of a skirt during Fridays before football games. But the girls get away with this because they're wearing something emblazoned with the school's mascot or if their individuality extended so far that they had abnormally short arms. The school only sponsors the truly individual girls by allowing them to break the rules.

The boys have to worry about other things in order to show off their individuality. Boys can wear certain T-shirts. If you want to learn the rules for these T-shirts, look at the sports page of your local newspaper. First, decide which sport has the most prominence at that time, football, basketball, or baseball. Never consider hockey the most important sport unless the local team has made it into the Stanley Cup playoffs. Once you know which sport is the most popular, you need to figure out which teams to follow. College teams work better then professional teams. You then go out to your local clothing store and buy clothes that point your allegiance to those particular teams even though you might know nothing about any of them. This helps with boys' individuality in two ways. First, by wearing the colors of the most popular teams, they show off their individuality. Second, they can also talk the talk of all the other popular individuals. They do this by always getting into an argument or an agreement about how the team they chose is one of the best that has ever played the sport. The fold of individuals will automatically bring them in and they are instantly popular. As soon as I figure out the right team's jersey to wear, they will bring me into this fold too.

Even though teenagers express their individuality better than anyone else, all teenagers hold onto a secret they never tell adults. They only put up a façade in order to look more together than they actually feel. They don't know a thing about themselves. They don't know what they want. The media and society easily influence them. Even though we may look like true individuals, we just follow a crowd in order to fit in.

It's like Macbeth. He didn't have an ambitious bone in his body. He could care less if they crowned him king of Scotland. He cared only about being a general and receiving the praise of those around him. He was like everybody before they reach their teenage years. Middle schoolers live in complete bliss and could care less what other people think about them.

But then high school comes along and all of a sudden people can influence each and every teenager. They get pushed this way and that to become something they don't want to be just so they fit into society. In Macbeth's case, his wife, Lady Macbeth, does the pushing. She acts like every teenager's parent, teacher, or commercial that happens to be on TV. Just like she wanted Macbeth to become king of Scotland, these influences encourage teenagers to become something they might not necessarily want to become. This crushes a teenager's individuality.

All of these pressures made Macbeth go insane. No person can overcome all of the pressure to become an individual. The ones who fight against these pressures go insane. The ones that decide to start wearing business suits, or in Macbeth's case, a crown, lose their individuality. No wonder teachers and parents consider teenagers complete nutcases. These people should stop playing Lady Macbeth and start to nurture the individuals that struggle to emerge.

So, in conclusion, even though teenagers only have one time in their lives to express their individuality, people in their lives crush that individuality. Or another way of putting it, all teenagers are insane.

. . .

For some reason, Mrs. Baker liked this essay better than any of the others I had turned in. She gave me a C on it, albeit a minus. But, considering I really needed to bring up this grade before my dad killed me, I would take it. She didn't even need to whisper when we had our conference. Oddly enough, when she praised me and told me all the wonderful things I did in my essay, the rest of the students in the class stopped listening to what she said and got to work on reading the final act of *Macbeth*. What a bunch of hypocrites. They will never pat the back of a fellow student who finally has done something well, but if they smell blood on the tracks, they will cluster around to watch the death and destruction. Bloodsuckers! They missed a lot of juicy notes, because Mrs. Baker still had some wonderful critiques for how to improve my next essay. She shrouded it in a "great job" statement followed by a "but" statement. It made me wonder what she really liked about my writing — the reasons for *good* writing or the reasons for *bad* writing. I barely listened to the notes, but paid more attention to her reading them to decide which one really got her off.

First, she told me she still really enjoyed my voice — great, a note I've already gotten on every one of my other essays, no change in facial expression, but she still wishes that I would stop using first and second-person pronouns. Her brow furrowed in frustration, and I really wanted to console her by saying that I wouldn't use them anymore. But I must've slept through that lesson in grade school, because I still couldn't point out a first and second-person pronoun to save my life. In fact, I have a hard time figuring out what a pronoun looks like. If some random word like "it" was a pronoun, I wouldn't be able to identify "it."

Secondly, she pointed out that I actually addressed the prompt about *Macbeth* this time. She said it showed that I had read the play. Actually, I had watched a version of it on PBS and halfway through I realized that it wasn't a strange, back-in-time episode of *Star Trek: The Next Generation*, so I decided to finish watching it. But she added that it took me a long time to get to this part, and I had scattered my ideas all over the place. She wished that I could keep my focus. She looked at me and smiled during this portion while she nodded her head up and down.

Lastly, it impressed her that I could connect the character of Macbeth to my own life. Her smile grew really large at this point, and she actually arched her back a little as pride welled in her bosom, but she needed to point out the fallacies in my argument, primarily that I talked about teenagers in the plural, being an individual, singular. Her look of pride took on a look of contempt that showed me it didn't take a genius to figure this out.

She wanted to leave me on a high note, so she told me about her pleasure that I finally got the heading right on my paper.

I've come to the conclusion that all English teachers are sadistic witches that spend all their free time analyzing television commercials and thinking of new ways to destroy the hopes and ambitions of every student who walks into their classes.

Chapter Eleven

I met Tessa up at Red Rocks. The weather had really started to turn, and even though I always knew it would come to Denver eventually, the first snowstorm always took me by surprise. Denverites hide under blankets, fluffy down jackets, and goofy-looking stocking caps. We dream of days when the sun will shine again and the winds won't tear through our skin, numbing our bones during the months of November, December, January, February, and sometimes March, and every once in a while April. I knew I would have to take these same precautions soon, but I could still squeeze what time I could outdoors while it was still available to me.

The weather wasn't that bad. The snow barely spat out of the sky. Big, fluffy flakes would float gently through the air to be gobbled up quickly by the still-warm concrete jungle humanity forged on the edge of the wilderness. The smarter snowflakes would gather on the grassy regions with all of their friends, only to wait for the sun to dismiss them when it poked its warm face through the gathering clouds.

Even Denver hid from view behind a layer of fluffy grey. It made Red Rocks the perfect quiet place to collect my thoughts and pick the mind of one of my best friends. A runner offered the only other noise in the place as he clopped his Nike shoes up and down the stairs of the amphitheater.

Tessa had already lit a cigarette and gently puffed away on it. "I don't understand your problem, Tristan."

There were times that Tessa frustrated me as much as Mrs. Baker because she wouldn't listen to my problems. Instead, she would blow them off as something not important. "What do you mean you don't understand my problem? I have to show downtown Denver to the one person I have been trying to avoid and I have to act excited about it. How can you not see what the problem is?"

Tessa leaned in closer to me. She stabbed each point she made with her smoking cigarette as if to emphasize its importance. "The problem is *you*, Tristan. You constantly hide. You run away from every situation that ever comes your way, and you blow even the smallest problem out of proportion like it's the scariest thing that has ever happened to anybody."

"You shock me, Tessa. After all we have been through, you act like you don't know me at all."

"No, Tristan, you are wrong. I do know you. I know you better than anybody else in this world, because you don't run away from me. If you have a problem with one of your teachers, you take all of the bullshit they throw at you, and then you wander back to your seat without stating your case. When you have a problem with your father, you hide behind a bowl of cereal and do whatever he wants you to do. And now here comes this guy, Thomas Edwards, and you do everything in your power to hide from him. You duck behind the line when he comes into the Burger House, and then you pretend to puke and go rushing out the back door. When he shows up at your confirmation class, you skate out of the building before he has a chance to talk to you. And now when you could have a good time with him, you hide behind some girl you barely know. You know what the saddest thing is?"

I don't know if she expected me to answer her or not, but I sat there and stared out into the cloud that blanketed Red Rocks.

"You hide from yourself."

I turned and stared at Tessa as she sucked another drag off her cigarette. She blew out the smoke and let it collect with the cloud that surrounded us. Eventually, she looked over at me and said, "What? It's true, Tristan. You hide from your true self all the time."

I don't know why I sat there and listened to her advice, because she never gave me anything I could use anyway. I got up from the seat and looked over at her. "That's the most insulting thing I've ever heard. How dare you sit there and pretend that you know me so well? I don't know why I come to you for advice, because you give me nothing but crap. I'm done listening to your shit."

I walked away into the cloud. Unfortunately, I could hear her voice rebounding off the perfect acoustics of the amphitheater. "Thank you for proving my point, Tristan."

Needless to say, Tessa and I didn't talk as much after that night.

. . .

I now needed to prove Tessa wrong. How dare she claim that I just go along with what others want me to do? Does she think I run away from any controversy thrown in my path? I needed to show her that I was a bigger person than her by not hiding from confrontation. I went to the Sixteenth Street Mall to meet Lauren and her cousin, Thomas.

The Denver Tourist Board claims the Sixteenth Street Mall as one of its biggest attractions. They boast that the outdoor mall stretches for a little over a mile through the heart of the city. They block cars from traveling down the street, and all of the fanciest shops and trendiest restaurants operate here. You can find the latest bargain, or some of the best food Colorado has to offer. You can also pass the time there by people watching. People from all different walks of life go there to hang out. Businessmen after a hard day's work, head to one of the many bars to unwind. The theater crowd hustles off to performances in the nearby Denver Performing Arts Center. The teenage crowd looks for other teenagers to hang out with. The sports crowd cheers on their teams in the many sports bars or heads off to the many stadiums that surround the mall. Even the homeless look for a free handout or a game of chess at one of the many concrete tables that line the middle of the mall's street.

I couldn't find a more perfect location to meet Thomas and Lauren because the hustle and bustle of the crowd would not allow Thomas to confront me. He would have to be on his best behavior, and I would get off scot-free. *Stick that in your pipe and smoke it, Tessa.*

I even arranged for the perfect place to meet them, Union Station. It stood a little bit off from the mall, but the Light Rail made its last stop there. It is also the place where trains leave from Denver, so a lot of foot traffic stomps through the building.

I got there a little early to scope out the place before Thomas and Lauren arrived. I was very happy with what I saw when I got there. People crowded the place celebrating the first night that Denver christened the ski train for the season, an event that always brought many people out. Skiing hadn't really started yet, but the train offered a scenic ride through the mountains to Winter Park, one of Colorado's more idyllic mountain towns. Many people dressed up in nice clothes to enjoy their trip, and I found a nice bench near the Light Rail stop. This way I could see Lauren and Thomas before they could see me.

I kept watching the Light Rail trains pull in and out, and I started wondering if they would even make it. People would load off the trains and mingle into the crowd or make their way into what the night had to offer, but I never saw either Thomas or Lauren. I started to think I could get off easy, when suddenly I saw Thomas looking out the window of one of the Light Rail trains. He smiled and waved at me. I smiled back, but something felt out of place. I couldn't see Lauren anywhere. She wasn't sitting next to him on the Light Rail. I couldn't even see her standing somewhere in the background.

My heart started to beat a little faster. How could this happen to me? I started to wish I had read that John Steinbeck novel assigned to me during my freshmen year in high school. Somehow it related to my plans, but I couldn't figure out how. My plans were going to Hell. They shifted to an even deeper plain of Hell when Thomas stepped off the Light Rail train and the announcer of Union Station said, "*Now boarding the ski train to Winter Park. Now boarding the ski train to Winter Park.*"

All of a sudden, the crowd stood up and moved off towards another platform nowhere near the one I inhabited. I looked around as my security blanket disappeared and Thomas walked over. The closer he got, the harder my heart beat and the more the crowd dispersed. My mouth got dryer, and by the time he reached me, we were the only two people left in Union Station.

He waved again. "Hi, Tristan."

I waved back sheepishly and said, "Hi, Thomas. What happened to Lauren?"

"She ditched us because I asked her to."

"Why would you do that?"

Thomas walked up to me and stuck his face into my face. "Because I wanted to do this for such a long time." He grabbed the sides of my face and kissed me.

Part Two

God

Chapter Twelve

A smell, a sound, a taste, or a touch can take you back in time. They are actually all strong triggers. Like when I smell fresh-baked bread, I'm transported back to younger days when my mom would make me a peanut butter and jelly sandwich with a loaf of Wonder bread, just opened. Or if I hear the Beatles' "Yellow Submarine," my memory transports me back to my first grade music class where Mrs. Giess taught us how to sing that song. Every time I have the powdery goodness of an "elephant ear," I think about hanging out at Elitch Garden's Amusement Park and getting ready to ride the Twister for the first time. And every time I slip into fresh, clean sheets, I think back to the night I would snuggle under the covers in anticipation of Christmas morning.

My five senses have always triggered memories for me, but I didn't know how much power their combination could have. The faint smell of Thomas's cologne, the muffled groan he gave as his lips touched mine, the minty taste of his breath, and the feel of his soft hair as I ran my fingers through it, brought me back to that night a couple of weeks earlier when we met in the basement of some random house. The kiss swept me away. It felt so wonderful. It felt so right. Emotions of yearning welled up inside me, and I started to wonder why I had spent so much time hiding from this individual. He made me feel good, just like he had that night two weeks earlier. His tongue played with mine. Our embrace brought us closer together.

I don't know why, but Thomas must have used the same detergent to wash his clothes as the one in that laundry room. As soon as I got a whiff of it, I started to have the same reservations I had that night. Why does kissing another boy feel so right? I must have something wrong with me. They didn't teach me to believe this. My parents and teachers have told me to find a beautiful woman to help populate the earth with new Catholics. Can gay people impregnate women? What will my parents think? Will they accept this? Will they try to fix me? *Can* they fix me, or will other boys always excite me for the rest of my life? Am I condemned to live my existence in Hell because of this affliction? Will God no longer accept me as one of his flock? Will he send a gaggle of nuns with rulers after me to make my knuckles bleed? What was I doing kissing this boy?

On the night of the party, I pulled away from Thomas and his kiss. I looked him in the eyes, and he smiled at me. It sent all the conflicting messages in my head over the cliff, and I needed to escape. Luckily, I had my back to the stairs so I turned around and ran up the steps. I kept running from the party, down the street, and all the way to the nearest bus stop. I slowly figured out how to get home that evening. Tessa yelled at me the next day because I had left the party without telling her. She had driven and didn't know what happened to me. I had to text her halfway home to let her know where I was and that I would explain everything to her in the morning.

I pacified her easily, because she knew I had these weird thoughts running through my head. She always tried to tell me not to worry, but I could never accept it. She didn't know what I was going through. She has always attended a public school and didn't know the power of Hell, and God, and nuns with rulers. I still trusted her enough to tell her my darkest secrets. In fact, I have only told her and no one else about my preference for boys over girls. She kept telling me I should talk to somebody else about it.

She couldn't possibly understand what that would mean for me. Who in Hell am I supposed to tell? If I go and tell my parents, they will disown me. If I tell my school counselor, she will try to make me see the error of my ways. If I tell Father Brett, he will excommunicate me. If I act on these behaviors, then I just give into an antisocial attitude. It's bad enough that I don't belong to any kind of group at school, but now she wants me to talk about things that would alienate me even more.

No, I could not act on these behaviors, and I couldn't tell anybody about them. I needed to repress them until I could get over this phase in my life. I would grow out of it. I would emerge from high school as a perfectly normal heterosexual man ready to have sex with thousands of available women. Then why did that moment with Thomas feel so good?

It was too much for me to deal with as I stood on the platform of the train station. I pulled back from him. It forced me to look again into those beautiful brown eyes. He smirked. My past revisited me, and I did the only thing that made sense to me. I turned around and ran off to the nearest bathroom so I could puke.

. . .

I don't know what I expected, but I never thought Thomas would chase me into the bathroom. He did, but not to cause problems. He came to see if everything was alright. I know I looked like a complete fool as my lunch and breakfast burst forth from my mouth. I could feel the acid burn the roof of my mouth as bile coated my tongue. I didn't have to worry about Thomas wanting to kiss me again. If he had, I would've started to worry about his sanity. What he did instead was endearing and kind. It made me look at him in a new light.

He patted me on the back. He stroked my hair. He provided me with comforting words until I got everything out of my system.

When my stomach stopped flipping over, I looked into the toilet and saw chunks of food floating around. Spit dangled from my lips, and snot bubbled from my nose. I could feel sweat on my brow from the exertion my body went through during this violent act. I knew if I stared into the toilet bowl much longer, I would start the process all over again. I reached up a weak hand to flush the toilet, and I turned over so I could sit in the stall and relax.

I closed my eyes and tried to steady my breath. You would think my ability to puke on cue would prepare me for the way it could wipe me out, but for some reason that time in Denver's Union Station it took a lot out of me. This might have happened because I hadn't brought it on through my own willpower. Instead, it came through more honest means.

My energy started to return when I heard a voice above me, "I thought you might want these." I looked up to see Thomas holding a wad of paper towels. "You need to clean yourself up a bit."

I thanked him and grabbed the wad of paper towels. The snot, sweat, saliva, and puke stains wiped easily away, and it helped me feel a little better. When I finished throwing up and could look around at my environment, I realized how poorly they cleaned the bathrooms at Union Station. Yes, they scrubbed them every once in a while, but it couldn't take away the old stain on the floor tiles, or the scratched mirrors, or the bathroom stall doors littered with graffiti. I decided not to hand the used paper towels back to Thomas, because whatever I did with them wouldn't hurt the ambiance of the place anymore. They ended up on the floor of the stall next to me.

Thomas stood at the stall door looking down at me. He had his hand on his hip and a worried look on those amazing brown eyes. "You know, I'm starting to wonder if this thing between you and me will work out. I mean, you seem like a nice guy and everything, but I'm starting to wonder if you might not have some mental problems."

I tried to wave off what he said as something humorous, but he maintained his worried look.

He crouched down to look me in the eyes. "No, I'm serious. Of all the times I've run into you, you've only acted normal once, and only because Lauren was there. You ignored me one of the other times, ran out on me another, and this is the second time you've puked. Everything okay?"

I gave him a thumbs-up from where I squatted on the bathroom floor.

He tapped his temple. "No, I meant up here?"

I had the same question bouncing around my head ever since I kissed a girl. It didn't excite me like I knew it should've. And since I knew that wasn't a normal reaction, I had asked myself on numerous occasions if I was "okay." Now, somebody crouching right in front of me forced me to face the same dreaded question.

I hid my eyes in my hands. "I don't know."

I don't know what effect my reaction had on Thomas, but I knew I couldn't look him in the eyes to find out. I was really making a mess of the whole situation. I didn't really know what I wanted at that moment. One second, I wanted him to leave, and the next I wanted him to rub my back until the tears stopped flowing. Confrontation or comfort, I couldn't decide which one I wanted. My emotions were as messed up as my thoughts. I didn't know what to do with myself, but I knew for sure I didn't want to spend any more time on that dirty bathroom floor. I think Thomas felt the same way because he asked, "You've never kissed a boy before, have you?"

I lowered my hands from my face and shook my head.

He offered his hand to me and said, "Come on. Let's go get a cup of coffee and talk. I can help you with your problem."

I took his hand as he helped me up. As we walked out of the bathroom, he said, "By the way, do you want a piece of gum?

· · ·

Thomas surprised me even more because here I was, supposed to be showing this guy around town, but instead, *he* took *me* to a place

I never knew existed, a small café down by the river called Paris on the Platte. I had never seen a cooler place. Paris on the Platte housed itself in an old brick building with small tables squeezed into various nooks and crannies. Paintings from local artists hung on the walls. Bookcases held tattered copies of great pieces of literature. For the first time in my life, I wanted to pick one up and start reading. Cabinets displayed various games customers could play at any time. People lounged on comfy couches and drank tea or coffee.

Thomas led me to a small table in a corner to give us some privacy. I picked up one of the small menus on the table and started looking through it. A waitress came up and smiled at Thomas. "Good to see you again, Thomas. How have you been?"

"Great," he replied.

"Do you want the usual?"

"Yeah, that sounds good."

"And for your friend?"

I looked up from the list of weird-sounding drinks. The waitress stood there expectantly. "I —" My mouth hung open, not able to say anything else. I looked over at Thomas for some help.

He seemed to understand my dilemma, because he looked up at the waitress and said, "He'll have café mocha." He then looked back at me. "You like chocolate, don't you?"

"I —" My mind went blank.

Thomas looked back at the waitress and said, "He'll have café mocha."

The waitress left and I looked around trying to absorb everything. Even though this café mocha scared me, I really loved the place. None of the walls had televisions on them, and I bet nobody in the place ever heard of ESPN. Some bluesy tune with a simple beat played on the stereo and it automatically connected with my soul. I looked at Thomas and asked, "How do you know about this place?"

"Oh, I've been coming here since I moved to Denver. A couple of friends from Oregon knew about the place, and they told me it would feel like home."

"Does it feel like home?"

"Of course, I come down here all the time. I love the artistic feel of this place and I really like the fact that they don't focus all their attention on football or basketball or whatever sport the Avalanche play."

I looked back at him in astonishment. "Do you mean some places don't care about sports?"

He nodded. "Yeah, Oregon."

"I've got to move there someday."

Thomas glanced around. "Well, if you like this place then you would love Oregon."

The waitress returned carrying a tray with two large coffee mugs on it. Steam drifted off the top of them. She placed a white mug in front of Thomas and a milky-brown mug in front of me. I peered down into it. Whipped cream and chocolate sprinkles overflowed from the top. Even though it looked amazing, I still worried about the taste.

Thomas had already taken his cup and sipped out of it. He could see my hesitation and said, "Try it. You'll love it."

"What did you get me?"

"A café mocha."

"Yeah, I heard you call it that once before, but what did you get me?"

"A cup of really strong coffee blended together with hot chocolate."

The combination intrigued me, and I lifted the large mug to my lips. I took a sip of it. It tasted like a Hersey's chocolate bar with a twinge of bitter aftertaste. It warmed me up as it slid down my throat, and I could feel my eyes pop open as the power of the caffeine rushed through my bloodstream. I couldn't figure out why I had never tasted anything like it.

"So what do you think?"

"I think I've found love. Why haven't I tasted anything like this before?"

Thomas laughed. "I can see that no one has ever introduced you to Starbuck's before. Every middle schooler treats it like a rite of passage where I come from. You can't spit without hitting one of their stores in Portland."

I took another sip and it gave me courage. "I still don't understand."

Thomas looked at me questioningly. "What is there to understand? Portland has a lot of Starbuck's."

"No, about you?"

"Ah!" Thomas leaned back. "So we get to this part of the conversation!"

"Well, I'm a bit confused. If you knew about this place, then why did you need me to show you around downtown? I thought you just moved here, but you mentioned being here for a couple of months. Did you really just move here? What happened to Lauren? Why didn't she come down? Why do you always seem to show up wherever I am? It kind of creeps me out. Have you been stalking me? Why did you kiss me? That must mean you know about me. How do you know about me? Only one person knows about me, but somehow you knew about me. Do you have psychic abilities? That kind of creeps me out even more. Can you read minds? What am I thinking right now? Don't answer that because I don't want to know."

Thomas let out a long, heart-felt laugh. "How many questions do you have? You know I can only answer one at a time."

I started to weigh the questions in my mind. I really wanted to ask him one question in particular, but the answer frightened me. I asked one of the safer ones first. "What happened to Lauren?"

Thomas took another sip of his drink. "She stayed at home."

"Why didn't she come down with you?"

"Because that would've ruined my plan."

His answer hit me across the face like a sack full of quarters.

"Plan?"

"Yeah, we worked it out last week. I really wanted to get to know you, but you didn't seem very interested in me. I had to work out a way I could force you to talk to me. I knew I would see Lauren in class, and I thought maybe she could approach you first, and then draw me into the conversation afterward."

"You mean you manipulated me?"

"No, I would never do that. Drink your mocha before it gets cold."

I took another sip of my drink and my anger faded away as the hot liquid warmed my bones.

Thomas continued. "No, I waited out in the parking lot until I saw you enter the class, then I texted her so she'd know you had arrived. She then texted me back when she had made contact with you. This way you couldn't find an excuse to avoid me. Lucky for us, you showed up early."

"So she knew what happened at the party?"

"Yeah, I told her."

I couldn't wait any longer, so I blurted out the question that really bothered me, "How did you know about me?"

Thomas chuckled again. "The way you looked at me told me everything. You don't get that kind of look from somebody with more than a mild interest in you."

Terror shot through me. Could everybody see this? Did everybody know about my condition? He must've seen this in my face because he said, "Don't worry. I can recognize it in you, and other gay people have that ability, too. A few girls have it. Lauren said she knew about you in middle school."

"How could she have known about me in middle school? *I* didn't even know about me in middle school."

Thomas had a good laugh at that. "Most people don't realize who they are in middle school. They try to fit in too much. In fact, most people in *high school* don't know who they are. It's part of this journey we call life. We voyage out to discover our true identity, and sometimes we need people to help us along the way. Try to think of me as a navigator." Thomas patted my hand.

I pulled my hand back. "Well, I don't like the way you've helped me so far. I'm still trying to figure out all these feelings bouncing around in my head, and the last couple of weeks have made me even more confused."

Thomas returned his hand to his side. "I see. I moved a little too fast. I need to start thinking about you. I should've thought about how much I struggled with my identity when I first accepted who I really was. Maybe I need to take things a little slower so you feel more comfortable with yourself."

"I'd like that." Instantly, a huge weight lifted from my heart.

. . .

Even though I still hadn't discovered who I was, I felt more like me then I had in a long time. We walked around downtown Denver and watched as workers prepared for the holidays. City workers strung up lights on the Sixteenth Street Mall but none were turned on yet. Stores placed Christmas trees in their front windows, and signs exclaimed the wonderful deals shoppers could have on Black Friday. I know the event was still three weeks away and I would usually make some snide comment about how society had gone down the tubes due to the fact they barely let us get through Halloween before throwing a new holiday down our throat. But because of Thomas, the fact that stores were preparing for the inevitable didn't bother me that much. The night just oozed with awesomeness.

We laughed at the old folks as they tried to fit in with the younger crowds. We bargained with some bums to try and get some alcohol from one of them, but to no avail. We talked with the skaters and punks that hung out on the mall. We perused shops and restaurants and talked about which we'd like to visit later. When the night came to a close, we made our way back down to the Light Rail station. The *F* took him back to his neighborhood, and the *C* took me back to mine. My train showed up first. We gave each other a simple kiss goodnight and I hopped on the train. I waved good-bye to Thomas as the train pulled away, and he blew me another kiss. Our time together ended perfectly. He didn't pressure me into doing anything I didn't want to do, and I felt comfortable in my skin the whole evening.

I'd gone on other dates, and each time, awkwardness prevailed. I always worried about how I presented myself and whether I said the right thing or not. My date would comment on the awkwardness of the situation, and it would make everything even more uncomfortable. We would both laugh at nothing and sweat our way through the final moments together. I would go home and never hear from her again. Only one time did a girl call me the next day, and in reality that turned out all right, but I was still more comfortable never hearing from any of them ever again. If the girl went to my school, we would go back to ignoring each other in the classrooms and hallways. Some might consider it a strange existence, but I couldn't really see how my experience was much different from any other high school student.

I might have had a terrible time on these dates because they were girls, but I think I felt something more in this case. I felt a bond with Thomas. I could have gone out with a different boy, and I would have experienced something very similar to the dates I had with the girls. Something special came with Thomas. He took extra time to set up this date, even though I could've run away in terror. He assured me that life wasn't that bad, and if we took things slowly I could find some real enjoyment in this relationship. I felt like a human being around him instead of a jumble of nerves like I felt around almost everybody else. He accepted me for me, and I didn't have to put up a facade in order to get along with him.

I was at ease with the world for the first time in a long time. No teacher giving me bad grades on essays I had slaved over could hurt me. No program forcing me to believe in something I wasn't sure I believed in could touch me. Even my father didn't have any effect on me as I rode that train back home. I watched as the town flickered by and the tracks gently rocked the compartment back and forth. Before I knew it, I had fallen into a gentle sleep. The conductor woke me up when we reached the end of the line. Lucky for me, it was also my stop. I thanked him kindly and went back out into the cold November air.

Chapter Thirteen

I remember while going through Catholic school every year my theology teacher would introduce a new aspect of Catholicism to us. They did this so that when we reached the eighth grade, we would have a solid foundation of the Catholic faith. In the first grade, we memorized the Our Father. In second grade, we learned everything we needed to know to receive the holy sacrament of the Eucharist. The next year, we learned all about Mother Mary and topped it all off with the Hail Mary — not the moment the Pittsburg Steelers made it to the Super Bowl, but the name of the prayer they said to make it there. In fourth grade, we worried ourselves sick about having to confess our sins for the first time. By the end of fifth grade, they forced us to memorize the Ten Commandments, and in the sixth they asked us not only to recite the Apostle's Creed, but to understand its meaning as well. I really struggled in the seventh grade. They taught us the Beatitudes that year. The nuns forced us to not only memorize them, but to understand all of their contradictory messages.

Basically, the way the story went, Jesus decided to preach to a bunch of followers on a mountain of olives. I don't know why he decided to preach there, because no one had invented the martini yet, but he thought he should deliver his most important message while standing on a pile of fruit. These messages explained how we should live our lives, and Father Brett focused on these during his next lesson. I sat there and paid attention like a good little boy. Sitting next to Thomas made it easier. We didn't hold hands or give people any indication of our blossoming relationship, but it comforted me to know he sat right next to me through the lecture. It made the words Father Brett said clear for the first time ever. I started to understand these Beatitudes even though they still contradicted themselves.

We started off with, *"Blessed are the poor in spirit, for theirs is the kingdom of Heaven."* Basically, if you muddle your way through all the mush, it means that a person finds their treasure wherever their heart lies. It doesn't involve monetary possessions, but instead the true loves in our lives. Being popular doesn't hold any joy, but instead we should try to follow our hearts. I knew that I had this one down because my peers would never consider me popular.

Jesus's next lesson was, *"Blessed are those who mourn, for they shall be comforted."* Jesus wanted us to have compassion for our brothers and sisters and not be so concerned with ourselves. I didn't have this one down yet, but I don't think any teenager does. Some adults even have a problem with this one.

The famous *"Blessed are the meek, for they shall inherit the earth"* followed next. Jesus wanted to warn us against the most dangerous of all sins — pride. We should never think of ourselves as better than someone else. The type of person who follows this Beatitude does not over-compete or seek power. I could see most Americans having a problem with this one. It went against most of the founding principles of this country.

"Blessed are those who hunger and thirst for justice, for they shall be satisfied." I knew I had this one because at that moment I couldn't find any better satisfaction while sitting next to Thomas.

I really liked the next one. *"Blessed are the merciful, for they shall obtain mercy."* The phrase "What would Jesus do?" came from this one. He did not judge or condemn any one. After walking around hoping that others would not judge me, I knew the danger of judging others. I needed to reject no one. I had started doing this with Thomas and felt a joy in my heart unlike any I had ever felt. Father Brett even confirmed this belief when he said, "*Do not judge and you will not be judged; do not condemn, and you will not be condemned.*" Mrs. Baker could do with hearing that advice.

The next one made me think. "*Blessed are the pure in heart, for they shall see God.*" I had never seen God before, and it always bugged me. Father Brett assured me that the false front we put up causes this. I knew I put on a front every day, and by doing so, I lied to myself daily. Maybe God never revealed Himself to me because of this. I gave a sheepish grin to Thomas while Father Brett explained this to us. Thomas returned a knowing smirk.

Thomas epitomized the next one. "*Blessed are the peacemakers, for they shall be called the sons of God.*" Father Brett explained to us that we should look for the ultimate goal — inner peace. I knew I looked for this all the time. I hadn't felt inner peace since I tried to kiss a girl. How could I, a jumbled mess of conflict, help others with their conflicts? Fortunately for me, Thomas seemed to have his stuff together and maybe he could help me get mine together. I resolved that if I ever figured myself out, I would help people like me, just like Thomas does.

The last one always haunted me, and it haunted me even more the night Father Brett mentioned it again. "*Blessed are those who are persecuted because they are good, for theirs is the kingdom of Heaven.*" Basically, this meant I needed to find happiness with the cross God gave me to bear. I always hated it when they told me that, but I should stand up for what is right, even if that meant doing it alone. I sat alone a lot, but if I stood up, others might notice my plight.

Chapter Fourteen

Tristan Adamson
Literature and Composition
Mrs. Baker

Unsex Me

During the time that Shakespeare wrote, people placed the ideal of manhood on display quite often. Men needed to demonstrate their power. They would do this by puffing up their chests around women and fighting among themselves. They couldn't show their emotions, especially if it meant grieving for a loved one, because doing so would require reducing oneself to the level of a woman. An insightful woman could use this knowledge about men to her advantage. Even though society was supposed to have evolved throughout the ages, it still has not matured. Men need society to view them as powerful, and women know how to use it to their advantage.

The male characters in *Macbeth* needed to constantly show off their power. This happens in the opening scene of the play after the battle with the Irish invaders. The wounded soldier comes in to tell of the courageous foray. Duncan could care less about the wounded soldier; he cared more about who fought the greatest among the ranks of his men. When he hears about Macbeth and Banquo's tribulations during the battle, he gets all excited and decides to give the more powerful of the two a promotion. Duncan doesn't care about their intellect or their spirit, but concerns himself more with their physical prowess.

High school life in the boy's locker room after gym class is exactly like this. The king of the land, the gym teacher, will walk into the locker room and look around for the weakest one of the bunch. He can spot him easily, because the others have pushed him around. The gym teacher will walk up to this weakling who is trying to recover from either an asthma attack or the embarrassment of wearing only a towel, and ask him the name of the most triumphant participant during gym class that day. The weakling will wheeze away while pointing to the one who threw the most touchdown passes, or sunk the most three-pointers, or broke the most ribs. The gym teacher will congratulate the chosen one and then promote him to quarterback, or point guard, or lunchroom bully.

A strong man cannot show one's true emotions in Shakespeare's Scottish landscape. It doesn't matter how tragic the moment, a man must never break down and cry. Women do that kind of thing. Macduff makes this mistake. When MacBeth brutally murders his wife and children, Malcolm urges Macduff not to break down upon hearing the news. He wants him to take it like a man. Men live in a harsh world, because they cannot grieve for the loss of their loved ones due to some silly rule about manhood.

Society also forbids teenage boys from showing their emotions. When slugged in the head during gym class by a ball, or elbow, or floor, the gym teacher will run up to said boy and tell him to walk it off. If the boy begins to cry, the gym teacher will chide him to take off his tampon and take it like a man. Not wanting to look like a girl, the teenager will fall for this ploy and the gym teacher believes he has made the world a better place by molding the young boy into a man.

Women know about this dynamic. They know how to make it work to their advantage. Lady Macbeth shows wonderfully how women can push men to do what they want. They just question his manhood. All the terrible things that happen in the play are put into motion by Lady Macbeth. She does this because she wants to be married to a powerful, strong man, not some wimp satisfied with the generalship offered by his king. She would do all the dirty work herself, but why should she when she has a man who can do her dirty work for her. In fact, she believes that every man needs to live up to this civic pride by killing and maiming all the people that get in the way of his wife's ambitious plans. Lady Macbeth tells the audience she wishes to be unsexed so shouldn't have to rely on the slovenly ways of her husband, and she can do the work herself. This way she'd know the job would get done right.

Throughout the ages, women have not changed. They still use a man's need to be manly to manipulate him. This dynamic reaches it most impressively as seen between star football players and their cheerleading girlfriends. Much like the arguments about the gym teacher, star football players do not need much encouragement to act manly when it comes to sports. It gets even worse when girls in short skirts cheer them on. They will start to do everything in their power to crush, dismember, or kill anybody that the cheerleader tells them to maim. This causes said cheerleaders to gain quite the ego. They play a violent kind of video game where they control certain avatars, except with real blood. The cheerleaders don't even have to worry about hurting themselves just like a video game, because once again they are not really playing. This translates itself into the school's hallways. The cheerleader will walk down the hallway expecting people to clear a path for her, since she sits on the upper echelon of the social hierarchy within the school. A lonely freshman, who doesn't understand this dynamic, will stop in her way to pick up a piece of paper he dropped. The cheerleader sees this social faux pas and of course freaks out. No one can see her kicking this fool in the gut, so she tells her star quarterback boyfriend that the freshman was looking up her skirt. Of course, the star quarterback will have to save his girlfriend's honor. Therefore, the ignorant freshman will have to visit the school nurse. All of this because the girl knows how to manipulate her boyfriend.

This just shows that Shakespeare knew more about the dynamics of the world than anybody else that has ever lived. He first saw how men were being manipulated either by themselves or by the women they married, by having the manipulator question their manhood. It still holds relevance today as it did in Shakespeare's time. This just proves the timelessness of the themes in Shakespeare's plays. I get it. He's a genius.

. . .

Mrs. Baker sat at her desk grinning like a mad banshee when my turn came to go up and listen to what she had to say about my paper. It kind of creeped me out. I looked at the other students to see if they noticed the same thing. They all pretended to do work. Bastards. Why do your friends hide when you need them? I had to face Mrs. Baker's grinning face all by myself and it scared me.

She slid my paper out from the pile and pushed it, facedown, across her obnoxiously clean desk. When it reached the spot right in front of me, she flipped it over so she could present me with my grade, a C. She spread out her hands as if she wanted to leap across the desk to give me a hug. "My pride welleth over."

I looked down at the grade and thought to myself, why should I get excited about a C? The grade would help get Dad off my back, but it still didn't deserve some kind of freak-out by an insane English teacher with jazz hands. It also didn't help that this reject from the fall musical would instantly go into the things I still needed to work on with my writing. As much as the improvement of my grade in this subjective class did place a smile on my face, I didn't want to hear what I needed to work on in the future.

Mrs. Baker apparently couldn't see my apprehension about this meeting because she decided to dive right into her feedback. She first wanted to tell me how excited she was that I could stay on topic. She was also happy that I could relate it to the modern teenagers' life because it showed that I obtained a strong grasp of the material. I wanted to ask her why I got only a *C* if I had such a strong grasp of the material.

She went on to tell me she was disappointed that I still fell into the trap of the five-paragraph essay. I didn't quite follow her argument, because I had written more than five paragraphs and even pointed that out to her. Mrs. Baker told me she recognized that mathematically I wrote more than five paragraphs, but structurally I still had written a five-paragraph essay. I will never understand a class that takes the fundamentally inarguable principles of mathematics and throws them out the window just to prove a point.

The last thing she told me as she sent me back to my seat was to remind me that my use of first person pronouns needed to stop. I went back to my seat, still wondering what a pronoun was and why they only had one person.

Chapter Fifteen

Creepy, grinning adults seemed to follow me everywhere that day because when I got home from school I found my mom and dad with huge smiles on their faces sitting at the kitchen table. My first thought was that Mrs. Baker had called to tell them about my amazing *C*. Then my mind told me to run, because my parents never condoned such a mediocre grade. Something much worse had to have happened. Either something so bad that my parents needed to break the news to me with Cheshire cat-like grins, or they did something for me they thought I would enjoy. I could only hope for the tragedy.

My mom started off, "Honey, come in here and sit down. We have something very exciting to tell you." My heart just plummeted all the way to Hell because I knew they had good news for me.

I eased myself into a chair on the far side of the kitchen table and tried to plaster a grin onto my face, but I knew it just made the moment even more insincere. "What do you want to tell me about?"

As Mom patted Dad's hand, I could see his chest welling up with excitement. He exhaled so he could let out the wonderful news, "Tristan, do you remember Mr. Wood?"

How could I forget Mr. Wood? He came over to our house on numerous occasions. In fact, his family hung out with my family a lot while I was growing up. The Woods would come over on a regular basis. Mr. and Mrs. Wood would sit upstairs with my parents and they would drink and tell stories all night long. Their daughter and son would hang downstairs with me and we would play games. Some of my fondest memories had the Wood family in it. Unfortunately, Mr. Wood's job transferred him to New York and these gatherings stopped. My dad's question had sparked a new interest in me. Maybe what they were going to tell me wasn't as bad as I had thought. "Yeah, Dad, of course I remember Mr. Wood. Why?"

My mom's excitement bubbled over. "Well, it turns out that Mr. Wood's company has transferred him back to Denver."

This was good news. "Great, when do they move back?"

My dad got a little more serious when I asked this question. "Well, nobody can just pack up their things and move overnight. They'll move out here permanently in a couple of months. Mrs. Wood will stay in New York so they can sell their place and take care of any other loose ends. Mr. Wood has decided to come out here to start work next week. While here, he'll look for a place to stay."

My mom's grin grew even larger, and she squeezed her hands tight like a toddler the night before Christmas. "It gets even better."

"I don't understand. How could it get even better?"

My mom reached her hand across the table so she could squeeze mine. I started to get nervous again. "Do you remember their daughter Emily?"

"Of course I remember Emily. She's my age."

"And she is such a nice girl." All of a sudden it hit me. My mom only commented on a girl's niceness when she wanted to hook me up with her.

My dad took a more disgusting approach by raising his eyebrows and saying, "And you should see how cute she's gotten."

I can understand my parents' concern. They had a son whose days of high hormone production were coming to an end and they started to wonder when he would ever begin to show an interest in women. They probably had a lot of questions running through their minds. Should they concern themselves with some health problems I might have? Did some terrible accident occur while I attended middle school? One time, all the boys in school liked to run around and rack each other. Could something have happened then? Did those random events turn their son into a eunuch? Or the worst of all possibilities — was their son gay?

I know they had thought that before. I could see it in my mom's eyes when she talked about the day I would find a lovely young lady to marry and we would populate the world with many small Catholic babies. I could see it in my dad's eyes while we watched Bronco's games and he commented on the sexiness of the cheerleaders. I just never had the heart to tell them the truth. It would devastate them.

I knew eventually I would have to have a conversation with them, but I'd always hoped I could avoid it. Maybe I could strike it rich and move away to some remote island filled with good-looking men, and they would never be the wiser. I could come home on the holidays and pretend that I was a heterosexual. Afterward, I could go back to my fantasy island. I could tell them I worked for the CIA, and I couldn't discuss my private or professional life with them for fear of putting them in harm's way.

I know it wasn't a very realistic fantasy, but I enjoyed entertaining thoughts like this. My other fantasy involved all of us having a loud shouting match. This scenario usually played out in my mind right after a fight with them.

If I was throwing my own pity party, I would envision them getting into some horrible tragic accident before I could tell them the way I really felt. Everybody I knew at school and at work would feel sorry for me, and I would stand in front of all of them at my parents' funeral to state that my greatest regret was never being able to tell them I was gay. Everybody in the congregation would come up and pat me on the back and console me. They would tell me that they knew my parents would have loved me, just like each and every one of them did.

I liked any one of these options better than actually "coming out" and telling my parents about my homosexuality. I knew that in the back of my mind the right thing to do was just tell them. I might experience some pain and unrest in our happy home for a while, but I still couldn't face it at that time. I could have used the moment they spent describing Emily to me to tell them about my homosexuality, but instead I chose a different path.

I looked at my parents. I put on my winningest smile, and I said with the warmest of regards, "I bet she needs somebody in town to reconnect with."

.   .   .

My mom had set up a date with Emily on Friday night. It bugged me that all of a sudden they knew my schedule at work better than they ever had before. They must have called up Dan at the Burger House and asked if I was working on Friday night. I really got creeped out when Mom told me she had arranged for me to meet up with Emily on Friday night, right after I agreed to go out with her. Just like my confirmation, I apparently didn't have a choice in the matter. I had a date with Emily whether I wanted it or not. My mom had even arranged a reservation at a restaurant for us, one of her favorites, the Italian Bistro. She bought me a fifty-dollar gift card so I wouldn't have to worry about paying for the meal myself. I looked at the amount on the card and wondered why I would need so much. My mom explained that we should order an appetizer and dessert. I needed to go all out with this meal. With the amount of time and effort Mom spent to put this dinner together, I started to wonder if she hadn't already booked a reception hall for our nuptials.

All of these thoughts gave me a panic attack. My parents had arranged for me to go on a date with a girl on a night that I had already made plans with Thomas. I couldn't say anything about it because doing so would expose my darkest and most closely held secret. I needed to get away from this insane conversation. I needed to get away from my parents. I needed to get away to some breathable space. I needed to get to Red Rocks.

I assured my mom that I was excited to take Emily out on Friday night, but I needed to get some work done at the library. I grabbed my cell phone, my backpack full of school books, a warm coat, and rushed out of the house. As I drove away, I rolled down the window so I could breathe a little easier, even though a small flurry of snow started to fall out of the sky. The snow did not cause many problems on my drive to the foothills, but a fine mist of slush created by other cars forced me to roll up my window. It made the drive through rush hour traffic and unfavorable conditions up to Red Rocks totally worth it because it meant I had the place to myself.

If Red Rocks on the off-season emulates peacefulness and reflection, it builds up a higher degree of ambiance during a November snowstorm. November snows in Denver are during the warmer part of the season, so when it snows, it comes down wet. The flakes bulk up to the huge Charlie Brown's catch-on-your-tongue sizes. They float gently through the air because the brutal winter winds have not yet picked up speed. Each individual flake does two different things. They gather up any available light and rebound it off in magnified proportions brightening up even the darkest nights. Secondly, they take any noise and muffle it. In a really strong snow, you can say something and the snow will muffle the noise so it won't even reach your own ears. It creates a strange combination. The snow illuminates a spotlight on you, but at the same time it quiets what you say so it forces you into a kind of public solitude. The feeling is enhanced even more when you find yourself alone in a large amphitheater overlooking the city.

The snow does something amazing to the city as well, coating it in a warm, fluffy blanket. All living things retreat to the comfort and safety of their abodes. They stand at their bay windows and look outside as the snow gently piles up. The people drink hot chocolate and reflect on the peacefulness of life. They don't bother themselves with their neighbors; they just draw their families closer together. At least they did in my younger days.

Now, I look for any opportunity to escape from my family. It seems that life gets crazier and more hectic with each passing year. I feel that the complications of life take away from the moments I imagine people have on days like this. I hope that when I grow older, I don't become an adult who complains about the snow. I don't know why they do it, but I suspect it has something to do with the way their lives have gotten more complicated.

I didn't worry about those complications while enjoying the snowfall on one of Colorado's most iconic spaces. I pushed those problems aside and enjoyed what nature offered until I felt a buzzing in my pocket. I knew I should've left the ugly beast at home, but I could never leave behind my cell phone. Let's face it, no teenager can leave their cell phone behind. How else could they stay connected to every other teenager they know, might know, and never will know? It's a status symbol. The more expensive the phone, the higher the teenager sits on the social ladder. Not having one's cell phone is the worst thing that could possibly happen. It shows every other teenager out there that your parents have grounded you, or they don't make enough money to pay for a cell phone, or worse, that your parents want to try and teach you the value of a dollar. Even though I wanted no one to bother me and I knew no one could demote my social status if they found me without a cell phone in this location, I still carried it with me. It buzzed away in my pocket.

I pulled it out of my pocket and looked down to see that I had just gotten a text from Thomas. I knew I had to respond or things would only get worse. I hoped he would not want to talk about our date on Friday night. I opened the text and read, "*cant wait for r date on friday.*"

This sucked. I looked up as the snow gently floated to the ground. I imagined myself flying in a spaceship through a meteor shower. A meteor shower would be a lot easier to navigate than this text conversation I knew I had to engage in. At least texting allows you to think out a proper response before sending it.

I texted back, *"thomas im sorry."* I strategized that easing my way into the minefield would work best.

"wtf" from Thomas. Not the response I was hoping for.

I wrote, *"something came up"*

"what came up"

"my parents set me up on a date"

"didnt u tell them u already had 1"

"u dont understand my parents they would of asked questions"

"r u embarrassed about me"

"no"

"then who is the other guy"

"they think im straight."

"ur cheating on me with a girl"

Things had not really gone the way I wanted. I needed to explain myself before things got out of hand. *"im not cheating on u my parents set up this date they even set up a reservation at the italian bistro and bought me a gift card i couldnt refuse"*

"u could of"

"no I couldnt u dont know my parents"

I sat in the middle of Red Rocks letting the snow cover me, looking down at the screen of my cell phone. No reply. I tried to text him again and again hoping to get some sort of response. I even contemplated calling him, but I knew that if he wouldn't respond to my texts, he wouldn't answer my call. I just sat in the snow watching the glow of my tiny screen hoping something would change. The world snuggled itself tighter into the blanket of falling snow.

Chapter Sixteen

I don't know if I could explain how nervous my date on Friday made me. I wanted it to go perfectly which in my mind meant ending in disaster. My wish for a disaster came later and not in the way I had hoped for. My hope was that Emily would experience the disaster, not me.

My parents trembled with so much excitement about the date that they took my car to the local car wash and got the supreme wash. My car sparkled next to the piles of glistening snow, and they cleaned the inside so well that it embarrassed me to show it to anyone. No respectable teenager would believe I kept my car that nice. It showed I was trying too hard and I didn't want that for this experience.

My mother even found time to go clothes shopping for me. I couldn't even count the amount of times I would come home to find pants waiting for me on my bed. She always told me that because of my weird body type, she had a hard time finding pants that would fit me. So anytime she came across a pair that would fit, she had to buy them. I do appreciate that she does this for me, but to have her dress me for a date crosses the line. She tried to find something that met her standards of respectable, but at the same time something I might consider fashionable. I don't know how she came to the conclusion I could impress both a date and her dad with her taste in clothes, though. I suspect it had something to do with fashion magazines informing her of the hip trends at the time. What she came up with had me dressed like craptacular pop star on his way to the Video Music Awards. I had a sports coat with matching pants. She even bought me a T-shirt from Aeropostle that matched a brand new pair of shiny white high-tops. I'm surprised she didn't try to cut my hair in my sleep so Emily would think I was a huge Justin Bieber fan. Once again, it made it look like I was trying too hard.

On a positive note, it could've worked to my advantage. Maybe Emily would see through all the effort and decide I wasn't worth her time. It might even creep her out a little. If you think about it, some guy you hadn't seen for a couple of years going through so much effort to try and impress you would creep anybody out. She would have to wonder about the real story behind all the effort. I thought that if I could handle the situation right, I could use it to my advantage.

But my advantage ran away the moment I showed up at the Hampton Suites and knocked on the door to her room. Emily opened the door, and her outfit shocked me. She wore a navy blue sweater over a white collared shirt. She also wore a grey plaid skirt that discreetly hid her knees. A grey bow in her long brown hair and matching modest heels that accentuated her calves accessorized her clothes. She looked like the perfect daughter from some 50s television show. It screamed of somebody trying too hard. It was kind of weird for some girl I hadn't seen for a few years to try to impress me so much. But then I remembered that she probably had the same thought about me.

"Hi, Tristan, good to see you again," she said as she looked down at my shoes.

I couldn't resist the temptation. "What's with the outfit?"

It seemed to loosen things up a bit as she looked up from the floor. "I know. I feel like my parents have just enrolled me in some Japanese elementary school." She then had the opportunity to see my attire for the first time. "And what's with *your* outfit?"

I looked down at myself and felt idiotic for questioning her style choices.

"You look like a reject from that 80s cop show that my dad loves to watch."

I hadn't thought about it that way before, and it was better than trying to imitate Bieber, but not by much. I looked back at her and laughed. It broke the ice even further and she laughed with me. At the same time we asked each other, "Did your parents dress you, too?" That made us laugh even harder.

We stood in the doorway, recovering from the fit we just went through. I found myself having feelings I hadn't had for a long time. There was an "old shoe" kind of ease between us and I returned to that comfort I felt when I knew her at an earlier age. I started to think that maybe I was wrong about this dinner. Just because I took her out to dinner didn't mean it had to lead to a romantic relationship. We had a wonderful friendship in the past, and maybe we could rekindle it again.

I offered Emily my arm in a gentlemanly manner and asked her, "Would you like to go to dinner, young lady?"

She grabbed my elbow and said, "With pleasure." We walked down the hallway of the hotel, laughing the whole way.

. . .

I pushed aside the thoughts my parents had about Emily and me dating, and went out to dinner with a good friend instead. I hate to say it, but I really enjoyed myself, and I think Emily really had a good time, too.

We arrived fashionably late, and as the hostess quickly escorted us to our table, we laughed at the throngs of people stuck waiting for the restaurant to call their names. People are always at their worst while waiting in the lobby of a restaurant. Their stomachs and their attitudes growl for attention, and it doesn't make the situation any better when they see a new name being called off the list and it's not their own. The lucky couple gets whisked away to a beautiful dining experience. It adds insult to injury when the hostess takes somebody who apparently only had to wait mere moments to their table long before the hungry people. I hate being one of those people who have to wait for a table, but I love gloating when I am the one being escorted to one.

It made me look even more important when I walked up to the host stand to tell her that we had a reservation. The little blonde girl ran her finger down the list until she saw my name. "Yes, Mr. Adamson, we have your table ready. Right this way."

She grabbed two menus and led us to a nice, comfortable table overlooking the mountains with the sun gently setting, creating a perfect picture for the ultimate dining experience. The meal was also perfect. There is no other place better for two hungry teenagers than the Italian Bistro. They will make sure to stuff you with food before sending you on your way. Emily and I enjoyed a wonderful appetizer of calamari, followed by the salad with the famous Italian dressing on top, and hot, steaming breadsticks. We got more breadsticks and salad as I enjoyed lasagna, and Emily had the manicotti. Even though we couldn't shovel another morsel down our throats, we made sure we reverted back to hungry teenagers by sharing a tiramisu for dessert. It worked out perfectly. I didn't even need to spend any of my own money. I put it all on the gift card my mom gave me. I even had enough left over to give our waiter a five-dollar tip.

If the food wasn't enough to make the evening perfect, Emily and I got along famously. Our friendship picked up right where it left off when they so rudely transferred her father to New York. We laughed, we reminisced, and in general, we had a wonderful time. I had lost myself completely in the evening. Looking back, I can probably pick out the signs, but during the dinner I didn't notice anything out of the ordinary.

Nothing was ever strained between us. During the appetizer, our eyes locked as we talked about the good times our families used to have. During dessert, I actually patted her hand to console her for the difficult time she had to endure when moving out to New York. Then just when she started to feel comfortable in the big city, she had to pack everything up again and come all the way back to the place she once left behind. I could see that she knew I had a genuine concern for her plight.

Because the evening had started out on such a formal note, I had continued with that theme throughout the whole evening. I opened the car door for her before we left, when we got to the restaurant, when we left the restaurant, and when I returned her to the hotel. I pulled her chair out for her at dinner and then pushed her into the table to make her feel comfortable. I thought of it more as a joke between two old friends and I assumed she had felt the same way.

When the evening ended and we stood in the lobby of her hotel waiting for the elevator to arrive, we talked uncomfortably, hoping the night wouldn't have to end. When the doors to the elevator dinged and slid open, I gave her a good-bye hug, which she returned. As the stainless steel of the doors started to show my reflection, she offered a sheepish wave good night. I returned it with a satisfied smirk. That was the last impression I left her with.

I walked out of the lobby feeling pretty good about the evening. I know I had gotten into a fight with Thomas, but I knew I could set things right. After he heard about the innocence of the night, I knew he would forgive me. I would even be able to introduce him to Emily to see there was nothing romantic going on between us. It would happen quicker than I thought, because during dinner she informed me her parents had enrolled her in the same confirmation class that Thomas and I were in. I knew I was in for a bumpy ride on Sunday, but at the same time I felt confident about it. For the first time in my life, I saw that I could set right all the things that had gone wrong.

Chapter Seventeen

My life turned into one big mess on Sunday night. I wish I had known this in advance because I might have done things differently. Instead, I walked through that door to my confirmation class with more confidence than I've ever had in my life, feeling like nothing could tear me down. I should've known better. God would never allow me to have such a wonderful life. He had to knock me down to a more humble level, or I would've gone on believing no other person who ever lived could achieve my greatness.

When I walked into the building, a large group of congregating teenagers had already formed. Thomas was already there talking to Lauren Mueller. His hands animated his thoughts and she tried to calm him down. I assumed their conversation revolved around me. The old me would have taken this opportunity to slink out of the building before either one could see me, but breathing in life made me confident, more than I had been in a very long time. I felt like I could do no wrong and I could easily explain to Thomas what happened the night before. He would have to understand my point of view. If he didn't, than Emily could confirm everything I was telling him. I looked around to see if Emily was there yet, but I couldn't find her anywhere. I knew she would arrive shortly, and until then I could deal with the situation, so I walked up to Thomas and Lauren.

I came from behind Thomas, so Lauren saw me before he did. I heard the end of Thomas's, "...*I just wish he would grow a backbone. I don't think he could stand up for himself, even if he tried.*"

I tapped Thomas on the shoulder as I saw Lauren try to hide a grin. She and I became quick partners in crime in Thomas's upcoming embarrassment. Thomas turned around to face me. "Well, speak of the devil. Are you here to whimper about your parents for a while before running to the bathroom to puke?"

I deserved that. "I owe you a huge apology."

I don't think he expected this because he stammered out, "You... you... you're damn right you do."

"Listen, can we go someplace private to talk?"

It gave Thomas the opportunity to show what kind of backbone *he* had. He turned around to Lauren to look for an indication of what he should do. Lauren nodded her head in assent. "I think you should go ahead, Thomas."

Thomas turned back around to face me. He pointed an accusing finger at me and said, "I'll go, but don't think this means I've forgiven you."

"Fair enough." I motioned for him to follow me, and I took him to the one place where I knew we would have some privacy. Across the parking lot and down a short dirt path sat a baseball field. During the spring and summer people used it regularly, but nobody used it this close to winter. I knew nobody would think of looking for us in the dugout. Classmates moved in the opposite direction towards the confirmation class and didn't notice us. I could see a couple of cars straggle into the parking lot as I led Thomas down the path. We ducked into the dugout and I looked through the chain-link fence into the field covered in a light layer of snow. I brushed away the snow that settled on the metal bench and motioned for Thomas to sit down. He folded his arms before he complied and said, "You have a long way to go to win me back."

I leaned on the edge of the dugout, across from him, and started. "I think you will see things my way shortly, but please hear me out before you say anything. First of all, I can't apologize enough for the other night. The girl I went out with was an old friend of the family. Her family moved out to New York about five years ago, and they were just transferred back here. My parents couldn't contain their excitement about it and they want to renew the friendship we had with these people. I don't blame them either, because I also have a lot of great memories with the family. Emily was a really good friend back in those days.

"Now what does this mean? Yes, I did have a wonderful time with her Friday night. I know you don't want to hear that, but the time we spent the other night had nothing to do with a romantic relationship. It was purely platonic. In fact, it felt like going out to dinner with my sister or a cousin I hadn't seen for a while. I picked her up. We ate. We laughed. We had a good time. I took her home. Nothing happened except we renewed an old friendship. In fact, her parents also enrolled her in this class. I can't wait for you to meet her because she'll tell you the same exact thing.

"Did I want to go out with Emily Friday night? No. My parents bullied me into doing something I didn't really want to do. You're right about me needing a backbone because I have a really difficult time standing up to my parents. At the same time, I can't tell them who I really am, yet. Someday, I'll let them know, but you have to let me do that in my own time. Otherwise I'm just being bullied around by you, and that doesn't really help me grow a backbone either."

I walked the two steps across the dugout to sit next to Thomas. I patted his hand resting in his lap. "What did I want to do the other night? I wanted to spend it with you. Why? Because you excite me, Thomas. You make me feel comfortable in my own skin, and nobody has ever done that for me before. I want to be with you, Thomas, and I want you to want to be with me. I'm excited about this relationship and where it could end up. Could you go with me to find out where this journey will end?"

Thomas looked directly at me, and his eyes softened as he leaned in. I leaned in to meet him halfway. Our lips connected. This kiss sparked even more magic than the other two we shared. Lights flashed behind my closed eyes, and choirs of angels sang in the heavens above. I think they sung Beethoven's "Ode to Joy."

．　．　．

I started to understand what was meant by a make-up kiss and why most people consider them so amazing. I wanted the moment to last forever. Here I was showing an expression of affection to someone who excited me. We truly conveyed how we felt for each other. We had just gotten over our differences in order to draw closer to each other, making the kiss magical. It made me want to run into the building and tell everybody that I really, really liked Thomas Edwards. I didn't care what they thought of me afterward.

When I pulled away from the kiss and looked into Thomas's dreamy eyes, I knew then and there I couldn't commit to a relationship "outside of the closet." I would hide out among the coats and scarves a little longer until the outside world was not such a scary place to venture into, but in this dark abode I wanted to dive back into the arms of the boy sitting across from me.

Reality sunk in, and I realized that if I jumped into my wish, we would miss class. This would raise even more questions and maybe even expose the secret I wanted to keep hidden. I needed to attend class, so I offered Thomas the one thing I promised him. "Do you want to go inside and meet Emily? She must have arrived by now."

Thomas considered this suggestion for a moment. "You know, I do want to see if your claim is true. Only a complete moron would set up something like this, expecting the worst."

That omen should've rung in my ears and I should've stayed in the dugout during class just to stay warm in Thomas's arms. Instead, I got up from that cold metal bench and led him back inside. We held hands until the bright lights of the parking lot shined down on us. We wound our way through the last of the stragglers and made our way into the building. Father Brett hadn't started class yet, and groups huddled together talking about the events of the past week. I looked around the room for Emily and finally saw her in the corner. She tried to look inconspicuous, but that just brought more attention to her. A hollow look emanated from her eyes. At the time, I assumed she was having a hard time adjusting to being in such a large group of strangers. I thought it would help by waving at her. A look of terror shadowed the expression of joy I expected from her. My eyes followed her running out of the room. I turned to look at Thomas. He gave me a quizzical look. I thought about chasing after her, but Father Brett entered the room at that exact moment and told everybody to take a seat. He wanted to get started on the evening's subject — the Holy Spirit.

I grabbed a seat in between Thomas and Lauren. I continued to look around the room for Emily, but she had completely disappeared. I couldn't figure out what had happened. Emily and I had renewed our friendship, and now when I could start introducing her to some of my new friends, she ran off. I don't know what could've happened in the past forty-eight hours to make her act this way.

I kept looking over my shoulder, wondering where Emily had run off to. Apparently, Father Brett didn't like the fact that I wasn't paying attention, and decided to use this moment to make an example of me. "Tristan, is it?"

I turned back to face him. "Uh, yes?"

"We'll let you out of class at the appropriate time, but until then you might find this experience much more rewarding if you actually paid attention to what was going on up here." He made a circular motion with his hand in front of him and then stepped into it. He smiled at me as if he had just made some witty remark. Instead, his actions reminded me of a Shakespearean fool.

"I'm sorry, Father. I'll do a better job of paying attention."

He said, "Thank you," then continued babbling on about his inane subject.

His singling me out pissed me off. Why did he pick on me?

Pretty much everybody in the room had given up on his lecture. Girls busied themselves by either putting on makeup or texting somebody lucky enough not to have to suffer through this torture. The boys had gotten the glazed, "I'm-not-really-a-zombie" look, pretending to understand the lesson but in reality their brain rested on a planet other than Earth. A couple of the guys were even reading sports magazines. Did Father Brett really care about my paying attention to him or did he see weakness in me? Did he believe that by making an example of me, everybody else would fall into line? Did he not notice that one person had run out even before the class had started and still had not returned? Didn't he care about her safety? All of these questions ran through my mind as I pondered Father Brett's hypocrisy. I gave up on them and decided that maybe listening to what he had to say would take my mind off of Emily.

I caught up with him babbling on about the seven gifts of the Holy Spirit. I had a hard time understanding how such an obscure figure in the Bible had seven gifts to give each and every one of us. Why hadn't I spent the time to write him a thank you letter for giving them to me?

"The Holy Spirit gave us the first gift — knowledge."

Suddenly, I understood why I hadn't taken the time to write the deity a note.

"You need to know about the facts of life."

I was still waiting to know about the facts of life. Every time I thought I had it figured out, somebody would come along and fuck up my perception.

"We use the Holy Spirit's second gift, wisdom, to apply the knowledge we gain."

It sounded like the traits of a Dungeons and Dragons character to me.

"The next one He bestowed upon us — understanding — we use to see the true meaning of any situation."

I don't think I've ever known the truth in any situation. Anytime

I came close to understanding the truth, somebody proved me wrong. Father Brett's lecture demonstrated a perfect example of this.

"The Holy Spirit then gives counsel, so that we may know what to do or say next."

Okay, now this was truly insane. I have never heard some tiny voice in my ear telling me what course of action I should take next. I would love for that to happen. I never know what to do in any given situation, because in every situation I tend to do the wrong thing. Maybe I should just start doing the opposite of what I think I should do, but I know deep in my heart that I would still do the wrong thing.

"We can group the first four together in a category of knowing, and the next two form their own category of being. Piety would be the first in this group. This is basically a deep love that you have for God and all that He has created."

I got confused at that point. I thought the Holy Spirit gave us these seven gifts. This last one sounded more like a gift I gave rather than received.

"This also ties in with the fear of the Lord. Through this fear we won't hurt the ones we love and by doing so we will show respect for God."

I almost stood up there because these gifts started to sound ridiculous. First of all, the Holy Spirit gives me a bunch of gifts about *knowing,* which I have never experienced in my life, and then he gives these gifts of *being*, which sound more like chores. I don't know about most people, but I don't really consider the bestowing of chores as a gift.

"The last one falls into a category all by itself — doing."

Oh great, all of a sudden according to the Holy Spirit, I just can't *be* anymore. Now I have to do something.

"The last gift, fortitude, allows us to endure difficult times and allows us to stand up for what we believe in."

I could really have used this gift. I have had to endure many difficult times, and even though I don't know what I believe in, I still want to stand up for it. I started to wonder if maybe I hadn't received these gifts from the Holy Spirit yet. Maybe when I did, things in my life would get better.

Chapter Eighteen

Tristan Adamson
Literature and Composition
Mrs. Baker

Friendship

The great Bob Marley said it best, "The truth is, everyone is going to hurt you. You just got to find the ones worth suffering for." And in a sense, nothing ever said about friendship has more truth to it.

Friends are the people you allow to hurt you. You will let them talk behind your back. You let them knock you down so you can get back up, so they can knock you down again. You let them cut open your chest cavity, surgically remove your heart, sauté it on a grill, place it back in your chest, and shock it back into pumping again just so they can dive in and eat it. A true friend will of course raise his or her head and ask the heart-eater if perhaps they wouldn't like some salt to go along with their meal.

In order to be a good friend, you must prepare to allow your new friend to walk all over you. A person desiring a friendship not only looks for someone they can hang out with and share spectacular moments, but also for someone to provide them with whatever their little heart desires. People make friends with other people just so they can be sure to have lots of people bringing them presents on their birthdays, Christmas, Valentine's Day, or any other made-up holiday the greeting card industry creates. The more friends they have, the more presents they get. If they don't get enough gifts at these events, they now have a network of people they can mooch off of at any given time. They will never do without soda, chips, candy, pencils, paper, or even money. A collection of people to manipulate is the first reason to have friends.

To be a good friend, you also must allow your friends to beat you up so they may feel better about themselves. You can only get so much mileage from material belongings. Any moron can tell you that. You also need to feel good about yourself. By putting people down, you can do this. To find the best people to put down look to the ones closest to you. This is why you need friends. If you don't like the way you look in a mirror, you make friends with an ugly person so you can look better. If you have packed on a few extra pounds, you make friends with a fat person. The dumber the person, the better to make a friend because you can belittle them at any time, and they will have a difficult time figuring out how to defend themselves. When somebody else feels small and insignificant around you, you feel like a bigger and better person. You make friends so you can feel better about yourself.

Lastly, you make friends in order to devour each other. When you become friends with another person you open your heart to them. You allow them to look around the private aspects of your life. They can see what makes you happy and what makes you sad. They witness the deepest secrets you have, and you allow this so they can use all of this information to their advantage. They can bring you up to the highest happy pinnacle, just so they can dash your dreams by exposing your deepest secrets and forcing you to feel the deepest despair. They will gnaw out your jugular so they can drink a mighty chalice of your warm blood. They will chew on your veins like a mad dog on a killing spree. Then they will pin you down and eat your entrails for desert. They will gorge themselves on your meat like a cheetah in the wild. Their stomachs will bulge from their torso, like a pregnant woman. You will lie there helpless as your lifeblood pools out underneath you, and the only thing left for you to say is, "It sure has been nice being your friend."

So we should all listen to the wise old reggae artist and understand that friends only hurt us. I know I will take this to heart from now on. I shall never want again for a friend. I will hide my heart and protect it from now on. No fucking bitch will ever have access to it again. They will only squat over my heart in order to defecate on it. So if you ask me for my friendship, I shall give you the proverbial finger because there is no fucking way I will ever make friends with anyone again. The assholes of this world have created friendship so they can treat others like shit. Don't put up with it.

∎ ∎ ∎

I found myself sitting in front of Miss Chompord, my high school counselor, when I should have been in my English class. She was asking me, "Do you have a plan?"

"What?"

She pulled my essay out of her desk drawer and placed it in front of me. She displayed it like a confession of my guilty mind. Miss Chompord looked down at it as if to explain why I was in her office.

I looked down at the paper, then I looked back at Miss Chompord. She raised her eyebrows and looked down at the paper and then looked back at me. I could feel her trying to search my soul for some deeper understanding. "You've still lost me."

She reached across her desk, patted my hand, and gave me a knowing nod. "I think you know what I'm talking about, Tristan. Do you have a plan?"

I pulled my hand back into my lap. "For what?"

She pulled back her hand and looked at me. "I think you know for what?"

"If I knew for what, I wouldn't ask, so for what?"

"For suicide, Tristan," she said very sternly.

That statement shocked me. "*What?!*"

"Tristan, do you have a plan for suicide?"

"Why would you think I would have a plan for suicide?!"

"Tristan, I need you to calm down."

I stood up and started to pace the short distance between the walls in her small office. "How do you expect me to calm down? You asked me to come to your office during the middle of class, you show me my essay, and then ask if I have a plan for suicide. Do you expect me to take this casually?"

"It would make my job a lot easier if you did."

I stopped pacing and looked directly at her. "It would've made your job a lot easier if you hadn't called me down here in the first place."

Miss Chompord crossed her arms. "Tristan, what do you expect me to do? You turn in this depressing essay the same week that social media has your face posted all over. We're concerned about your emotional well-being, and we need to know if you are thinking about doing anything rash."

I slumped down in the chair again and put my head in my hands. "Don't tell me the whole staff saw that picture, too?"

"Tristan, I think everybody in the whole town has seen that picture."

The picture explained a lot about the weird behavior Emily displayed on Sunday, because she took the picture. She had pulled into the parking lot at the same time Thomas and I made our way down to the baseball diamond. She didn't hesitate to follow closely behind. By the time she had made it down the hill, I was in the middle of my explanation of why I wanted to spend more time with Thomas.

Apparently, what I took as signs of friendship at our dinner the other night, she took as being more romantic. She had just gotten over a volatile relationship back in New York City and she saw something more stable in me. It broke her heart, though, when she heard me say that it would never happen between us. It shocked her even more when she discovered that I would rather spend time with another boy.

It so happened that during the exchange, she had her iPhone in her hand. She raised it up in perfect time to take a picture of Thomas and I enjoying that special moment together. The flashing lights I thought I saw were really the flash of the picture being taken and the ringer on her phone, "Ode to Joy," played as her mom called to see if she had found her way to class.

Of course, being a teenager, she immediately posted it to Facebook. Her parents saw Thomas and me in a lip-lock and quickly e-mailed the dirty evidence to my parents. Other friends of Emily passed the photo along as well, and it kept getting passed around. Because of that, all of my friends, enemies, and now, apparently the whole staff at my high school instantly viewed it. Even if I wanted to come out of the closet, I definitely didn't want to do it this way. Whether I wanted to or not didn't matter anymore because now the picture forced me to face it.

All of a sudden, everybody treated me differently.

If girls weren't talking behind my back, they came to tell me how brave they thought I was. I couldn't really decide which made me more uncomfortable, but I wanted to go back to being invisible to them. The boys at my school acted completely different. They either kept away from me, sometimes going to the extreme of turning around and heading in the opposite direction as if I carried some plague, or they looked at me with threatening eyes. By the end of the week, I knew the school would find me as some bloody pulp in a random corner of the building. The teachers treated me a little differently, too. Now that I found myself in the counselor's office, I finally figured out why.

The only ones who hadn't talked to me yet about this turn of events in my life were my parents. I couldn't wait until that conversation happened.

Finally, I lost it while in Miss Chompord's office. The reminder of the picture sent my mind reeling. Would I have to have plastic surgery and change my name to Raul so nobody would recognize me anymore? Would I have to move and never see anyone I knew ever again? Maybe I could find someplace where they would accept a freak like me, like France.

I looked up from the floor, surprised to find myself still sitting in Miss Chompord's office. She sat across the desk and stared at me. "Well?"

I was confused by the question. "Well, what?"

"Do you have a plan?"

"For suicide?"

"Of course, for suicide."

Feeling despondent, I looked down at the floor again. "No, I don't have a plan."

Miss Chompord let out a sigh of relief as if this were the only thing she wanted to hear. "That certainly takes a load off my mind. You had me really worried there for a second. I thought I might actually have to do something. You can go back to class now."

"What?"

"Go back to class, Tristan. You're missing out on an important learning opportunity. Oh, and take this essay with you."

I wish I had come up with a plan, because then maybe somebody would listen to my troubles.

Chapter Nineteen

I knew at some time I would have to face my parents about the picture. I knew they knew, because they acted really strange the last couple of days. My dad wouldn't look me in the eye anymore, and he would find any excuse to leave the room as soon as I entered. My mom behaved even worse. She would attempt to talk to me about something mundane, such as the weather, dinner, or school, but instead she would break down and start crying. She would lock herself in the bathroom, thinking the door would muffle her sobs. It would only take a short amount of time before they got over their awkwardness about this unexpected news and sit me down to have a long talk about what they would expect from me. I dreaded that moment probably as much as they did. This explained the reason why they didn't give me much grief when I told them I had schoolwork to get done at the library. They didn't question it or ask when I would come home. Of course, I didn't have any work I wanted to get done at the library; I just wanted to spend some time on my own. I drove my car up the hill to Red Rocks and snuck into the amphitheater.

The days started to get shorter, so by the time I got there, the sun had already dipped below the horizon. No clouds hung in the evening air, and the dark Colorado sky blanketed the seats of the stadium. A full moon rose, illuminating all the perfections and imperfections of the night. I had the whole amphitheater to myself.

I avoided sitting in the stands, but instead climbed on the stage to face an imaginary audience. I could see them sitting quietly, staring at my presence up on the stage. They had their hands folded in their laps and they had their eyes opened wide. Most importantly, their ears stood attentively waiting for the sweet message I would deliver.

I walked to the edge of the stage to lessen the distance between them and me. It didn't give me the confidence my speech teacher told me it would, but then again, I did imagine them. I thought maybe if I imagined them in their underwear it would help. I shut my eyes tight and let the mental image come to me. When I opened my eyes again, an imaginary, *nude* audience filled up this historic amphitheater. Except for one guy in the back — he wore a green shirt, khaki pants, and a weird, wide-brimmed hat. Even though the power of my imagination couldn't disrobe this member of my imaginary audience, the rest of the naked people put my mind at ease.

"I would like to thank you for coming out tonight."

The audience sat there and stared at me. I started losing the confidence I had just gained, so I went back to what my speech teacher had taught me. If I could loosen up the audience with a joke, then it would loosen me up as well. I tried to go through my mental rolodex until I came up with a joke that would fit with what I had to say. I chose to tell this joke:

"So this guy has this insanely hot wife. I mean other guys go completely nuts every time they see her, and it makes this guy proud that he married this hot woman. He has this problem though. He always thought his wife was cheating on him, and he needed to find out for sure. So one day, he pretends to go off to work, and comes home around lunchtime. When he gets there, he sees his wife wearing nothing but this skimpy bathrobe with her hair all messed up. It confirms his suspicions. He demands to know where his wife was hiding this guy she slept with, but his wife sticks to her story. Of course he doesn't believe her. He goes tearing through the house looking for this guy. He goes up to the second floor to the kitchen, and sees a guy sitting on a moped outside the front of his house. He thinks he has found the guy, so in his jealous rage he picks up the fridge and throws it out the window to hit the guy. Before he can determine if it hit the guy, he has a heart attack and dies right there on the spot. So off to Heaven he goes. He sees St. Peter standing before the Pearly Gates, and the angel asks him to explain the reason he has arrived there. This guy tells the holy apostle that he had a heart attack while throwing a fridge at the guy sleeping with his wife who tried to get away while sitting outside his house on a moped. St. Peter doesn't have any sympathy for him because this guy attempted to kill another guy, so St. Peter pulls a lever to send him down to Hell. Well, St. Peter remains standing at the Pearly Gates wishing he had an iPad to while away the time when another guy appears. He walks up to the Pearly Gates and St. Peter asks him to state his business. Well, the guy says he was just sitting on his moped when — *wham!* — a flying fridge hit him in the head and he died. St. Peter tells the guy that his reputation has preceded him and pulls the lever again. This guy gets sent to Hell, too. St. Peter can't help but feel pretty pleased with himself. Here he is, having a pretty slow day, but he still found the time to banish two obviously evil people. He could feel the pride of the Lord's grace upon him. All of a sudden, a third guy shows up. St. Peter looks this guy up and down and asks him to tell his story. The guy says to the holy apostle, 'I was minding my own business hanging out in a fridge when this guy comes along...'"

My imaginary audience goes into hysterics, except for that one guy wearing all of his clothes. The laughter's wave drowns me in its energy, and I ignore the freak that won't loosen up.

I continue on with my speech. "You see, even a saint can make large mistakes when he starts to become too judgmental. That guy on the moped didn't deserve an eternity of pain and misery just because some guy's dumbassity mistook him for the real culprit in the case. But St. Peter hears some rumor and automatically believes it. People need to quit doing that."

I could see my message starting to get through to my imaginary audience. They leaned in closer to hear more of my wisdom. Except for that one guy, he leaned further back.

"Just look what happened to me. They victimized me here. People started to spread rumors about me, and it destroyed my reputation. Well, I didn't really have much of a reputation to begin with, and you can't call it a rumor if it's true. Scratch that — bad example."

I thoroughly confused everybody in the audience including the one clothed guy. I needed to regroup before I lost them for good.

"I have been victimized in this case. I was the innocent bystander. Some mad, crazy person came running along and threw a fridge at me when I really didn't do anything wrong."

I could see I had them again. Now, I just needed to explain myself further.

"I just wanted an innocent kiss, even though my parents can't see it that way. My classmates won't see it that way either. I would also suspect my priest would have a problem with that kiss as well. So okay, maybe that kiss would make Beelzebub proud!"

My passion with the subject really got the audience's attention, even the dressed guy. They all leaned in closer.

"Okay, so maybe *innocent bystander* doesn't describe me best. But don't compare me to the creep hiding out in the fridge. I haven't sinned that big. You can't call me a liar either. Well, maybe I have lied about what I've done, but I'm not hiding from people. Well, I am hiding my real self from my family and friends, but can we really call that cheating? In a way, it is cheating. I'm cheating myself the most by not really embracing my true self. I should start prioritizing honesty in myself, and I need to quit hiding in the fridge. I can't do it for them, but I have to do it for myself. Because of this, I have asked you to come here today so I could tell you the truth about myself."

The audience sat on the edge of their seats. The guy with clothes on even tilted his hat back further on his head so he could get a better look at me. I closed my eyes before I shouted out, "*I am gay!*"

I opened my eyes again to see their reaction. My imaginary audience had disappeared, except for the guy with the clothes on. He looked down at me and said, "Have I sat here this whole time to hear that?"

It really amazed me that not only had I imagined a whole audience of make-believe people, but I also created a defiant one who would talk back to me. What did it all mean?

The defiant audience member stood up and walked to the stairs heading out of the amphitheater. He started to walk down to the stage. "Listen here, Gay Boy. I hope you're finished because I'd appreciate it if you would leave. That way I can close up the stadium for the evening."

I didn't have as good an imagination as I thought. It didn't deceive me enough to allow me to ignore the real person listening to my rant. I hid my face in my hands and slunk out of the amphitheater before the guy could say anything else.

Part Three

Nuns with Rulers

Chapter Twenty

The brochure lay on the table when I got home. My parents probably couldn't hide their joy that I hadn't come home at a reasonable hour. This way, they wouldn't have to talk to me face to face about the issue. I found it a little ironic that my dad, who found it so easy to push his beliefs and ideals on me, could not talk to me about an issue so dear and close to my heart. Granted, I really didn't want to talk to him about it either, but that wasn't really ironic because I never wanted to talk to him about anything.

Of course, my dad turned to the one thing he always turned to in times of crisis – God. I could just picture him as he saw that incriminating picture.

His jaw probably hung open for a while, and then he ran off to his closet where he hid a red phone with a huge blinking light on it. He picked up the phone, slammed the button down, then he waited for somebody to pick up on the other end. Halfway across the world, some wrinkled old man heard a similar red phone ring. He walked over to the phone and answered it, "Ciao." In a sweaty panic, my dad babbled, "Cardinal Gocci, I need to talk to the Pope right away." The old man got a puzzled look on his face and asked, "Perche?" My dad fell to his knees and cried to Heaven, "Because my son is gay!"

Apparently, the solution by the Catholic Church to this dramatic scene was to send my dad a brochure. Instead of my dad presenting it to me himself, he thought it better to leave it on the kitchen table so I could stumble upon it later. I've never seen such a courageous person. I also knew that just because my dad didn't present it to me that night, didn't mean that he wouldn't want to talk about it later. I needed to know the material in it, so I could come up with a plan of attack.

I picked up the brochure. The cover held a picture of a smiling nun, and it didn't help to convince me of her message when they placed a ruler in her hand. I started to wonder if the first thing they did to a woman as she entered the convent was superglue a ruler to her palm. Underneath her smiling face, the name of her organization was listed as Sister Correggio's Apostolate. So far, I was very skeptical of the idea, and the more I delved into it, the more I wanted to run away. But I found strength in myself to continue on.

I opened up the brochure and read,

"Leviticus (18:22, 20:13) reminds us, 'You shall not lie with a male as with a woman; it is an abomination... If a man lies with a male as with a woman, both of them have committed an abomination; they shall be put to death, their blood is upon them.'"

I could tell right away that Sister Correggio didn't believe in the business of comforting. I pictured Sister Correggio bludgeoning me to death with her ruler. After my exploration of this brochure, I had a feeling that the Catholic Church had not yet emerged from medieval times. Even if the Bible told them that they could put me to death, the United States government might see it a different way. At least I hoped so.

I opened up the brochure to a group of smiling teenagers, sitting in a group and laughing with each other. Whatever solution presented itself, this one did not look so bad. At least I hoped they wouldn't laugh at the homosexuals they threw to the lions. On the top of the page, large, bold words read,

ARE YOU ATTRACTED TO MEMBERS OF THE SAME SEX?

Now, it seemed like they were talking to me. The print got smaller as Sister Correggio's Apostolate attempted to answer this question.

"Don't worry. Many people out there have the same urges you do. The Catholic Church states that for most, they are just going through a stage. As long as you do not act upon these desires, then God will not subject you to the pains of Hell that He can surely throw you into."

I started having flashbacks to all of the Catholic guilt piled onto me by my parents. They surely hit upon the major three – Hell, and God, and nuns with rulers.

"Think of it as a test of God's love. He gives you this cross to bear. By giving into temptation, you will, much like a drug addict to their drugs, fall deeper into the sin of homosexuality. But by being a stronger person, you can overcome this temptation and find salvation with God. This phase, too, shall pass."

I started to question this brochure. They tried to tell me that my attraction to other boys was nothing more than a phase. Apparently, I would outgrow it as I got older. Someday, I would lust after women, but until then I had to bear the cross God had given me.

"For a few select individuals, these urges never pass. Sister Correggio's Apostolate can teach you how to cope with these feelings so you never have to act upon them. This way, you can find your salvation in the everlasting love of the Lord."

This last phrase really set me on edge, especially the part about never having to act upon my urges. Basically, this brochure was telling me I was just going through a phase, and that a good, healthy woman could cure me. Or, if incurable, I would have to live the rest of my days in chastity. Either way I looked at it, it made me extremely mad. I almost wished I *could* go back to medieval times so they could put me to death and I wouldn't have to worry about these urges anymore.

. . .

I avoided my parents for the next couple of days, but the brochure did not end my woes. I really shouldn't have thought it would end them, but I did everything in my power to try and make sure they wouldn't bother me much. Before school every morning, I woke up extra early to make sure I could run out the door before my dad sat down to breakfast. I would mumble some excuse as I ran out of the house, and I prayed he accepted it. He always tried to stop me before I slammed the door, and after years of pretending not to hear what he had to say, it made it really easy not to hear what he had to say as I scurried off to my car. I had an even easier time after school. I would leave some message on their voice mail saying I had picked up a shift at work, or I had some school work to do at some imaginary friend's house. I would avoid home at all costs, and when it got late enough I would go back to my neighborhood and sit outside my house and wait for my parents to turn off the lights. I would still wait a little longer afterward because I knew Dad would get out of bed to talk to me if he hadn't fallen asleep yet. I would wait an hour to make sure I wouldn't have to discuss Sister Correggió's Apostolate.

You would think I'd be really tired, getting up so early and going to bed so late, but not so. I didn't go to the library, or work, or some imaginary friend's house. I took my car up to the one place my parents would never think of looking for me — the Red Rocks parking lot. I had parked there so many times that I bet casual passersby started to believe that whoever owned it actually worked for the amphitheater. I would pull out the blanket I kept in the backseat, push the seat into a reclining position, and curl up to catch some sleep. With all the time I slept at home, during class, and after school, I was catching up on the sleep I had missed when I thought going to bed sucked.

Now I know you're wondering how somebody could sleep so much, but don't forget the power of sleep to a teenager. If you ask a group of teenagers what they most like to do, you'll get a list that includes hanging out with friends, eating, playing video games, and sex. But you will find that every one of them has *sleep* on the top of their lists. In fact, most if not all, teenagers believe they can perform this act very proficiently.

Teenagers can sleep in any position, anywhere in the world, at any time. It is the one thing that schools teach us to do really well. The teachers almost expect us to fall asleep in their classes. They come up with subjects that bore us to death, so we have no choice but to nod off. Maybe if they started talking about hanging out with friends, eating, playing video games, or sex, they would interest us enough that we would stay awake.

For this reason, I hate social studies classes the most. I think they invented them just to torture teenagers. They created these classes for the sole purpose of showing us the importance of a good night's sleep. First of all, they assign some meathead to teach each of these classes. This meathead thought when they praised him for all of his exploits on whatever sports team he belonged to in high school — usually football — that he would someday excel in that sport. When he got to college, this meathead came to the realization that he had no real future in sports. He needed to find some other means to make ends meet. He would think back to his high school days, and try to emulate someone. This would cause him to think of that other meathead who taught him all the exciting stuff in that one class. After thinking really hard about what class that was, he would get the pup tent of joy in his pants, and eventually arrive at the answer — social studies. This would amaze the new wannabe teacher, because that same meathead who inspired him also happened to coach whatever sport he excelled at, once again usually football. The meathead who finally learned the lie that sports told him in high school found a way he could relive his glory days. He could become a coach at a high school, and teach social studies on the side.

The social studies teacher never has anything useful to say. They teach the same thing every year, no matter what they call the class. In U.S. History, of course, they teach U.S. history. In Civics, they teach U.S. history from the perspective of our government. In Sociology, they teach about how America contributed to this prestigious field. Geography centers on learning all the states and their capitals. Even Western Civilization focuses on how they first created the U.S. so we could come and save Europe's butt during World War Two. The sad thing is they cover the same thing every year but from a different perspective. And for some reason they believe that nothing ever happened after World War Two, because they always end up there.

They have taught me this same thing since I started school. At first, I had fun playing with construction paper while we created hats and learned about the pilgrims, but sometime around middle school it started to get redundant. Yes, of course I think America is the greatest country ever. How could I not? They've beaten it into my brain ever since first grade. I just wonder why we need to cover the same material over and over again. What do they expect me to really learn in a class like that?

What I do learn is how to sleep while looking awake. It takes a little practice, but anybody can accomplish this feat. You need to first open your notebook in front of you. Then you need to position your writing hand above it with a writing utensil in it. Then you lock your other arm into position where your elbow rests on the table and your hand covers your eyes. This way it looks like you are busily taking notes while the teacher drones on about whatever era of America they are talking about that week. Don't worry about the notes. They hold no importance because first of all, you've had this information before. Second, if you don't already know what the teacher is talking about, they cover it in the textbook so you can get it that way instead.

I have perfected this art of sleeping in class. I've even taken it to other aspects of my life. In fact, I don't feel fully refreshed unless I've had at least ten hours of sleep a day. This doesn't have to come continuously. I can get it through catnaps, and daytime snoozes, or going to bed for the entire evening. Most of my sleep, I get while going to school, specifically history class. So when I get an opportunity to curl up on a comfy car seat to take a nap, it is pure heaven. Even though the crumbs of my life slipped through my fingers, I found plenty of time to get the sleep I needed by parking in the Red Rocks parking lot.

Chapter Twenty-One

I thought I was doing a really good job of avoiding my parents. After all, they are stupid people, and it doesn't take much to fool them. Every once in a while, though, they can surprise me. They obviously wanted to talk to me about Sister Correggio's Apostolate, but I just didn't want to have that conversation. I figured if I avoided it long enough, it would never happen. According to my thinking, it wouldn't take too long. My dad had grown pretty old with a susceptibility to heart disease. If luck was on my side, he would keel over with a heart attack sometime in the next couple of years. At worst, he would only last another five. Also, I have read somewhere that when one spouse passes away, it only takes a couple of months for the other to follow. After doing the math, I would, worst-case-scenario, only have to wait six years to avoid this conversation. My chances might even improve with the stress I put on them when they found out about my homosexuality.

I was not that lucky. In fact, they had caught on to my game quicker than I thought. On Thursday night, I had stayed outside of my home, watching for that moment I knew my parents would go to sleep. They had stayed up later that evening than the previous one. I knew I could outwait them, because both of them had to get up and go to work the next morning, whereas I just had to get up and go to school. They needed their beauty sleep for work, but I had plenty of time to catch up on my sleep while at school (see previous chapter). Even if I didn't catch up on my sleep, I had spent a lot of free time doing just that over the last couple of days. In fact, I had just come back to the neighborhood after a nice, long nap at Red Rocks.

While I waited down the street for the lights to go out at my house, I kept a close eye on the time. It progressively got cooler as the night wore on, yet the lights stayed on at my house. Midnight had passed when I started to worry. My parents had already tried to get in touch with me via my cell phone, but I kept ignoring the ringer. I could always claim later that the battery had died and I never got their message, but I would have a harder time explaining why I came home so late since my parents knew the library closed at ten o'clock. I started to worry they knew exactly what I was doing staying up progressively later each evening because of it.

So I continued to play the waiting game, even though it looked like I would lose. I couldn't hang out in my car, because that would look weird with it parked on the street while I wasn't home. I had it parked a couple of blocks away, so my parents wouldn't think I was waiting for them to go to bed. I then hid behind a bush down the block that looked over at their bedroom window. This way I could see the exact moment that their lights went off for the evening. I remember God had blessed me on that Thursday with a cold November night. The temperature had dropped quickly, and I longed for the warmth of my bed. If things hadn't changed soon, I might have lost this war of attrition.

My parents finally gave up and turned off the lights. Usually I would have waited an hour before I pulled my car up and quietly entered the house, but the cold really started getting to me. My nose started to run. My ears started to ache. I needed some real warmth and I needed it quickly. After fifteen minutes, I left to go retrieve my car. I pulled into my parking spot on the street and snuck in through the front door. I had taken off my shoes even before I slid my key into the lock. With my backpack slung over one shoulder and the same hand holding my sneakers, I tiptoed up the stairs toward my bedroom. As I made my way down the hall, I avoided the creaky spots in the floor so as not to alert my parents to my presence. I knew I would be safe as soon as I made it to my room.

I snuck into my room, but I didn't turn on my light until I knew I had shut the door completely. I turned the knob on my door so I could silently shut it without making the mechanism click like it would if I had closed it normally. I then turned on the light and spun around. Sitting on my bed, apparently waiting for my return, were Mom and Dad. He had a stern look on his face, and she was evidently crying, because she had a handkerchief hiding her red eyes.

Being outsmarted by my own parents was one of the most embarrassing moments of my young teenage life.

. . .

Dad sat on the bed with an earnest look on his face. "We've missed seeing you the last couple of days, Tristan."

Mom took the more dramatic approach of sobbing my name into her handkerchief.

My mind reeled with options I used to be able to talk my way out of this mess. I came up with the best excuse I could think of. "My car needed a jump, and I would've called you, but my cell phone's battery died."

A ringing came from my pocket. My dad held up his cell phone to show me he had just speed dialed me. He looked at me and asked, "Do you want to try again?"

"I didn't get any reception at the library," I threw out, hoping it would work.

My dad crossed his arms. "Odd, because when I tried to call you from the library, I had perfect reception."

Now I knew I stood in it up to my neck. "You went to the library?"

"Yes, Tristan, and strangely enough I never saw you at the library. I looked all over the place, ran into some of the kids from your school who know you..." Everybody at the school knew me now with my picture plastered all over Facebook.

"...and they told me they never saw you at the library tonight. For that matter, they haven't seen you there all week. I found that really odd because you told us you'd been going there to get school work done."

My mom looked up long enough from her handkerchief to ask, "Where have you been going all week, Tristan? What have you been doing?"

I knew I could come up with some new lie, but that would take a lot of energy. It wouldn't help me to keep lying, because my parents wouldn't believe whatever I told them anyway. I wondered if they would even believe the truth, but I had nothing left. I sat down in my chair and said, "I didn't go to the library."

This gave my dad the opening he had hoped for. He stood up from the bed and started to point his finger at me. "Where have you been going all this time, Tristan? It is becoming painfully obvious to me that you've been lying to us for quite some time now. Your recent exploits on the Internet and your grades prove that."

I knew I should've listened to his rant, but his nicely groomed fingers kept distracting me. I sat in that chair, looking for an answer that would get me out of trouble.

The silence hung in the air right next to my mother's sobs. She finally broke the spell by asking, "Have you had intercourse with that boy?"

"*Mom!*"

My dad sided with her. "Well, have you, Tristan?'

"Dad, how could you even think that? We've only gone out on one date."

My dad turned away from me in disgust. "Oh, but you've thought about having sex with that boy, haven't you?"

I just sat there with nothing to say. Mostly, I just felt numb.

My mom shook her head back and forth. "Tristan, where did you get this crazy idea about being gay? Television? Music? Public school?"

"Mom, it has nothing to do with any of that. I just like boys."

My dad turned around to face me again. "No, Tristan, you do not just like boys. I will not have a gay son. Do you hear me? You are not gay. You're just going through some phase. We can fix you and you will want to get fixed."

I didn't get it. Did I look like a dog to my dad?

I looked up at my dad, and tried to implant my wishes deep down into his eyes. I couldn't believe he had just said something so offensive to his own son, but then again he had always treated me this way. He pushed me around and forced me to do whatever he believed in. I just followed along like a dutiful son. I could see the perfect image he had in mind for me — a successful businessman with a lovely wife and two kids that he could spoil during Christmas time. As long as I lived up to that image, then pride would swell in his chest. Until then, it was his duty to make me into the image he desired. I looked hard into those eyes, searching for any kind of sympathy, but the hard line I always found looked back.

My dad pushed his well-manicured finger once again into my face. "Starting on Monday night, you will attend Sister Correggio's Apostolate to get the help you need. Otherwise, you are grounded. You will not go out for any other reason until the counselors at the apostolate tell us you have recovered enough to act like a normal member of society. You will quit your job tomorrow, and the only place you will go to is school, church on Sunday, and your confirmation class. Do I make myself clear?"

I sat in that chair fuming. I wanted to stand up for myself once and for all. I wanted to tell my dad off. I wanted him to understand the person I've kept hidden for so long. But did I do any of this? No. I turned away from his gaze and muttered the words, "Yes, sir."

He pulled the finger out of my face and said, "Good, then let's all go to bed."

Chapter Twenty-Two

My life was officially over.

My parents woke me up promptly at six-twenty a.m. They required me to take a shower, eat breakfast, brush my teeth, and take a seat in my dad's car. They had confiscated my cell phone and locked my car keys in their dresser. I couldn't even pee without it being scheduled first.

Dad drove me to school that day. Usually, the upcoming weekend would have excited me, but my mind kept wondering what horrors the weekend would bring being stuck at home with two parental figures sorely disappointed in their gay son. I could just picture family game night, followed by a discussion of lady-parts, and wrapping up the evening with a glass of warm milk and the latest issue of *Playboy*. I couldn't even imagine what my dad had planned for the weekend.

Luckily, my dad didn't talk at all during the drive to school. He didn't try to lecture me on the virtues of heterosexual intercourse. I bet he never had to prepare himself for this situation. Somewhere in his closet, my imagination could see binders full of various lectures he had written over the years for all of the different situations he would face while raising a good, old-fashioned American boy. He knew how to talk about relationships, drinking, drugs, grades, sports, the virtues of the Catholic Church, the dangers of Hell, and why I should listen to my teachers even though their rulers were so scary. He had thought all of this through, but he never fathomed in his lifetime that he would discuss with his son the need to have sex with women. I know it made the ride to school extremely uncomfortable, but not nearly as uncomfortable as it would have been if he had decided to talk to me about the issue.

He dropped me off in front of the school in complete isolation and humiliation. I could see the other juniors and seniors hanging out in the parking lot, whispering about me. I had now completed the perfect picture of "freakdom." Not only did my picture still make the top ten list of high school gossip, but now everybody saw my parents dropping me off at school. The only thing that could make it more humiliating would be having everyone know that my parents had taken away my cell phone. I prayed I could make it through the day without anyone noticing its absence. I took the lonely walk to the front doors of the school through the throng of freshmen and sophomores. I had nothing in my pockets. I didn't have my iPhone. I didn't have the keys to my car or house. Judging by the looks I saw while walking into the building, I didn't even have my dignity.

I spent the whole day trying to make myself inconspicuous and small. I never had a problem doing that before. Even when I tried to get noticed, nobody would comply. But now people talked about my plight more than the record of the football team. I could feel the eyes following me wherever I went. I kept hoping the day would end quickly, but then I remembered that my mom would pick me up promptly at the final bell. I would then have to spend the rest of the weekend with my parents. I started to think that the pictures in the children's Bible had some inaccuracies. Those books shouldn't depict Hell as the land of fire and brimstone filled with anguished people being chased around by red men with pointy tails and horns upon their balding heads. No, Hell is a teenager's life after their parents have grounded them for something that everybody knows about.

Just to prove my point, my mom picking me up from school was the epitome of Hell. I would've welcomed the burning flesh and pitchforks. I had gathered all of the books I would need over the weekend and slung them on my back as I shuffled through the groups of students excited about all the fun the weekend offered. I walked outside to join the freshmen who waited outside on the curb of the building for their parents to pick them up, and quickly searched for my mom's car. I didn't see it in the long line of idling cars. Parents sitting in those cars would yell for their son or daughter to come over so they could get out of the exhaust cloud and go home. Luckily, I couldn't find my mom anywhere in this pathetic display. I started to think she had forgotten to come and get me. I started to have visions of me dropping my backpack and running off toward the football field. I could skip through the cool and dying grass on my way to the Highland Canal, a sanctuary of trees and water that wound its way through the suburbs of Denver. I could hide among the tree's roots, eating berries and whatever squirrels I happened to kill. People would know me as that crazy guy who lived along the canal. Girls could pass by safely, but boys would need to beware. It gave me a sense of freedom, and I almost considered dropping my backpack and doing just that when I heard the voice I dreaded the most.

"Tristan!"

A voice familiar to me since the womb rang out behind me. I turned around to see my mom standing next to the principal of the school, waving at me. "Tristan! I'm over here talking to Mr. Grant."

I tried to avert my eyes to make it look like I didn't know this crazy woman making such a scene in front of everybody at the school. I hoped that if I ignored her, she would ignore me as well. But I should've known better, because no mother on the face of the earth will ever let that happen. I could see through my peripheral vision, my mom putting one hand on her hip and wagging a finger at me, "Tristan, you have already dug yourself a deep enough grave, and you should not ignore me right now, young man."

"Yeah, Tristan, we wouldn't want you to get into any more trouble, would we?" someone shouted from the after-school crowd gathered outside. A wave of laughter started to cascade over the crowd. I wanted to crawl further into the shell of my T-shirt.

My mom didn't understand the true intent of the sarcastic remark. "You should listen to your friends, Tristan." The crowd burst into even more laughter.

I swallowed my pride and went over to my mom in an attempt to lessen the humiliation. I took the walk of shame for the second time that day. If they didn't know me before, the spreading whispers confirmed what they already suspected — this was the guy caught on Facebook tangled in a lip-lock with another guy. I wished against all reason I could go back to being the one guy who blended into the background that nobody talked about, but I knew I had become an overnight celebrity and I would never have that luxury again. I just wished I could embrace the spotlight, and then this experience wouldn't be as bad.

I walked up to my mom and she gave me a hug. Just when things couldn't get any worse, she planted a kiss on top of my head, followed by more laughter and whispers from the crowd. My mom looked at the kids gathered out in front of the school and smiled. "You run quite the jolly school here, Mr. Grant."

He responded with a polite thank you. I had spent most of my high school career avoiding Mr. Grant. He had no idea who I was. As a high schooler, you do not want to be on a first name basis with the principal, but it appeared that in one fell swoop my mom destroyed all the years I had avoided this. "Mr. Grant and I were having the loveliest conversation before you came out, Tristan."

I tried to compose some sort of dignity by looking up at Mr. Grant. "Well, glad to hear that, sir."

"I told him all about your situation, and how we might have to pull you out of school here."

I clearly heard the message she was sending me — Catholic school. I turned and looked at my mom with my best hurt puppy dog look. No matter how miserable public school got, Catholic school would always be worse. I couldn't let my mom do this; pull

135

me out of Heaven just to throw me into a Hell run by nuns with rulers. My knuckles would be in danger of being bloodied every day if I went back there. I delivered a small prayer to God promising him whatever he wanted as long as Mom didn't pull me out of public education.

"But Mr. Grant has assured me that this school delivers a quality education."

I slumped down in relief.

"He also assures me that he will keep a closer eye on you so that you won't fall into temptation again."

I looked up at Mr. Grant. "You need to stay on the right path, Tristan, and you will find that in the future, the choices made for you right now will keep you on that path."

"But just so you know, Tristan," my mom continued, "we haven't taken Catholic school completely off the table. If your dad and I don't feel you are living up to your side of the bargain, we will pull you from this school and send you off for a more conservative education."

My mom looked over at me to be sure I heard her message loud and clear. I nodded in time with the sound of the threat ringing in my ears.

∎ ∎ ∎

My humiliation didn't end at school. I entered the car to see my work uniform nicely cleaned and pressed, lying in the back seat. Another stop on this trip of shame stared back at me. My mom drove me to the Burger House so I could relinquish another aspect of my freedom. My parents wanted to make sure to cut off all my lifelines while reconnecting me to the ideals they believed they could trust.

I didn't really listen to my mom as she prattled on during the drive. It had something to do with her and my dad deciding the best course of action for me. She knew I wouldn't like it and it hurt her, too, because she always thought she could trust her only son. I didn't see why she couldn't still trust me. I never got drunk or crashed the car. I didn't steal from anybody. No court ever convicted me as a killer. I didn't even get some teenage girl pregnant, even though at that moment, I believe my mom probably wished for that problem instead of the gay one. I just let some urges welling up inside of me take over. Just because I kissed another boy I had to lose my cell phone, my car keys, and my job.

Did we all move back to the 1950s, or had we moved ahead as a society to a better place? Why did everybody treat me differently? The thought of this being my life if I didn't change my evil ways scared me the most. I could see myself as a fifty-year-old man still being driven around by my now near-blind mother to another job I would have to resign from because she caught me kissing a fifty-year-old man. She would scold me as she traversed two lanes, "*Your father, bless his good Catholic soul, would roll around in his grave right now if we had not cremated him. You need to understand that you can't kiss boys. I can't trust you to do the right thing, so now you must resign as CEO.*"

I would slouch in the seat and mumble, "I'm sorry, Mom."

She would reply, "*You shouldn't apologize to me, but instead to all of those good heterosexual individuals without your guidance at the Apple Corporation.*"

After I put in my resignation, she would drive me home and pull out the good stationery. I would have to sit at the dining room table and write an apology letter to each individual that ever worked for me. I would have to include my indiscretion with the fifty-year-old man in each letter. My mother would hope that this punishment would make me never want to kiss another fifty-year-old man ever again. But each letter would remind me of that one magical kiss, that moment that Thomas and I shared in the cold dugout outside my confirmation class.

Actually, my thoughts had returned to Thomas time and time again. I hadn't been able to talk to him since all of this blew up. I had texted him a couple of times and even called him once. I only got one text in reply, "*I think we should play it quiet for a while until this blows over.*" Otherwise, I was on my own, literally, with my parents.

Tessa could have been there for me, but she was still mad at me for walking out on her at Red Rocks. We would still laugh and have a good time at work, but she grew a little more distant each time I saw her. When I explained my situation, she told me it was probably for the best, and it was about time my parents found out. The remarks did not comfort me at all, but in reality Tessa never held back her punches. I did realize she could help me get in touch with Thomas before Sunday, because she would be working at the Burger House while I dropped off my uniform. If I could get her a note, she could deliver it to Thomas, then maybe he would come to my rescue.

I tuned my mom out even more as I tried to think of what I could say to Thomas. I knew I could get him the message without too much difficulty. When I went into the back to resign, my mom would have to stay in the lobby while I explained to Dan why I had to quit. During that time I could write a note to Tessa and slip it to her as I left. My mom wouldn't know anything had happened. I just didn't know what to write to him.

While I tried to think of what I could say, we pulled into the parking lot. I grabbed my clothes from the back seat and opened the car door. A little more luck presented itself to me when my mom didn't open her door. I looked over at her and asked, "Aren't you coming in with me?"

My mom pulled her lipstick out of her purse, and twisted it preparing to apply some. "No, Tristan. Even though you betrayed us, we need to start placing some form of trust in you again, or our relationship will never heal. I believe you will do the right thing." I stared at her in disbelief as she applied a new layer of red goop to her lips. I couldn't believe she wanted me to quit work because she couldn't trust me anymore, but then told me she would start doing just that. These conflicting messages started to confuse me, but I had more important things to worry about. I couldn't turn down this great opportunity.

I strolled through the front door for what I thought would be my last time ever. I could see Tessa in the back, preparing for the night's rush. She yelled at Dan in the back. I couldn't really tell what she shouted, but I bet it had something to do with the fact that he needed to get off his lazy butt and help her get ready for the evening. They engaged in this dance during every shift. You would think things would change eventually, but Tessa continued to yell at Dan for being lazy, and Dan continued to hide in the back.

I took a deep breath to build up the confidence I needed to get this over with, and I walked in the back toward the office. I crossed into the kitchen, and Tessa looked up from her work. "What are you doing here? You don't work again until tomorrow night."

It broke my heart when I realized what I needed to do. This would cut me off from my last friend. I gulped deep, ignored Tessa, and headed back toward Dan. Tessa went back to her work and I could hear her mumble, "*Whatever,*" as I walked away.

Dan sat, talking on the phone, begging someone to come into work for him. Desperation clung to him. "We just had a coach of a football team call us, saying they'll stop here after the game. They'll slam us at nine, and I desperately need your help, man." I could see he was getting nowhere. "Well, don't come begging for a day off the next time you want to go to a party when I've scheduled you to work." He slammed the phone down and rubbed his face in frustration. "Could today get any worse?"

I decided to knock on the door then. Dan looked up and his face lit up. "Tristan, thank God. I really need your help."

I gave Dan a sheepish grin and said, "Dan, your night just got worse."

Dan's smile faded. "What do you want, Tristan?"

"Well, Dan, you see, my parents got really mad at me the other day, and because of that, well, they've forced me to do certain things, and I really don't want to do them, but I still live under their roof, so I still have to follow their rules, and based upon a whim they make up new rules, and new punishments, and this has to do more with a punishment than it does with a rule, because they never stated the rule, and I don't know how they expected me to know that I shouldn't do what I did, but anyway, you see, because I should have..."

Dan interrupted me. "Tristan can you get to the point. I got a lot of crap going on."

"Dan, I need to quit."

Dan stared at me dumbfounded. "Fucking teenagers. I should've worked harder in high school. Great, leave your uniform on the desk, and get out. Sorry I don't have time for pleasantries, but I got a shitload to do right now."

I remembered the other thing I needed to do, and knew I needed to stand up for myself or I wouldn't get what I wanted. "Uh, one more thing before I go."

"What?"

"Can I borrow a piece of paper and a pen?"

Dan slammed a pen and a scrap of paper on the desk, then picked up the phone and started dialing the next number. After placing my uniform on the desk, I took the pen and paper out of the office. I looked at the blank piece of paper, trying to think of what I wanted to say to Thomas. It had to be meaningful and poignant so Thomas would understand all of the pain and despair I went through without him.

I scratched on the paper:

Thomas,
Sorry for all of the trouble I've caused you. Now, you see why I couldn't tell anybody about my situation because of what would happen to me. Please, Forgive me.
Tristan

I looked at what I wrote. I knew I could do better, but my mom had finished putting on her makeup, and it wouldn't be long before she got restless and started looking for me. I knew I didn't have a lot of time so I scribbled on the bottom,

P.S. I miss you.

And I folded up the note.

I walked up to Tessa as she threw a box of burger patties in the side freezer next to the grill.

"Hi, Tessa."

"What do you want, Tristan?" she asked as she ripped open the box.

"Could you do something for me?"

She stopped working and faced me with her hands on her hips. "What?"

I held out the note to her. "Could you deliver this note to Thomas?"

She turned away from me without even taking the note. "Do it yourself, Tristan."

"I can't, Tessa. My parents grounded me and won't let me do anything. I'll lose something special if I don't get this note to him."

Tessa looked at me skeptically for a second before grabbing the note out of my hand. Before I could tell her not to read it, she had it open and did just that. I had mixed emotions about her reading the note. It was meant for Thomas's eyes only, but at the same time I wanted to know if what I wrote would help me solve my problem. The later was probably better than the former as I eagerly waited to hear what Tessa had to say. The reaction Tessa gave me did not meet my expectations.

Tessa laughed. "Oh, look, another relationship you've ruined just because you won't admit to people your true self." With that she crumpled up the piece of paper and threw it in the trash can. "Tristan, you need to realize that the longer you hide your true self, the more miserable it will make you."

Right before I could respond, I heard my mom shout at me from the front counter, "Tristan, you've had plenty of time. We need to go, now."

Tessa looked at me and said, "Yes, Tristan, you need to go back to doing what your mom and dad want you to do."

I wanted to respond to Tessa's bitter statement, but my mom was waiting.

Chapter Twenty-Three

Tessa's words rang in my ears all weekend. It didn't help that I had to spend that time with the people she patronized me about. All weekend long, I tried to make my parents as miserable as I felt. I moped around the house, giving monosyllabic answers to their questions, but it didn't seem to dampen their spirits. They were just happy they didn't have to worry about me running around with some crazy boy committing some outrageous act that would bring shame upon the family. They could find me at all times. They had control of the whole situation. There is nothing worse than having what little freedoms you've obtained taken away from you.

My greatest desire all weekend was to be by myself at the confirmation class. The one thing I dreaded doing more than anything in the world had become my only salvation. Not only would I get to escape my parents for a while, I would also have a chance to talk to Thomas. I could fix all the problems I had caused the week before. I figured he had started to wonder why I hadn't texted him or called. He must've started feeling pretty guilty for ignoring me. I could see him sending me text messages while I shuffled around my house trying to find ways to avoid my parents. I should've taken this strategy in the first place. Maybe ignoring Thomas drove him crazier than bugging him all the time. I couldn't wait to see the effects on Sunday night as Thomas came groveling back to me. Of course I would take him back but it would be more on my terms then his. Considering the situation I found myself in, he would have to wait until I turned twenty-one and could make my own decisions before we could start dating again. He might not wait that long, but at least I could dream he would.

Thinking about various scenarios like this offered me my only escape all weekend. I held it up as my salvation. Sometimes salvation doesn't come the way you intend it. Sunday night came, and during dinner my mom and dad had a conversation about who would take me to the confirmation class. I thought it a little silly that they would discuss such a thing since I could easily drive myself, but of course they wouldn't listen to that logic right now. I assumed that one of them would want to drive me to the meeting. What I didn't expect was when Dad said, "I know it is two hours out of my weekend, but I guess I could take him this week."

That threw me off a bit. We only lived ten minutes away from the school. Why would driving me to class take two hours out of my dad's busy night? It made me question their logic. "Excuse me, Dad, but why would it take you two hours to drive me back and forth to the confirmation class?"

My mind raced with various answers, but none were as horrific as the one I got. "I'm going to class with you." Visions of my dad sitting next to me throughout the whole class, pointing out that I needed to take better notes, filled me with a terror that the Taliban could never achieve.

"What?!"

"Your mother and I have decided that because the moment of your indiscretion happened at the confirmation class, we would have to attend it with you to make sure this behavior does not occur again."

I sat there with terror racing through my veins. What would this do to my relationship with Thomas? How would this affect my already poor reputation? *How could my parents do this to me?*

"Why worry about how I act during class. Just pull me out of it."

My dad pinched the bridge of his nose and breathed deeply.

When he got his boiling temper under control, he opened his eyes and said, "Tristan, how could you even ask a question like that? You know that you confirming your belief in the one, true God is one of the most important ceremonies in your young life. You need to receive this sacrament, and considering the lies you've told your mother and me over the last couple of months, it leaves us no other option but to attend the class until you've completed it."

I tried to plead with my dad, "But..."

He slammed his hand down on the kitchen table. Silverware, plates, and water glasses jumped from the table. "That is enough, Tristan. It's been decided."

We all returned to our dinner and uncomfortable silence for the remainder of the meal. I had come to the realization that even though I didn't believe things could get worse, that evening proved that things always could.

·   ·   ·

The older you get, the more embarrassing your parents become. The possibility of them always embarrassing you might have something to do with it. You might get smarter the older you get, or they might just get dumber and not realize how embarrassing they've become. I'm suspecting it's more the latter than the former. Growing up, I have fond memories with my parents and many moments when I have enjoyed their company in public. Sometime around middle school, I wanted them around much less, but they didn't comply. They always told me to grow up, but how could I do that if they watched my every move? Right around high school, they started to get the hint and would accompany me less and less, but anytime they lurked in the shadows, they became even more embarrassing. They must have felt some of the embarrassment — I don't know how they could avoid feeling it. The night my dad accompanied me to the confirmation class must have embarrassed him as much as it did me.

We arrived at the class five minutes before it started. It just meant all the other teenagers had already showed up to mill around and talk to each other. I could hear the conversations and laughter coming from the classroom as I got nearer. I walked a lot faster than my father because I thought that if I entered before he did, then nobody would connect him with me. They would just wonder who the guy was and why he had shown up for their class. Maybe, my dad would even give me a little break by ignoring me for the rest of the class and stand in the background.

I had outpaced my dad by a good ten steps when I entered the classroom, but I instantly lost the advantage I thought I had gained. The room became instantly quiet upon my arrival. At first, I wondered why they had stopped talking, but then I remembered the previous week. Everybody in this room had probably seen the picture of me in social media cyberspace. I focused so much on the agony I had to endure with my parents that I had totally forgotten about all the agony of my social life. The two combined in one glorious moment when my dad entered the room and put one of his meaty paws on my shoulder. The conversations didn't start up again, but a couple of snickers emerged from the back of the classroom. My only relief came after a quick scan of the room. I didn't see Thomas anywhere. At least, he couldn't feel vindicated for my pain.

My dad didn't seem to notice the uncomfortable situation. I couldn't see how he could miss it. "Come, let's go find a seat."

I instantly trained my eyes to the ground, trying to avoid the stares, and made for a seat in the back. My dad stopped me before I could grab one. "Not there, Tristan."

He took me by the hand like a little toddler that needed help getting across the street, and led me to the front of the room. "You always take a seat in the front. Studies have shown that students sitting in the front of the classroom retain more information." I just wished the room wasn't so quiet and he wasn't so loud, so the amount of chuckles that emerged would not have been so audible.

Luckily for my dad, he found two seats in the front row, right in the center. Somehow I suspected he always found these seats. One advantage to this spot was that I couldn't see the stares everybody gave me. That didn't mean I couldn't feel those stares boring into my back.

I decided to avoid all of this by reading my confirmation book until class started. It would please my dad that I took such an interest in a subject he approved of so highly, plus it would distract me from all the uncomfortableness in the room. Fortunately, it only took a couple of minutes before Father Brett entered the room prepared for the night's lecture on the Apostle's Creed. I hoped he would jump right into the lecture, but the older gentleman sitting in the front row of his class took him by surprise. It only took Father Brett a couple of seconds to recognize the old man sitting beside me. I could see the light of recognition pop on which depressed me even more. It just meant he had seen the same picture everybody else had. I didn't have a chance to escape from this humiliation.

I felt like one of the apostles. After the Romans had killed Jesus, they hunted down his followers like rebels. The Romans believed that if they allowed Jesus's followers to continue to preach his message, then all of mankind would turn against the Romans and the mighty empire would collapse. Because of this, the apostles needed to hide themselves or get stoned, crucified, or worst of all, persecuted. They lived a miserable existence, never allowed to express their true feelings. I guess the important lesson to learn from the apostles is to never express your true feelings, because if you do, you'll experience persecution. I sat there quietly in the front row and diligently took notes on Father Brett's lecture.

Father Brett went through the Apostle's Creed line by line and explained each of them to us. It reminded me of English class. It still amazes me to this day how much bullshit one person can read into each line. Sometimes I think they just make things up so others believe they're smart. I wondered if Father Brett felt the same way as my English teacher, because he basically retold the Gospels with each line until he got to the part about Jesus descending into Hell. Now I know I have no expertise on the Bible, but I don't remember any of this during the Easter part of the story. It just basically talks about Jesus being crucified and then buried. After three days, he rises again, and does a whole bunch of crazy stuff that some people would call magical.

Apparently, they left out what happened to Jesus in those three days after his death. He went to Hell. You would think that with Him being the son of God, His dad would've broken that original sin rule and would've let Him come back up to Heaven, but God's eternal plan didn't include that. You see, God needed Jesus to go down to Hell so Jesus and the devil could have this epic battle.

This blew my mind. Why would they exclude this epic battle from the Bible? They could hook so many more people if they included that part. They could even make it into a really cool movie with Brad Pitt playing Jesus. I'd watch that. But no, they had to stick to the part about the apostles hiding in a house instead. Apparently, the Bible could have used a better editor.

The other crazy thing about Jesus going down to Hell is that God did it as a sacrifice for all people of all ages. Honest to God, Father Brett told me that. I liked that so much I wrote it my notes and underlined it twice, because all people of all ages should include *me*. If Catholics should believe this, then why was I being treated like the plague by everybody in this room? If Jesus cared enough about me, then shouldn't everybody else? Christianity claims to work this way, but it doesn't.

As I contemplated this thought, Father Brett supplied me with an answer. "*Christ will judge each of us on how we loved and served God and our neighbors while on Earth.*"

My point exactly. In fact, Father Brett went on to explain, "*God judges us on the way we behaved to others in need.*"

Wasn't I one of these people in need? And didn't these people treat me like the stuff they found on the bottom of their shoes? They made me believe I had done something so horrific that by being in the same room with them, they would all contract some terrible disease and would die of homosexuality by the end of the week. They treated me as if household junk held more importance than me.

"God doesn't make junk," Father Brett explained next. I really needed to start figuring out how he infiltrated my brain all of the time.

"The Catholic religion does not try to force everybody into one mold." That really confused me. I quickly thought of Sister Correggio's Apostolate brochure and wondered how the Catholic Church did not force everybody into one mold with that institution.

In fact, Father Brett explained to me that Webster's dictionary defines Catholics as all-inclusive. I started to think of this church as an all-inclusive group of people with the same beliefs, and they would accept you into their fold as long as you thought like they did. People did live out there who would accept me for me and include me in their fold. I just didn't believe I could find it in the Catholic Church. Oddly enough, I was starting to wonder if I really even wanted to belong to Thomas's group.

Chapter Twenty-Four

Tristan Adamson
Literature and Composition
Mrs. Baker

Paradise Lost

They say that absence makes the heart grow fonder. In direct contrast, that should mean that presence makes the heart grow harder, especially the smothering kind of presence. You need a break from people because if you see them all the time, the littlest things will start to annoy you.

Think about it this way. When you don't see a person for a long time, some trait of theirs becomes endearing, but that same trait becomes extremely annoying if you see it day after day. Take, for example, that boy that everybody is freaking out about because I kissed him. I didn't really know him very well to begin with, but because of this terrible act I haven't seen him much since. Even though I just started to know him as a person, one endearing trait would always draw me closer to him. When he walked, he had this confidence that just oozed out of him. It caused his long bangs to bounce in front of his eyes. You would get little glimpses of those dark beautiful orbs. Each passing flicker would just melt your heart. It was so endearing, and because they cut me off from him, that one image sticks out in my mind. It makes me yearn for him even more.

At the same time, if I saw him every day, I would probably get sick of the way he walked. I would start to think of it as being a little too cocky, even though I doubt that because he walks with confidence, not cockiness, and I like confident people. It shows what I lack and what I wish I could emulate. But I might want him to cut his hair and update it a little and it would allow me to see more of those beautiful eyes. Then again, that bouncing hair and that little tease make me desire another glimpse even more. I don't think I could ever get tired of looking into those eyes. I could spend the rest of my life looking across a table and losing myself in that deep brown. I guess you need to throw out the thought of me getting tired of Thomas as a bad example, but I do have a wonderful example with my parents. My best transition ever, if I do say so myself.

I have spent the last forty-eight hours with nobody but my parents. They followed me around wherever I went because they grounded me (see earlier mention about boy I kissed and you'll know why), but even if they stopped following me around all over the place, I've still spent my whole life getting to know them. I know every annoying thing about them, things they don't even know about themselves. For instance, I sat at the dinner table eating, trying to avoid my parents. I knew that if they started talking it would turn into another lecture about how I needed to quit throwing my life away on an absurd notion, and that in the eyes of God, this notion is nothing more than an abomination.

Of course they started a conversation with me, and I tried my best to ignore it. We talked about this movie we had watched as a family the night before, and I found it pretty interesting. Even though they never brought up their disgust with my being "thrown out of the closet," I could see those thoughts running around in the back of their minds. It made the moment so annoying. I knew they wanted to talk about it. They always want to talk about the things that are wrong with my life. Of course, we don't have these conversations. They would rather have the ideas stew around for a while in my brain before they spring the trap. The day they do, nothing will be worse, and that's my point.

I know my parents so well that I know the thoughts they don't even know about. It annoys me that I can do this. In fact, I don't see how anybody can see that trait as endearing. I guess they see it that way because they have spent so much time together and haven't gotten sick of each other yet. Either that or they're so stupid that they just don't know what the other person thinks. But that's what happens to people who are together all the time. They must build up such a tolerance for it that they can stand each other for the rest of their lives. I guarantee you that each one gets annoyed by the other, just as I do by both of them.

And that proves my point. We need to lose paradise every once in a while; otherwise, we can no longer live in paradise. It becomes the most annoying thing in the world, and so routine. If you want to stay in love with someone, avoid them every once in a while and you will always care about them. It sounds crazy, but I can guarantee this as the only real truth out there.

. . .

When Mrs. Baker went through the list of people to talk to about their essays, she skipped right over my name. Of course, I didn't even notice. I pretended to read some long-ass poem by some guy named John Milton, who wrote around the same time as Shakespeare. I couldn't understand a single thing this guy was talking about, and the pictures in the book accompanying it disturbed me. It reminded me of a well-drawn children's Bible, except all of the pictures depicted Satan and Hell. It made me wonder about the concept of separation of church and state and how they needed to apply it in this case. Even though I spent a moment pondering this, I spent more time worrying about being condemned to my own personal Hell. The pictures reminded me of the things happening in my life. I worried so much about this that I didn't even notice when Mrs. Baker skipped over my name.

Toward the end of class when I started to notice, it made me worry even more. I started to wonder if she had lost my essay, giving her an opportunity to yell at me for not turning one in. I started to think that maybe I did forget to turn one in. Or worst of all, if I turned it in, she graded it and now needed to have a special conference with me about it. As with all things in my life, it turned out the worst possibility was the one I had to face. As the class rolled to an end, she pulled me aside and said she needed to speak to me after class. No other words strike more fear into a high-schooler than those. I had no choice but to comply.

After everybody had filed out of the classroom, I stood dutifully at the edge of her desk with my hands folded politely in front of me. Mrs. Baker pulled my essay out of a drawer and threw it on top of the desk. The big, red letter *F* stared back at me. I know it should have scared me, but with all the other crap going on in my life, I could care less about the *F*.

Mrs. Baker seemed to care more about it than I did. "What in the world did you give me?"

I looked down at the paper and said, "My 'Paradise Lost' essay."

Mrs. Baker slammed her hands on the top of her desk, framing my paper with her fingers. "I know damn well this is your 'Paradise Lost' essay. But what does this essay have to do with John Milton's *Paradise Lost?*"

"What's that?"

Mrs. Baker looked flabbergasted. "What's that?! We've only focused on it in class for the last week, Tristan. You know the story of how God threw Satan out of Heaven?"

"Oh, that helps explain those pictures. That story has me lost. It sounds more like Greek mythology. It really confuses me because it has nothing to do with Christianity, yet you say it does."

Her frustration must have escalated, because she rubbed her eyes with the heel of her palms and grunted. "If you didn't understand the prompt, why didn't you ask me about it? You know I don't have a class after this one. I could have helped you with your problem."

I waved off the idea as absurdity. "I just figured I would write about the paradise that I lost, and if I created a great enough argument, then you would understand and give me the appropriate grade."

She motioned to the paper. "I did give you the appropriate grade."

"You must not have liked my argument then."

She closed her eyes and breathed deeply. She exhaled before saying, "Let me put this another way, Tristan. You desperately need to improve your grade, and it would take a miracle for you to pass. This miracle will not come from God either. This miracle must come from you. I will not assign any more essays this semester, but I will give you one more for extra credit. Do well on it, and you can pass my class. You have two weeks. I based it on an American literature prompt, but I think you'll find it appropriate. It will require you to do some research, but I really think you'll get something out of it. I recommend you start working on it tonight, so you can make it the most amazing thing you have ever written."

With that, she handed me a sheet and told me to get to my next class.

Chapter Twenty-Five

Now, I know I should've taken Mrs. Baker's advice and read the prompt that night, but I didn't have the opportunity because I had to attend my first night at Sister Correggio's Apostolate. I found it odd that my parents punished me for not doing well in school, lying to them, and being gay by sending me to more classes. They must've figured that education could fix anything. My dad drove me to the apostolate and waited in the car, making sure I entered the building before he drove away.

The apostolate hid itself in the back corner of a strip mall. They had painted the large front windows with pictures of Jesus nailed to the cross. I couldn't look inside to see its interior because of these paintings, so I opened the door hesitantly and crossed into a warm inviting room. Someone had laid out rows of folding chairs all facing the same direction. At the very end of the room stood a podium next to a table full of doughnuts and bottles of soda. A group of young men and women stood collectively around this table eating the doughnuts and laughing. Considering my fear of social outings, I avoided making eye contact and took a seat in the back row.

I concerned myself with making sure nobody noticed me but I had failed to notice the person hiding in the shadows behind me. This presence announced itself by *ahem-ing*. The sound sent back a repressed vision from my grade school experience, and I turned around to see that repressed vision incarnate — a nun dressed in full black habit. I quickly looked at her hands to see if she held a ruler, but they were behind her back and I couldn't see their knuckle-cracking potential. This made me even more nervous as I plunged my hands in my armpits.

When the nun had my full attention, she addressed me, "You must be new here."

I cleared my throat, preparing my best speaking voice. "Yes, sister, this is my first time at one of these meetings."

"Well then," she said as she pulled her hands out from behind her back. My worst fears came true. In her left hand she held a ruler, a foot-long variety with the metal edging still attached to insure bloody knuckles if properly cracked. In her other hand she held a perfectly round wicker basket. Inside the basket I could see various bills — mostly fives, a couple of twenties and even a hundred-dollar bill. The nun took the ruler and tapped the side of the basket, grunting softly.

At first, I couldn't figure out what she wanted from me until she tapped the side of the basket again. It dawned on me that the good sister held a collection plate. I had a quick thought of what would happen if I didn't donate some money. Would they let me stay, or would they kick me out of the class? I would have considered testing this theory if her hand held something besides a menacing ruler. I pulled out the only money I had in my pocket, a twenty dollar bill, and threw it into the plate. I wished I had a smaller bill because I wouldn't have much money left over after that twenty left my possession, and I had no way to make any more now that my parents forced me to quit my job. You can't ask for change back from a nun. A look of surprise etched itself on the nun's face.

"A twenty?" she admired as she returned the plate and the ruler behind her back. "How very generous of you. Do you have a sponsor yet?"

"A what?"

A kind smile came over her face. "A sponsor, my son. Someone to help guide you through all of your troubles."

I shook my head and said, "No, my father just brought me here and I really don't know what to expect…"

The sister interrupted me by snapping her fingers at the group gathered around the table of doughnuts and soda. I wondered what happened to the collection plate as the group quieted down and directed their attention to the nun. In unison they all said, "Yes, Sister Denaro."

"Theodore, can you come over here please?"

A boy in the back quit smiling, put his head down and shuffled over to us. He kept his head down as he addressed the nun. "Yes, Sister Denaro."

She responded by using the ruler to gesture at me. "Theodore, meet a new member in need of a sponsor."

Theodore looked up excitedly. "Do you really think I'm ready?"

Sister Denaro hid the ruler and smiled kindly at Theodore. "You have been making wonderful progress, Theodore, and I believe we should move your rehabilitation to the next level. This experience will make you a stronger person."

"Thank you, Sister Denaro."

"You're welcome, Theodore. Now why don't the two of you get acquainted?" She backed up into the shadow of the room, disappearing from view.

Theodore mumbled at her departure. "Wow, me a sponsor. Who would have thought?"

I think he forgot about me because he stood there with his mouth open, staring at the place where Sister Denaro once stood. I nudged him to jar him out of his reverie. "I would never have thought it."

He turned to look at me. "So you just started here tonight?"

"I guess so."

"Well, I'm Ted," he said as he offered me his hand.

I took his hand and tried to think of a way I could make casual conversation. "So, are you gay, too?"

157

A look of shock came over Ted's face. "Gay people don't come here."

I couldn't believe it. Not only had I given my last twenty dollars to a nun threatening me with a ruler, but I had given it to the wrong nun. I went to the wrong place, and I admitted my homosexuality to a complete stranger. The people here probably had drug addictions and I let them know about my gay struggle. I hid my head in my hand and groaned, "I can't believe my dad took me to the wrong place."

Ted quickly corrected me. "Oh, you're definitely in the right place, but there are no gay people."

I looked up through my fingers. "I don't understand."

Ted sat down next to me. "Everybody here has an affliction with same-sex attraction."

That really confused me. "I thought all gay people had an affliction with same-sex attraction."

Ted let out a little laugh. "No, people afflicted with same-sex attraction only have an attraction to people of the same sex, whereas gay people act on those feelings. The people in this room have good Catholic restraint. We help each other here."

"Unh?"

"Think of it this way. You sit in a room full of hot, tantalizing men. They all wear nice, form-fitting shirts and pants a little too tight that reveal the size of their packages. One of these guys has amazing hair, haunting blue eyes, and luscious, succulent lips. You start fantasizing about sucking on those lips for a while, and then you think about what it would feel like to have that package inside you. You start fantasizing about it." Ted closed his eyes. "Yeah, Mike, I know you see me thinking about you." He started rubbing the inside of his thighs, and I looked around the room a little uncomfortably to see if anybody else noticed. All of a sudden, a large ruler came out of the dark and smacked Ted's knuckles. I never saw where the ruler came from or retreated to, but Ted shrieked, and woke up out of his fantasy. He looked around the room and remembered where he was. "Consider that temptation. But here at Sister Correggio's Apostolate, they give you a sponsor to work with. When you have those temptations, you can call your sponsor and he will talk you through that feeling. You'll never have to act upon it."

"Wow, it sounds a lot like Alcoholics Anonymous."

"Oh, you have a problem with alcohol, too?" Ted asked me, but I couldn't answer because a different nun entered the room and walked up to the podium.

She tapped the top of the podium with her ruler and said, "Children, let's call this meeting to order. Please take your seats."

Ted quieted down and faced forward as all the other people in the room put down their doughnuts or sodas and found their seats.

■　■　■

When the group had quieted down, the nun looked at someone seated in the front row. "Neil, you can start the meeting now."

A young man dressed in a fashionable suit stood and walked up to the podium, as the nun blended into the background. He looked over at the nun and said, "Thank you, Sister Correggio."

She gave him a slight nod to proceed.

"Good evening folks, and welcome to the regular meeting of the Denver chapter of the Sister Correggio Apostolate. My name is Neil and I have an affliction with same-sex attraction. At this moment, I would like to open the meeting with a moment of silence followed by the Prayer of the Faithful."

He bowed his head and everybody else followed suit. In contrast, my head bobbled around. I couldn't believe the way everybody else acted, and I vowed to never act the same way until my eyes made contact with Sister Correggio's. She glowered at me with a disapproving frown while smacking her ruler in the palm of her hand. It felt better to just go along with the crowd. I bowed my head. As soon as I looked involved in meaningful prayer, the rest of the group broke out in unison.

"Oh Lord, we call upon You in our time of sorrow, that You give us the strength and will to bear our heavy burdens, until we can feel the warmth and love of Your divine compassion. Be mindful of us while we struggle to comprehend life's hardships.

"Keep us ever in Your watch, 'til we can walk again with light hearts and renewed spirits."

Everybody raised their heads and said, "Amen." I joined in with the Amen and looked at Sister Correggio for approval. She smiled and my heartbeat calmed. Neil continued the meeting. "At this time, we would ask any new members to introduce themselves."

Nobody had told me I would have to talk in these classes. I thought it would be like any other class, I could sit quietly in the back, pretend to take notes, and leave with nobody the wiser that I had ever entered the building at all. I didn't expect this new wrinkle. The fact that apparently no other new members had signed up that night made it completely unfair. Everyone in the room had turned around to stare at me, expecting me to say something.

Ted nudged me in the side of the ribs and whispered harshly in my ear, "Dude, you have to introduce yourself. Don't ruin my opportunity."

Not that I cared about Ted's opportunity, but I knew I needed to stand up and do what they asked of me so they would stop staring. So I stood up and waved at them. "Hi."

I could hear Ted hissing at me, "Tell them your name, dude."

"My name is Tristan."

I began to sit down again even though everybody continued to stare at me. Ted helped guide me even further, "Tell them a little bit about yourself."

"Oh!" I stood back up. "'I grew up here in Denver and I go to Arapahoe High…"

"No, dude," I heard Ted grumble, "the *reason* that you're here."

"Oh!" I smacked my head in embarrassment and looked out in

the group. "I came here because I'm gay."

I could feel the air rush away from me as a collective intake from everybody shook the room. One person in the front put his hands over his ears and shrieked, "Make the bad man stop saying the evil things."

Ted quickly corrected me. "Dude, what did we just talk about?"

I flashed a sheepish grin. "Sorry, I meant to say that I have an affliction with same-sex attraction."

The collective breath exhaled, and everybody said in unison, "*Welcome, Tristan.*"

I took that as my cue to sit back down. Everybody turned away from me, and Ted whispered, "We have to work on your introduction." I hoped that I would never have to go through that experience again. It just made me happy to get that over with.

Neil continued the class by asking if anybody would like to come forth and tell their story. The guy who called me a bad man raised his hand and Neil called on him. Neil sat down as the eager participant walked up behind the podium.

He started off, "Hi, my name is Kirk."

"*Hello, Kirk,*" everybody said in unison.

"Thank you for letting me make this little update in my life. As you all know, except for Tristan." Kirk said my name while giving the quotation marks sign with his fingers and rolling his eyes. "I have been exploring the heterosexual option in my life. Through the guidance of Sister Correggio, I have worked with many proven methods to excite myself about the opposite sex. I have looked through the library of materials and have taken home many *Playboy* and *Penthouse* magazines. I even took home a copy of *Hustler*. Though it piqued my curiosity, it didn't convert me to the heterosexual lifestyle."

At this moment, Kirk bowed his head in shame. The crowd gifted words of encouragement toward Kirk. He found the courage within himself and looked up to continue his story.

"I'm proud to report that these setbacks did not discourage me.

I set out to find other ways to find heterosexuality within myself. I started asking girls at school out on dates. Well, that didn't work out so well either because they all knew I had an affliction with same-sex attraction, and none of them would go out on a date with me."

The crowd sighed, feeling the same pain that Kirk felt. I found myself sighing with all of them at the same time. I had no idea I could fall into line so easily.

"But I found a new way to meet girls — the Internet. I went on to Christian Soulmates, the site that claims they've helped over a million Christians find a spouse. Well, only after a day of posting my information, some girl contacted me and we went on a date."

Everybody, including myself, leaned in closer.

"Well, I went on this date last Friday night. We went out to dinner, and things went really well. My heterosexual friends tell me that she is definitely attractive and she lives by the same Catholic values that I do. We really enjoyed each other's company, and we plan to go out again this Friday night. The best part was at the end of the evening when I dropped her off at home and we shook hands."

The whole room gasped at the scandal.

"And I think I felt something move inside me."

I started to think that if Sister Correggio's Apostolate could help Kirk, it might be able to help me with my problem.

Chapter Twenty-Six

Ted and I exchanged information so I could call him if I ever felt the temptation of my affliction for same-sex attraction bubbling up. I went home feeling better about myself. In fact, that feeling continued the next day at school. I started to believe I could lick this problem with my affliction. I could even end up living the normal life my parents had always envisioned for me. I just needed to keep a positive attitude about my situation and believe in the therapeutic methods developed by Sister Correggio's Apostolate. I could even convince Thomas that he would want to go this way as well. After all the drama had settled, a really good friendship could grow. As I was beginning to get one of my life problems under control, I knew I needed to work on the others as well. The next biggest issue my parents bugged me about was my grade in English, and I knew how to take care of that. I just needed to get the most amazing grade ever on that essay Mrs. Baker gave me to write.

On Tuesday night of that week, I looked at the assignment for the first time. This way I could get a head start on writing it. I couldn't do anything else because of all the restrictions my parents placed on my social life, so this turned out to be the best thing I could do to avoid my parents. I had the added bonus of making them happy because I was focusing on my schoolwork, and not spending so much time shuffling around the house in an obvious depression.

That night I psyched myself up to get a jump on this

assignment. I pulled out the ratty piece of paper from the bottom of my backpack and read the prompt for the first time. My joy at being ahead of the game quickly disappeared when I read the title on top of the page. Printed on the top was a word that I'd never heard of and had no idea what it meant — Transcendentalism.

I became even more discouraged when underneath the word, I saw the prompt:

All men should strive
to learn before they die
what they are running from, and to, and why.
~James Thurber

There was nothing else written on the paper. I turned it over to see if there was anything written on the back. I didn't understand the prompt. What the hell was I supposed to do with this? Did I miss some other instruction some place? Was this a joke, and was someone recording me right now so Mrs. Baker could exploit me on YouTube later? I knew the best thing I could do, would be to talk to Mrs. Baker about the prompt, but I decided to Google the word instead.

After 575,000 results, I went with the most reliable one, *Wikipedia*, and clicked on it. I read the brief description, and it surprised me that any public institution would allow me to study something like this. My parents would blow a blood vessel in their collective brain if they knew that my teacher wanted me to write a paper about transcendentalism. I started formulating plans for using this information to get Mrs. Baker fired, but the thoughts about transcendentalism intrigued me. So I didn't run downstairs waving the piece of paper in front of my parents. I read on about this new idea.

Basically, they made the idea for this philosophy, as they called it, really simple. It combines Eastern thought with Western religions, whatever that means. But this one guy, Ralph Waldo

Emerson, got sick of preachers telling him what to do and how to act, so he revolted against them. He traveled the country advising people that listening to preachers would produce nothing but evil thoughts for a person. This made me wonder about his hypocrisy, but I excused it because I found truth in his words. He said the greatest evil in the world was organized religion, because religious leaders have an agenda and would do anything to impose that agenda upon other people. This Emerson guy said that if we wanted to find the truth to our spirituality, we had to look within ourselves. Also that we just needed to stop listening to all the distractions life had to offer, and listen to our inner beings (I tried to listen but it sounded like blood pumping). He went on to explain that we needed to get away from society if we truly wanted to connect with ourselves. We could do this by devoting more time to nature. This thought made me long for the moments I could spend up at Red Rocks and how I truly felt at peace there. I started to think that everything I learned in English class wasn't a complete waste of my time.

I just couldn't figure out how the quote she gave me had anything to do with the assignment, and what the assignment was really about.

. . .

I spent the rest of my week the usual way — blending into the background while trying at the same time to explore the true meaning of this quote and what it had to with transcendentalism. I would avoid socializing at school all day to get in touch with my real being. Of course, it didn't feel any different from any other day at school, except I now had some purpose behind my avoidance.

It still didn't help. I had no idea how to write this. At night, I would try to bang away at some idea and still never reach any true insight. I would go to bed every night more frustrated than the night before. And in the back of my mind, my grade in English kept nagging me. If I didn't do well on this essay, then I wouldn't pass the class. My parents would get even angrier with me, and if my punishment over the last couple of weeks proved anything, they would send me away to some boarding school where the nuns would harass me with rulers on a regular basis. I needed to do well on this essay, and I had to turn to the only person who could help me out — Mrs. Baker.

By the time Friday rolled around, I swallowed my pride, and I went to talk to Mrs. Baker about what exactly she wanted me to do with this assignment. I stayed after class, patiently waiting for everybody to exit before I asked for help.

"Tristan, good to see you. I hope you're working on that assignment."

I pulled the assignment out of my back pocket, hoping it would give me some courage. "Yes, that's part of the reason I'm here right now. I'm struggling a little with the assignment. Could you help me out?"

"Sure thing," she said as she motioned to the chair I always dreaded sitting in. I sat down anyway. "What can I do for you?"

"Do you remember the assignment you gave me?"

She nodded quickly at my question. "Yes, the one on transcendentalism. Have you been working on it?"

"Well, not exactly."

"Tristan, you need to get a really good grade on it if you want to have any chance of passing this class. I would recommend not waiting until the last minute."

I tried to calm her down before she got out of hand. "I understand that."

"Then I suggest you get started on it."

"I would. In fact, I've tried, but I keep getting tangled up in the logistics."

I could see a light go on inside her head. It surprised me that teachers, the pillar of wisdom within our culture, could be so dense sometimes. "Oh, what's your difficulty?"

I gave her the assignment sheet as if that would demonstrate my frustration with it. "The prompt has me confused. I don't understand what you want me to do with it."

Mrs. Baker pulled the assignment closer to her and looked it over. A smile grew on her face as if some long-lost joke had just come back to her. She pushed the piece of paper back across the table toward me. "I can see how this prompt might cause you some difficulty."

"Well, what do you want me to do with it?" I said with all the sincerity of my heart.

She bluntly replied, "Figure it out."

"What?"

"Tristan, all semester long, I have given you prompts about life, literature, and our society, and you have written whatever you wanted, no matter what I asked you to write. Sometimes, you base your essay so loosely on the prompt that I have trouble understanding the thoughts bouncing around inside that skull of yours. I chose this prompt especially for you, hoping you would take the time to write a beautiful essay based on what you find. If you decided to ignore it, I wouldn't have a problem with that. I would just give you the grade you deserved. But if you would ponder this nugget of wisdom for yourself, then brilliant things might start happening for you. It comes down to you. I don't want you to think about your boyfriend, your parents, or your friends, or even about Heaven or Hell. No, Tristan, this is about *you*, and I hope against all my good judgment that you figure this out."

"Thank you?"

"Sure. I'm glad I could help. Now you better run off to your next class before the bell rings." She turned her back to me, and started doing some work on her computer. Once again, I had a conversation with my English teacher and learned nothing at all.

. . .

I spent most of that weekend staring at the cursor on my computer screen. I would look at the prompt, hoping to find some inspiration there. My fingers had run over the page so many times that I wore it down, but no wonderful insight ever came. The more I thought about this essay, the more it frustrated me. I wanted to take the prompt and shove it into a fire and watch with glee as each individual word burned down to a piece of insignificant ash. I knew I couldn't do that, though, because if I did I would have no chance of finishing this essay.

I began to see this as a regular occurrence throughout my high school career. They would force me to retake this English class over and over again until I passed. My grade would struggle along until Mrs. Baker would pull some crazy quote out of her butt and demand I write an essay on it. My ultimate downfall involved figuring out what I was running from, to, and around. Mrs. Baker would end up handing my paper back on the last day of school and tell me, "Well, I guess we'll see a lot of each other again next year?" I would then go out and drink myself stupid at some bar, because by then I would have turned twenty-one.

At least my parents believed I was working really hard because I spent so much time in front of the computer. I wonder if they would have felt the same way if they knew I spent an hour writing nothing but, *Fuck, fuck, fuck, fuck, fuck, fuck, fuck...* on one page before deleting it. I bet if I double spaced it and turned it in to Mrs. Baker, she would give me a better grade than anything else I could've come up with. Many times I thought about doing just that, but away in a corner of my mind some consequence I hadn't thought about tugged at me. I tried to come up with something more appropriate.

On the bright side, staring at that cursor gave me something more exciting to do than hang out with my parents. Every once in a while I would get so frustrated that I'd walk downstairs to look for something to eat or catch up on a little television. I quickly regretted that decision because my dad had planted himself on the couch with the remote firmly in his hand, and Mom was puttering around the kitchen preparing dinner. Both would look up at me expectantly hoping conversation would sprout out of nowhere. When I realized that their hopes might actually come true, I quickly slunk away to my room where I could continue with my other frustration. The nuisance of the essay pained me, but not nearly as much as a conversation with my parents would have.

Even though this essay bugged the hell out of me, it wasn't the worst aspect of the weekend. It was the sense of isolation I felt. Now I know I'm not the most social person in the world, but I feel a certain sense of relief when surrounded by my peers. I feel a certain kind of connectedness, even if they don't think anything like me.

Most of this isolation came from being separated from Thomas and Tessa. I didn't leave either one on the best of terms, but I still missed the interaction with both of them. I didn't know which one I missed more, but I felt the emptiness in my heart.

I knew that Tessa was still mad at me, but if I could talk to her I could work everything out. We had been through too much together for her to ignore me. She needed me as much as I needed her. I longed to hear her wisdom about my troubled life, and she needed me so she'd have somebody to worry about. Her true nature forced her to have somebody to look after. If she couldn't look after me, she would seek someone else to look after. She had done that before she met me and always ended up finding some boyfriend who treated her like garbage. She wouldn't get rid of that person because she felt if she did, he would fall completely apart. Tessa would stick through a terrible relationship until I came around, and in me she found someone she could help. I know it sounds selfish, but I have a more honest relationship with her than I do with anybody else, and I think Tessa would feel the same way.

As for Thomas, I just yearned for his touch. He took a chance on me, and I was eternally grateful for it. I knew these thoughts went against the teachings of Sister Correggio, but sitting there by myself in front of that blank computer screen, these ideas kept creeping back into my brain. The devil kept trying to tempt me into an unholy life. I needed to stop having these feelings. My hand went into my pocket and thumbed the card with Ted's number on it. I thought that might help me with my cravings. But even if it helped, it didn't matter because I still hadn't heard from Thomas since the incident. I kept wondering if his parents had isolated him much the same way my parents had with me, or if he just had no desire to see me again.

These thoughts ran through my lonely mind and drove me crazy. It just made me madder at these stupid transcendentalists. They seemed to have all the answers in life, but I bet none of them ever had to spend his life in isolation. If they had gone through that experience even once, then maybe I would have trusted their beliefs.

Chapter Twenty-Seven

Sunday's class returned me to the uncomfortable world of teenage social life. All the whispering that circulated when I entered a room didn't create this feeling. I knew they whispered about me, but I also knew I could do nothing about it. If I fretted about what they said then I would live a miserable existence, so I just didn't listen to their crap and went about my business.

My mom's turn to join me for class didn't make me uncomfortable either. I was also getting used to one of my parents accompanying me everywhere I went. It embarrassed me, but once again I could do nothing about it. If I threw a tantrum, it would've just brought more unwanted attention to me, and if I tried to avoid my parents, they would find a way to make their presence more obvious. I just needed to accept that they were going to follow me for a while and eventually they would tire of it and leave me alone.

Even Thomas didn't make things difficult for me. He missed the class again. If he had shown up, it might have been weird, especially with me sitting in the front row with my mom. I started to come to the realization that the relationship I had with Thomas might be over, and I should just accept that. It hurt me to think this, but my parents, my classmates, my religion, and most of society kept telling me I had sinned terribly when I cultivated my attraction to another boy. I needed to start listening to what these people told me instead of believing I could find the answer somewhere within me.

You would think that one of these things would make me feel uncomfortable during the lecture that night, or maybe a combination of all of them together, but they didn't. The subject of Father Brett's lesson, on the other hand, did. His lesson was about free will, sin, forgiveness, and grace. Father Brett must have put together that night's lecture with me in mind. It really started to annoy me, the way he could always connect his little talks with the problems occurring in my life. He probably thought he could get through to me and by doing that, it would ensure his place in Heaven. Either that or he just enjoyed watching me squirm in the front row. My mom bubbled with joy about the subject. She even put down her cross-stitch so she could focus her attention on it. Now you can see why Father Brett's lecture made me uncomfortable.

Father Brett began by saying that even though God has a great cosmic plan which will always remain a mystery to us, this great cosmic plan comes at the whim of free will. God didn't want a bunch of mindless worshippers wandering around doing good things. Rather, He wanted all of humanity to choose to do good, and by doing so they would show their love to Him. This sounds like a really great idea, but it did come with a risk because with all this freedom He granted us, we could always choose to do wrong. Father Brett summed this idea up best by stating, *"Freedom comes with great responsibility."* I wondered if that quote came directly from one of the *Spiderman* movies.

He talked about how this choice was the key to the confirmation class. *Choice* is a very adult idea. Even though we have gone through many of the sacraments, we had not made the decision to receive those sacraments. Our parents and our community guided us to the right decision. Things had changed though. We had made it to the point in our lives that we needed to make the decision about our faith — for ourselves — not with the help of our parents, confirmation teacher, or even priest. Father Brett wanted us to know that the more we made the right choice, or chose good over evil, the freer we would become. And the best choice at this time was to become confirmed in the Catholic Church, so we had better choose it.

He put it another way for us. Father Brett referred to all the countless hours of cartoons we had all watched. Every cartoon character sees a little devil sitting on their left shoulder while an angel sits on their right shoulder. We should consider the same dynamic happening with every decision we make. If we listened to the devil, he would lead us to an eternity in Hell, whereas if we listen to the angel, we would eventually reach a life of eternal freedom. We just needed to listen to the voice of the angel, or as Father Brett told us, *Father Brett.*

I could almost start to see how this *was* a choice for ourselves. My mother seemed to have grasped this concept because she patted me on my left knee and said, "Listen to what he has to say."

Father Brett did explain to us that even though God gave us a choice to do good, every once in a while, we make mistakes, or sin. We didn't need to worry if we sinned because everyone had done so at some point in their life. We just needed to do the right thing after we recognized our sin. We needed to ask for forgiveness, and in order to receive this forgiveness, we must first acknowledge we have sinned.

Father Brett paused to allow us time to contemplate this thought. I tried to understand his circular logic, but when I looked up, Father Brett was staring down at me. I can't think of a creepier moment in my life. At first, I couldn't understand why he gave *me* all this attention, but then I remembered what he had just told us. Did he want me to confess my sin? Did he want me to stand up in front of my peers and explain to them about the awful thing I had done? Hadn't this class embarrassed me enough? Did I have to subject myself to the humiliation Father Brett asked of me?

I looked over at my mom. She also grinned eagerly at me, probably thinking I would do the same thing Father Brett hoped I would do. I started to understand what it meant to have free will in this world.

I looked back at Father Brett and made a small motion with my hand for him to continue with the lecture. At first, I don't think he got the hint because he stood there staring at me like a pretentious prig. I opened my eyes wide and cocked my head slightly for him to get the hint. He still persisted. *"When we ask for forgiveness, we realize our imperfections. We can start to accept ourselves as a productive member of society, and self-esteem starts to grow."*

He looked at me again with that same expectant grin. I could see Mom out of the corner of my eye. All the hope in the world oozed out of her. I just sat there with my arms crossed looking up at Father Brett.

He tried one more time. *"The only sin that can't be forgiven is the one we don't ask forgiveness for."*

I closed my eyes and shook my head to indicate that he wouldn't get what he wanted. He finally got the hint and continued on with his lecture.

"Next, we need to talk about the two different types of sin, venial and mortal..."

Chapter Twenty-Eight

Tristan Adamson
Mrs. Baker
Literature and Composition

Running Culture

The great Transcendentalist, James Thurber, once said, "All men should strive to learn before they die what they are running from, and to, and why." Obviously, people regarded Mr. Thurber as a very intelligent man; otherwise we wouldn't be quoting him today. Millions of people have analyzed and admired his ideas for years, and those ideas have helped them become better people. This essay will explain why.

First off, James Thurber talks about running. I don't run much. In fact, I engage in more of a sedentary lifestyle. I do enjoy watching television, and every once in a while curling up with a good book. Neither of these activities involve running. Because of this sedentary lifestyle, I've grown out of shape. Maybe if I ran a little, it would help me get into better shape. I could think of worse things to do. I've been told that after a while it actually starts to feel pretty good. Then you start to feel pretty good about yourself. This could be what James Thurber was talking about. He must have run a lot because he definitely felt so good about himself that he published his ideas for all of humanity to read for many generations.

This brings me to my second point, knowing where to run from and where to run to. Nobody just runs aimlessly around unless in gym class, but I don't think you want me to get started on that. A gym teacher will make students run around aimlessly in circles with no real discernible purpose except for the fact that I think gym teachers enjoy seeing young teenagers suffer. I believe this has to do with some deep-seated emotional disturbance generating from some daddy issues they had while growing up. Why this translates into running I will never know. But I digress.

Except for the aforementioned case, most people know where they are running from and to. A runner must have a place from which they start their run, so of course they know where they are coming from. They also need to have a destination in mind. If they don't, they could easily get lost. It would be like running blindfolded down dangerous alleys and into unknown situations. It could be very detrimental to any runner. Runners have their courses plotted out so that they won't run into danger.

This leads us to the question of why people run. I really struggled with this concept for a while. I see people out there running, and every time I see them I feel sorry for them. I wonder why they would subject themselves to so much pain and agony. They never look happy while running. In fact, some of them even look like they might die. So then, why do they do it? Obviously, some of them do it because they want to get in good shape. Some of them do it for the glory because they might want to compete in races at some time. Some of them might do it just to get out of the house instead of dealing with a crazy parent. Some of them do it because a big sweaty gym teacher on a golf cart motivates them. Whatever the reason for somebody to run, it is personal. Nobody can convince a person to engage in this solitary activity, which makes running an act of transcendentalism.

Apparently, if you really want to find yourself, you need to become a runner. Nobody knows themselves better than runners. I don't know if I will ever know my true self, because I don't like to run. If some other activity came along that helped me discover myself and didn't involve sweating, I would happily do that instead. Until then I will just try to figure it out. Go Transcendentalism!

. . .

I sat in my usual seat in Mrs. Baker's room quietly waiting for her to tell me about my attempt on the essay. She looked through it carefully while I waited for her feedback. I had a feeling she would consider it brilliant. I think I really nailed this Transcendentalism thing, especially the conclusion. Who wouldn't love that conclusion? She would love my conclusion and essay so much that she would disregard everything else I had done in her class up to that point and she'd give me an *A* for the whole semester. Mrs. Baker would forgive the fact that I hadn't quite gotten any of the other literature we read because I understood this one item so well. Transcendentalism just happened to hold so much importance that nothing else would matter.

Mrs. Baker finished reading the paper and put it on the table. I smiled my most confident grin. Mrs. Baker shook her head and looked down at her desk where my attempt at an *A*-style essay sat like a guilty confession.

I tried to defend my case, but it came out whiny. "What now?"

Mrs. Baker looked up from her obvious grief and pinched the bridge of her nose. "Tristan, you missed the point completely."

"What are you talking about? For a not very athletic person, I think I described the culture of running very nicely. Personally, I don't know why you gave me a prompt about running. Obviously, I don't run often..."

Mrs. Baker raised her hands up to stop me. "Since when did you become such a babbler?"

"What?"

She leaned in closer to explain. "Tristan, you've sat in my classroom for half a year trying to hide in the background. You don't want anybody to notice you, and even when I have you sitting up here to discuss your paper, I can't get more than a couple of words out of you. But now, you sound like a middle school girl with a crush. When did this start happening?"

She didn't know anything about me because I always considered myself a babbler. She should have noticed it by now. I tried to get her back on the more important subject. "What about my paper?"

"Sorry," she said, and returned to my last vestige of hope sitting upon her desk. "Tristan, you missed the whole point about the quote. Some stuff in this paper I could look at as a metaphor, but I'd have to stretch it a bit. This quote has nothing to do with the running culture."

"Then why does he talking about running?"

"Tristan, he's not talking about running when he mentions running."

"Then what is he talking about?"

Mrs. Baker pinched the bridge of her nose again. "How do I explain this? Think of it as a metaphor."

"Oh!"

"Does that help?"

"Yeah, a metaphor for what?"

"For *life*, Tristan! James Thurber wrote a metaphor for life and the way you live it."

"Oh, that makes sense," I told her, even though I still had no idea what a metaphor was.

I looked down at the assignment sheet as James Thurber's quote loomed back at me. Even after Mrs. Baker's explanation, I found myself completely lost with this assignment.

Chapter Twenty-Nine

Mrs. Baker believed I had made a breakthrough with the assignment. She sent me home with the expectation I would work on it that evening. I didn't have a chance to touch it, though, because I had to attend my second meeting at Sister Correggio's Apostolate. In fact, since that evening, I didn't look at my essay again for a while.

I know what people might be thinking. What horrible thing could have happened that I wouldn't work on the one thing that could have saved my English grade? I've got you now thinking about all the horrible, terrible, no-good, rotten things that could happen to me, and I bet whatever you think, the worst possible thing has not yet crossed your mind. Go ahead. Close your eyes. Picture the worst possible thing you think could've happened to me at Sister Correggio's Apostolate. Do you have that image in your mind? Now, imagine that thing as a hundred times worse. You can't do it, can you? Probably because you can't imagine something worse when you've already imagined the worst. But after I tell you what happened, you will have no choice but to agree that what happened equates to a hundred times worse than what you thought was the worst.

The meeting started off pleasantly enough. Dad dropped me off again and I walked into the same scene as last time — kids looking for help and solidarity, gathered around a table, laughing, drinking soda, and eating doughnuts. Ted saw me and waved me over to join the group. As I started over, Sister Denaro emerged out of the background with her collection plate. This time I came ready with a five-dollar bill. My dad gave it to me before dropping me off for the meeting. The good sister looked a little disappointed, but what did she expect from somebody my age without a job. It should satisfy her that she got anything at all.

I went over to the table to partake in the sodas and doughnuts. Ted introduced me to a couple of people, and we chatted before the start of the meeting. I really didn't get to know anybody better, and nobody felt any more comfortable, but we couldn't ignore the formalities. You could taste the tension in the air that nobody wanted to talk about but everybody knew was there. It could've come from the struggle we all experienced with our attractions to people of the same sex. It could've come from standing in a group of people who happened to all be the same sex. It could've come from the rising barometer and the threat of the year's first blizzard. Wherever it came from, the tension hung in the air. Before it got to the point that one of us would explode, Sister Correggio tapped the edge of the podium with her ruler and motioned for Neil to get the meeting started.

Neil walked up to the podium. He said the same prayer to a chorus full of bowed heads. I bowed my head like a good Catholic boy afflicted with an attraction to the same sex. I didn't say the words because I didn't know them, but I mouthed the word *watermelon*. The nuns never noticed the difference.

Then Neil asked for any new members. I was pretty sure that Sister Correggio wouldn't get any new members for a month or two. The Apostolate couldn't possibly find a new member every week, because if they did, they would pack the place. But despite that logic, a new member did stand up that night. I didn't see him because he sat in the back row and I was sitting toward the front. Apparently my dad's ideals were starting to rub off on me. I didn't even notice that most of the people had turned their chairs or heads so they could see this new member. I didn't really pay attention until I heard a familiar voice say, "Hi, you really shouldn't consider me a new member because like the prodigal son, I have returned to these meetings."

I couldn't believe my ears. I had held that voice up on a pedestal for the past couple of weeks. I started to think I would never hear it again, but here, in the one place I thought it could never enter, I heard it. I turned my chair to confirm with my eyes what my ears already knew. There he stood with his beautiful brown eyes hidden behind those luscious locks of hair.

"My name is Thomas Edwards, and I have an affliction with same-sex attraction."

I didn't know if this recent development should have excited me or scared me. Conflicting emotions attacked me. I had hoped for so long that I could have at least one word with Thomas so I could explain my side of the story, but at the same time I had found a safe haven at Sister Correggio's Apostolate. Should I jump on the opportunity that God had given me? Or should I shy away from the temptation that Hell had presented? Fortunately, Thomas's introduction solved that problem.

"At one time I believed this treatment had cured me. I hadn't felt an attraction to a boy for a very long while. In fact, I appreciated women for the first time in my life. I even dated a few."

Kirk chirped from the other side of the room, "You go, brother."

"Thank you," Thomas conceded before returning to his story. "You see I just moved here from Oregon. Back home, I had a lot of support for my affliction. I had a sponsor, and I even sponsored a couple of people. This program helped me a lot."

This praise seemed to please the nuns because knowing smirks started to appear on their faces.

"Like I said, I started to date girls. In fact, there was one girl I dated pretty consistently. I guess you could call her my girlfriend. I understood the true meaning of the word *love* with her, and it felt so wonderful and so right. It felt completely different from the hollow relationships I had with boys."

The last statement stung me deeply. I never considered the short relationship I had with Thomas as hollow.

"But then my dad got a new job in Colorado. We had to pack up our stuff and move out here. I had to leave my girlfriend behind. My dad said I would find love again and there were just as many girls out in Colorado who would love me the same as they did in Oregon. I didn't think my affliction would cause any concern when I came out here. I thought I had it under control. Until I met *Him*."

He obviously didn't know I sat in the audience because he went on talking about me as if I couldn't hear him. It made me feel good because I could learn more about his feelings for me. Maybe I had misjudged his previous statement. Maybe he didn't find our relationship hollow. Maybe he had hollow relationships with boys until he met me.

"He saw me at a party and I don't know how he knew I had an affliction with same-sex attraction, but he knew. I sat there minding my own business. I even talked to a girl I felt I could cultivate some good Catholic feelings with, when He came up to me."

Maybe he wasn't talking about me. I didn't remember this story the same way. He had been talking to two other guys when I first saw him and I don't ever remember going up to talk to him.

"He gave me a couple of compliments and convinced me to go downstairs to this laundry room."

If he wasn't talking about me, he ended up in the laundry room a lot.

"While down there, he attacked me. His hands covered my body. I remember them distinctly caressing my butt."

The story had a profound effect on everybody in the room. The boys leaned in further, hanging on every new word coming from Thomas's mouth.

"His other hand danced in my hair."

Boys struggling with same-sex attraction held hands. Rulers emerged from behind the nuns' backs.

"I had feelings well up inside me that I hadn't felt for a long time."

The nuns began to lose control of their meeting as they exchanged worried looks among themselves.

"He firmly kissed me and his tongue tickled my esophagus."

I sat there, confused. Who was he talking about? I felt a little twinge of jealousy.

"The experience weirded me out. I had fallen victim to this affliction earlier in my life and I had worked really hard to overcome it. I avoided my old friends because I knew I would fall back into that lifestyle once again if I hung out with them. I dated women and formed a strong relationship with one of them. I was well on my way to leading a normal lifestyle when this individual — this temptation sent to me by the Devil — came into my life and brought my cross painfully back into my existence."

When I first met Thomas, I had the same kind of thoughts running through my head, even though I never considered him a devil.

"It confused me and scared me so much that I could do only one thing. I pulled away from Him, turned around, and ran out of the party."

Sporadic clapping pattered from the audience. I tried to place where I had heard this story before.

"I thought I had escaped from a terrible tragedy. I felt proud of myself. I believed I had found the right path to salvation. But for us who know the persistence of the Devil, he doesn't allow you to escape that easily. This temptation started to show up at my work. He showed up where I would go to relax with friends. He even showed up at my confirmation class."

The crowd gasped at the audacity of this devil. I gasped because I suddenly knew where he had gotten his story.

"He pursued me until eventually I gave into temptation. He forced himself upon me and I kissed him back. I feel terrible and I hope by returning to the apostolate I can find guidance. I hope your strength will give me strength."

The crowd started to clap in response to Thomas's rendition of my story. I felt such a flow of rage course through me. I knew I could not let him get away with this. I stood up to face him through the forest of applause. Thomas looked over and saw me. I could see terror flash behind those beautiful brown eyes. I could see my anger reflected in that fear, and I wondered if Thomas would change his story and report the truth. I did not expect him to do what he did next.

"*The Devil!*" he said as he pointed at me.

"Me?"

The whole room stared at me. I could see by the way they looked that they would never believe anything I said.

"He's even trying to tempt me during my return to counseling. He won't leave me alone until he has me in his grasp. Somebody do something. Help me!"

I stood there trying to work up a defense against his onslaught, but he added to his fiction of pain by flopping down in his seat, pretending to cry. The rest of the group got out of their seats and crowded around me. Their questions flew at me accusingly.

"*How could you treat him that way?*"

"*Don't you know the trouble you've caused him?*"

"*Can't you see his innocence?*"

When I never answered any of the questions, the accusations became more violent.

"*Maybe you are the Devil.*"

"*We should do something so He can't do this again.*"

"*Tar and feather him.*"

"*No, draw and quarter him.*"

"*I don't care how you do it, just kill him.*"

"*No, castrate him.*"

Before they could make a eunuch out of me, Sister Correggio had pushed her way through the crowd to where I stood. She pushed her arms out and parted the crowd like the Red Sea. The finger-pointing quieted down. I never thought seeing a nun would make me so happy. From somewhere in the folds of her sleeve, she pulled out a ruler and pointed it at the unruly mob.

"Let he who is without sin cast the first stone," she reminded all of them. They bowed their heads showing their shame. The good sister turned to face me, and before I even realized it, she whacked me in the ear with the ruler. A ringing reverberated in my head, and my ear went instantly numb. The mob cheered her as if this had turned into a world-class wrestling match and the powers-that-be had cast her as the good guy.

She looked me deep in the eyes as I rubbed my ear. "I think you need to leave." She took the ruler and pointed it toward the front door. I shuffled my way there, wondering what I had done wrong. The mob jeered and hooted as I took my walk of shame. Before I made it to the front door, I looked over at Thomas as he sat in his seat. He smiled at me.

. . .

I don't know what I expected to see my dad doing when I came out of the meeting, maybe reading *The Wall Street Journal* or something like that. I would see him flip through the pages not suspecting anything wrong happening at the apostolate. He would concern himself with the little numbers in their little columns. He wouldn't care about how his son would be getting along with others who had an affliction with same-sex attraction. While busying himself with the financial page, the door to the apostolate would burst open, and I would come running out. In my imagination, he still wouldn't notice me. I would wave my arms and yell at him to start the car, but he would have just pulled out his calculator to make some computations. A group of depraved, mad, drooling boys afflicted with same-sex attraction would flow out of the same door led by nuns waving rulers around. I would dodge cars trying to find a parking spot, hop over kids in strollers as their moms took them shopping, and avoid bums looking for money to buy booze with — all the time trying to get my dad to divert his attention away from his silly newspaper. When I got close, he would finally see the mob, wielding pitch forks and flaming torches, and chasing after his son. He would throw his paper in the back seat, jam his key into the ignition, and start the car. I would slide over the hood, hop into the passenger seat, and we would speed away. While diving away from the crazy mob, my dad would pull me close, hug me, and tell me that he was sorry for forcing me to join that group of inconsiderate heathens.

At least I wished it had happened that way. It was nowhere close to that scenario.

I shuffled out of Sister Correggio's Apostolate with no urgency, no screaming mob, and no nuns with rulers. I didn't have to dodge cars, shoppers, or bums because the apostolate was in an obscure corner of the strip mall and the only people visiting that corner were the ones going to Sister Correggio's. My dad was busy with something and didn't notice me as I made my way to the car, but it wasn't *The Wall Street Journal*. Apparently, he had driven down to Mr. Chicken and was devouring a meal deal, even though my mother had cooked his favorite that night — pot roast. I stood there in the parking lot and watched as he consumed huge chunks of meat and stuffed his face from the cornucopia of fries in the passenger seat.

Snow began to spit from the sky, and I wondered what getting in that car offered me. Where would it take me? What argument would my father have with me? Would I accomplish anything by taking that option? Could I ever become the dutiful son he wanted me to be?

I looked up in the sky. Huge chunks of crystallized water landed on my cheeks and a cold wind melded them to my skin. For the first time in my life, I felt completely free. I knew what I had to do. I knew the clothes I wore were not conducive to the weather, but I didn't care. I knew where I could go, and I knew where it would lead me. As my dad shoveled food into his mouth, I turned away from his car and walked off toward the mountains.

Part Four

Transcendence

Chapter Thirty

I didn't make it very far because the storm blew in quicker than I thought possible. Even though I knew of its looming presence, I underestimated its might. By the time I walked a couple of blocks from the car, a full force gale with stinging snowflakes made me stumble along. I knew I needed to find shelter and quickly.

That was when I saw the beacon that became my saving grace. In bright red neon glowed my salvation, the Burger House. I knew people there that could help me out of my situation, and I didn't think my dad would ever look for me there. He believed I had finished my tenure with the Burger House forever. I had no reason to go back there. If my luck held up, then maybe the schedule that day would include Tessa and I could seek solace in her wisdom.

Tessa was working that night, but my luck didn't account for the large crowd of people who thought this would be their last night to gorge themselves on the fast-food lifestyle of America, because the storm would take over their lives. The place was packed. My luck didn't see Dan's inability to schedule the right amount of people for this unexpected occurrence either. Tessa worked in the back flinging juicy goodness to impatient customers. Sheryl struggled at the counter trying to take everybody's order and put them together in a timely manner. Of course, nobody could find Dan to help them out. I knew he was probably in the back calling everybody he could to try and get them to come in for a couple hours, but every phone call he made had to have been met with resistance.

I took a seat in the booth across from the counter and tried to get Tessa's attention by waving her down. She threw burgers under the heat lamp so fast that she didn't have time to look up. If she had any attention to spare, she directed it at the back office where I could hear her yelling at Dan to get off his lazy butt and help with the rush. I knew she would have more of a chance to win the lottery than to have that happen. At the same time, I knew it gave her comfort because at least she was able to voice her opinion. I also knew she definitely needed to get some help soon or that tiny thread she and Sheryl walked on would snap and the whole night would go to hell quickly. Suddenly, inspiration hit me.

I got up out of my seat and walked behind the counter. Sheryl turned to make some comment, but when she saw it was me, she went right back to helping the customers.

Tessa, on the other hand, got directly to the point when she saw me walk behind the line. She looked at my quizzically. While she continued to flip burgers, she asked, "What the hell are you doing here?"

"Nice to see you, too." I waved at her, but continued to walk to the back room. She stood at the line with a greasy spatula in her hand staring at me until Sheryl slapped the counter on the other side to get her attention.

"Tessa, I don't have time for one of your meltdowns. Can I get those burgers before I have a riot on my hands?"

Tessa snapped out of it and started pulling the burgers from the grill. I walked back to the office where, as I predicted, Dan panicked on the phone.

"Please, would someone just answer their phone?"

"They won't answer, Dan."

Upon hearing my voice, he let out a little yelp and dropped the receiver. He tried to recover by looking up at me and asking, "What the hell are you doing here?"

"Tessa just asked me the same question."

"And what did you tell her?" he asked as he picked up the receiver and put it back in its cradle.

"I didn't tell her anything."

"Well, then maybe you'll answer me?"

"Well, the way I see it, you've got a problem — a lobby full of hungry customers and not enough employees to give them the service they want."

He picked up the receiver again to dial the next number on the list. "Yeah, now you know why I was calling employees. You remember that word *employee*, don't you? It means somebody who works for a living."

"Like I said, they won't answer the phone."

"Why?"

"Because everybody has caller ID. When they see you calling, they won't pick up. Nobody will come out in this weather to work a couple of hours, but apparently they'll come out to eat fast-food. The way I see it, you're going to have to find help somewhere else."

"And where can I find that help?"

"Well, that brings me back to your original question, what the hell I am doing here."

■　■　■

I made a simple deal with Dan. First, I didn't have to wear the uniform. I hated the thing. I don't think anybody in the history of employment at the Burger House ever loved that uniform. There was no way he could get me to put it back on. When he saw where this was heading, he nodded yes and said that was a given.

Second, he would have to feed me. Since he fed every employee during every shift, he agreed. Even though, hunger hadn't attacked me yet, I knew my teenage metabolism would eventually catch up with me and then I would feel the pangs of starvation. I just wanted to make sure he didn't argue this point later on. For whatever lay ahead, I needed a full stomach.

Third, he would have to pay me fifty bucks under the table. This way I wouldn't have to wait for a stupid paycheck to come around with half of it taken out for taxes. I would have fifty bucks in my pocket, and I could avoid my parents a little longer. Dan wasn't too happy with this stipulation. This would mean the fifty dollars would either come out of his pocket or he would have to figure out a way to cook the books to make it look like the Burger House made fifty dollars less that week. I reminded him about his creativity, and I felt confident that he could figure out a way to make it work. He frowned at the price I offered. He knew at most I would only work about five hours and that put me way over minimum wage. I looked out at the swarm of people covering the lobby and told him he could take it or leave it. He took it, but he made sure I stuck around to do all the clean-up for the evening. It seemed like a reasonable trade-off, and it would keep me out of the bad weather.

My final demand almost broke the deal. He had to come out of the office and work the drink machine until the rush ended. He stared at me like a deer in headlights as the fear flooded over him. He actually might have to interact with customers. I could see the idea terrified him, but he wasn't killing his firstborn son because a burning bush told him to. I only asked him to quit hiding from stuff. I could see the wheels in his brain working overtime to decide whether he should take this deal or not. After a while he accepted, since what he was being asked to do wasn't that bad. He could handle the drink station during this awful rush and get an employee for the evening at the same time.

With everything in place, we went out to help with the rush. At first, Tessa couldn't accept my presence, but after ten minutes of working the fryer, we fell back into our old routine. Our separation disappeared into the past. Burgers and fries flowed out in record time, but no matter how hard we tried, we could not make a dent in the mad rush. Weather does weird things to people. You can never predict which way they'll go. A blizzard can do one of two things. It can keep people inside their homes hiding from the storm, or it could bring them out in droves to experience one more moment of freedom before the weather takes it away. The latter was in full swing that night.

Every time it looked like we would make it through the crowd, a new group of people would come waltzing through the front door. The night probably went down as one of the most profitable nights the Burger House had ever experienced. The best part was that for the first time ever I saw Dan help out in the restaurant. He actually seemed to enjoy working the drink station. It weirded me out, but as long as I could remember we couldn't find a single person willing to do that job. The instant that Dan, who never does anything, was put in that position, the heavens opened up and created the perfect match. Dan could be productive for once. He found a mindless job where he didn't have to interact with the customers, and it drowned out the time ticking away through the night. I think I even saw him smile.

Tessa and I grinned throughout the evening. Granted, at first, we could taste the tension, but after we fell into our routine, our unattended friendship renewed itself. It felt great getting back to that routine. Each of us welcomed the experience. We needed it in order to mend our relationship.

Around nine o'clock that evening things started to slow down. In fact, they seemed to stop altogether. The snow started to pile up outside and the roads grew more dangerous. You could no longer see lights of cars passing up and down the street. In fact, the only lights I saw in that night flashed blue as the snowplows tried to stay ahead of the storm. We had a pretty good idea that we wouldn't see any more customers that evening, but that didn't mean we didn't have a lot of work still ahead of us. The whole restaurant was a complete mess. Nobody had time to go out and check the trash cans or clean up the waste left on the tables by hungry customers. Grease splattered the stainless steel, and ketchup and mustard started to congeal in weird places all over the prep tables. The floor had turned into a grease trap waiting to take somebody's feet out from underneath them. A huge job towered in front of us, but at the same time I didn't mind because once again I didn't have any other place to go.

It made me think of my parents. I could just imagine how worried they were about me. It had to have been a strange moment for my dad when he started to see everyone file out of the apostolate. They probably ran to their cars quickly to avoid the impending storm. I wondered how long he waited there until he decided to go inside and check on me. He probably got out of the car, wiped the fry grease from his fingers on the legs of his pants, and went in to talk to the nuns. They probably gave him a weird look when my dad entered the building because he was a little too old to seek out their services. When he started to ask about me, the nuns must have gone into shock.

"You fathered Him?" they would ask.

He would look at them for a second, and then ask, "What has he done now?"

The nuns would line up and make the sign of the cross with their rulers. Sister Correggio would take a step forward and tell my dad, "We have sent Him on his way."

"Why?"

"Because Mr. Adamson, your son is the Devil."

He would look at them for a moment with tears threatening to stream from his eyes. He would fall down on his knees and look up to Heaven, screaming, "*Noooooooo!*"

. . .

"So, you haven't explained why you showed up tonight."

I looked up from my side of the kitchen to see Tessa leaning against her mop, smoking a cigarette. Even though I knew I hadn't officially clocked in, because of habit I snuck a look into the back office to make sure Dan wouldn't start yelling at us for slacking. The usual hypocritical smoke floated from the office, and I knew we had time to talk.

I leaned against my mop thinking of a way I could explain it to Tessa. I decided avoidance was the best option. "Are you seeing anyone right now?"

Tessa laughed. "Okay, I'll bite. No, I'm not seeing anyone. I did date this guy, Pete, for a while. We had fun together, and I thought he understood me. That didn't last long. He had a problem."

"What?"

She made the drinky-drinky motion with her hand while saying, "Glug, glug."

I had to laugh. "You broke up with a guy because he liked to drink? Pretty harsh, considering how much *you* drink."

At first I thought I might have crossed a line because of the way she narrowed her eyes, but she quickly warmed up to the conversation. We fell into our usual comfortable combative nature. "He liked to drink too much."

"Tessa, all teenagers like to drink too much."

"I understand that, but his love of drinking went beyond a normal teenager's indulgence. We'd go to a party and he would get stumbling drunk. At first, it made me laugh until he did it at every party we went to. I always ended up dragging him home and leaving him on the lawn. His parents never grounded him for it. I tried to help him, but he wouldn't listen to me. I tried to find other activities to do besides parties."

"Did it help?"

"At first I thought so. We went to the movies, out to eat, and played putt-putt golf. Once we went for a hike, and during that hike, I realized all the activities I had planned didn't stop him from drinking. About halfway up the trail, I took a sip out of his Nalgene bottle. He had mixed the perfect drink — fifty percent vodka and the rest Gatorade. Apparently, everywhere we went, he found a way to doctor his drink so he could continue his habit. Granted, he didn't get as sloppy drunk as he did at parties, but he couldn't do anything without drinking at the same time. It made him look a little pathetic, and I realized I couldn't save him."

"You can't save them all."

Tessa ashed her cigarette in the trash can. "Apparently, I can't save any of them, but let's talk about you. Good job of avoiding the subject, first of all, but you will tell me why you decided to show up here in the middle of a blizzard."

I started mopping again and said, "You know, I drove by and saw that you might need some help. I knew Dan would have trouble finding somebody to cover, and I saw the perfect opportunity to make a little extra money."

"So where did you park your car?"

"Over on the other side of the building."

"And your parents don't care?"

"Of course not."

"Do they even know you're here? I never saw you give them a call."

"I used the phone in the office to tell them."

"So you can leave the house again?"

"Of course. They un-grounded me up a couple of days ago."

Tessa ran her cigarette under a faucet before throwing it into the garbage can. "Cool, then we can hang out tomorrow night."

I stopped mopping. "Well, not exactly, because I have lots of school work to do, and church. You know, that confirmation class thing. Plus my parents still want me to go to Sister Correggio's Apostolate."

"What?"

"Oh, I forgot, you don't know about that. This place helps me with my problem."

Tessa raised her left eyebrow. "What problem, the fact that you're gay?"

"I have an affliction with same-sex attraction."

Tessa suppressed a laugh. "What? I have never heard a more serious pile of bullshit than that. I don't care what you call it — homosexuality, being queer, or an affliction with same-sex attraction — but it all comes down to the same thing. You're gay. The sooner you recognize that, the sooner you'll find happiness within yourself. You shouldn't let your parents try to change you, and you definitely shouldn't listen to what this Sister Crappaggio has to say."

The events of the night came back in a flood as I listened to Tessa's rant. I wanted to contradict her, but she made too much sense. Why was I trying to run away from who I was? Why couldn't I fight for who I am? It might isolate me from certain people in my life, but if I didn't do that, I would spend the rest of my life hiding in a corner. On the other hand, I kind of liked the corner. A lot of people out there had conformed to society and were happy. Why couldn't I do the same thing? Maybe I should start listening to Sister Correggio and develop a regular heterosexual lifestyle. I had a lot of questions bouncing around in my head, and I had once again connected to the one person who could help me out. I realized then that I could really use Tessa's help.

I leaned against my mop and looked at my best friend. "Tessa?"

She stopped her mopping and looked over at me. "What?"

"I lied to you. My parents don't know I'm here tonight."

"I figured as much, but that brings me back to my original question. What are you doing here, Tristan?"

"I walked out on my parents."

Tessa started laughing. It started off small, but rumbled into a full-belly roar.

"What's so funny?"

She pointed to a window where the snow plummeted in full force. The light reflecting off each flake shot out a brilliant display of darkness that my eyes could not penetrate. "You picked one hell of a night to finally assert yourself. Where do you plan on sleeping?"

I smiled my most charming grin.

"Fine. Let's get done here and then you can crash over at my place, but just for one night."

Chapter Thirty-One

Tessa was right. I had probably picked the worst night in the history of Denver weather to decide to assert myself. The drive to Tessa's house took us almost an hour when it usually took ten minutes. All the other cars had cleared off the roads, and the snow really started to pile up. The radio announcer, in-between classic songs from the eighties and new rock standards, told us that historians would record this blizzard as one of the worst Denver had ever experienced. Schools had already started closing. Of course, my school had not made that call yet. With my current situation, I didn't plan on going anyway. I could see Mom and Dad standing at the front doors of the school, waiting for me to attend. They would be holding a stack of papers with my picture on it underneath the word *Missing*. They would ask everybody as they entered if they had seen their son. My parents really knew how to embarrass me sometimes.

Tessa and I didn't talk much during the drive to her house. She had to continuously wipe a small hole in the windshield to keep the condensation at bay so she could see the road. I did the same thing to the side window so I could watch the snow fall.

Ever since early childhood, it amazed me when teachers told me that no two snowflakes looked alike. I couldn't help but think about that as I watched them fall. They pretty much fell in the same direction and at the same angle, unless a gust of wind came. Then, a small portion of them would swirl around for a few seconds until they came back to that same angle all their friends fell from. It also amazed me how every snowflake eventually hit the ground and then it didn't matter what they looked like to begin with. They instantly melded with all of the other snowflakes. Fate would decide what happened to them, depending on where they landed. Some of them fell on the road where plows eventually pushed them off to the side so they could eventually turn grey and melt quickly. Some fell on residential sidewalks where homeowners shoveled them on to various lawns in huge piles. These piles stuck around for a long time but eventually melted when the spring sun hit.

If a snowflake was really lucky, a child would come along and turn it into a snowball for a fight with other neighborhood kids. Those snowflakes would live a fast and furious life, but eventually end up on the dry pavement where they would quickly melt, and people would forget about them. Sometimes, a child would make them into a snowman. That child would treat them with loving care, and then it would slowly melt away. People would look at those last remnants of the past storms, long after the brutal aspect of winter had passed from their memories. In that snowman, they would still see the joy it brought a child. If fate decided that a snowflake deserved something special, it would become part of a snow sculpture designed by some artistic mind. Fate would give it the opportunity for greatness. People would take pictures of it so they could always remember it for ages to come. I couldn't help but wonder where I would land if fate had made me into a snowflake.

By the time we made it to Tessa's house, the lights on most of the homes had winked out. Everybody had curled up in their beds to sleep the storm away. Tessa's house looked like all the others. No light shined inside or outside, and her parents had obviously gone to bed. I knew nobody would bother me there because her parents rocked. They were laid-back, and they didn't care much what she did. You could see this by where they placed her in respect to themselves in the house. Her parents had the master bedroom located on the top floor of their three story house. They had so much space in the house that they gave their only daughter the basement as her room. They had finished the basement, and it stayed cool all year long. This sucked in the winter, and spiders emerged during the summer, but even with these disadvantages, the advantages greatly outweighed them.

Tessa had a huge room that not only held her bed and bedroom set, but also a couch, coffee table, and entertainment center. She had her own private living room in her bedroom. She could do whatever she wanted as long as she didn't disturb her parents. She could drink, watch movies in surround sound, or rock out to music, as long as she didn't get so loud as to interrupt her parents' watching television or sleeping. She insured that her parents would never come down to complain by drawing a red line on her stereo receiver so the volume never got too loud. I had gone from a semi-safe place at the Burger House to a completely safe haven in Tessa's room.

Tessa thought we needed to celebrate, because we had worked our way through a difficult time in our friendship: she no longer dated a drunk and ironically felt she could now get drunk herself; because of the snowstorm, she wouldn't have to go to school the next day; and most importantly, I had stood up to my parents. Because of these small victories, Tessa stole a bottle of vodka from her parents. I don't know how Tessa considered running away equal to standing up to my parents, but Tessa believed so, and I just wanted an excuse to drink. It would help me with my plan too, so away we went on our drinking binge.

We drank what we called "Dew drops," which was vodka mixed with Mountain Dew. Within an hour, we had gotten good and drunk. Around this time, we started having great philosophical debates.

"How did our parents get this stupid?"

I don't know what led to this but somehow we had found ourselves complaining about our parents' generation. I completely agreed with Tessa's sentiment.

"I know what you mean. They went through the same schooling we did and they've shared very similar experiences, but for some reason they walk around completely clueless as to what teenage life is really like."

"Yeah, they grew up in the golden age of being a teenager. They were born after the era where they had to walk through the snow uphill both ways just to get to school, but before the era where technology played an important part in what it meant to grow up. Back then, in school, you just had to listen to what the teacher said and then check the right box to show they had implanted it into your brain. Our parents didn't have to first gather the information for themselves and then apply it some way. Their parents gave them a car so they could get around, and they didn't have to worry about any other technology. They didn't need the fancy new cell phone. They didn't have to worry about computers, and social networking, and all the technological crap we have to deal with."

"I couldn't agree with you more, but you're forgetting about one thing."

"What?"

"The way adults gave them freedom to do what they wanted. They didn't have a ridiculous drinking age back then. They could smoke if they wanted to. They could eat anything they wanted, because nobody cared about their health. And let's not forget that their parents didn't overprotect them like our parents do, and let's face it, you need to blame all the news reports for that. Think about it. Do you see pictures of them riding their bikes with helmets on? Hell, I don't even think they had to wear seat belts growing up. The generation before them had it tough, and they didn't see a purpose for all of these useless protective devices like bike helmets and seat belts."

"Yeah, and they didn't have all of this stupid technology which they now use like a leash."

"God, our parents had it easy, and then they have the nerve to sit there and tell us that they know all about our pain."

Tessa poured more vodka into her glass with just a splash of Mountain Dew. She raised her glass in a toast and said, "Exactly, that's why I'm glad you finally stood up to your parents. You needed to quit doing everything they tell you to do."

I toasted her with my glass in a ceremonial clink from across the room. "I appreciate your admiration, but I don't know if you can say that I really stood up to my parents. You might want to call it more of slinking away without their permission or without them noticing."

Tessa walked over to me, dodging dirty clothes while trying to keep most of her drink in her glass. She didn't have much success. She flopped down next to me on the bed, and took a long pull off her drink. "It doesn't matter much what you call it. It matters that you actually did something to make your parents notice you are gay, and they better accept it."

I put my glass on the ground next to the bed and sat up so I could look at Tessa directly. "Actually, can you help me out with something?"

She pulled open her drunken eyes just a hair more and asked, "What do you need, buddy boy?"

I took her glass from her hand and put it on the ground next to mine. "I need your help deciding my sexuality."

She sat up. "How?"

"Kiss me."

That seemed to sober her up a bit. "Again?"

"Come on, Tessa, this has really confused me. You can help me put this to rest, once and for all."

She stood up and looked down at me. "We tried this once before, and it turned into a total disaster. Your confusion and responding all weird the last time we kissed really messed me up for months. When you decided you might be gay, I was finally able to get over it. I don't know if I could deal with that again."

Besides Thomas, my mom, and my grandma on my dad's side, I

had only ever kissed Tessa. I couldn't remember an uglier experience. I have read in all the books about the magical moment everyone experiences with their first kiss. It is something unexpected, but exciting at the same time. It makes your heart stand at attention and you should fall instantly in love. This did not happen when I kissed Tessa. I expected fireworks and lust to take over my body. I would fall victim to the passion and find myself with a baby nine months later, all the time not exactly remembering what happened. I had felt that way, well, everything except the baby, when I had kissed Thomas out in the dugout. But I felt nothing when I kissed Tessa. I wondered why everybody made a big deal about their first kiss. In fact, as far as exciting went, I could compare it with an algebra exam, something that made you nervous for the build-up with not a lot of payback at the end.

It had a devastating effect on Tessa as well. Because she hadn't ever kissed another boy before, she felt all those magical things the books promised. She fell madly in love, until I broke off the kiss and said good night. I then walked off to my car as if the moment didn't mean that much to me, which it didn't. Tessa thought she had some physical defect. Like many other teenagers she assumed that God blessed certain people with a kissing gene. She thought I had that gene, and she believed she didn't. She called me the next day, and the next day after, and the day after that, because she needed me to take her out on another date so she could prove to me that she also had the kissing gene. We went out a couple weeks later, but I was unaware of her plan.

I made things even worse on that date. We went and saw some corny, romantic comedy. During the movie, she tried to cuddle up to me. She hoped I would pull the "arm over the shoulder" routine, but I never took the bait. Afterward, Tessa tried to hold hands while we went out to the parking lot, but I kept my hands in my pockets. I drove her home and hung out in the car while I waited for her to leave. She leaned in for a kiss, making it completely obvious what she wanted. I had to stop her and tell her that kissing her made me feel uncomfortable. She reminded me of our last date and the kiss we had. I blatantly told her that the kiss really didn't do anything for me. She exited the car. I wondered what was wrong with me.

With the help of an underwear ad while on the porcelain throne a month later, I discovered my problem. After my fascination with the ad, my mind immediately turned to Tessa. I thought about the terrible thing I had unknowingly done to her. I called her with the happy news about what I had discovered. It took a load off her mind, but since that kiss she had taken up smoking and had turned into the bitter girl that made her my best friend for life.

I looked into the eyes of my friend at that moment, hoping she could find the courage to help me. Evidently, she needed more encouragement. "This will be nothing like the first time. You don't have as much risk. If you think about it, you can even brag that your kissing ability converted the gay."

She pondered this possibility for a second, and then put the palm of her hand next to her mouth so she could test her breath. The results apparently pleased her because she leaned in and said, "Okay, let's do this."

It started off slowly. Her lips gently brushed against mine. I closed my eyes to let the moment take its full effect. I could smell the lingering aroma of the night's work on her, a little burger grease, and some cleaning solution. She pushed in further, and I could hear her taking in my scent just as I had hers. It also forced me to open up my mouth just a little so I could breathe easier. That effect was quickly replaced by the tip of her tongue tickling the tip of mine. Her breath tasted of the tang of Mountain Dew's citric juiciness. When she decided I tired of the chase, she went full force wrestling her tongue with mine. We stroked each other's tongues for a second before she pulled back, closing her mouth. Pulling back from each other with a wet pop, I opened my eyes. I saw her gently open her eyes seductively.

"So?" she asked me.

I looked at her and said, "Nothing, sorry."

Chapter Thirty-Two

I woke up the next morning without being able to feel my arm. Panic forced me to raise my head. I quickly regretted that decision when the feeling I should have had in my arm transferred itself to my head. I popped my eyes open, hoping that would control the pain. A light left on the night before invaded my pupils, making every red blood cell in the whites of my eyes explode. I debated with myself which one caused more pain, my head or my eyes, but in the meantime, blood rushed back to the numb arm. Pins and needles shot through my arm now, causing a new sensation that my body wasn't ready for. A queasy feeling in my stomach added the final note. A rock band played in my body with none of them in time with the others. I needed relief from the pain quickly.

I knew Tessa always kept a bottle of extra-strength Tylenol in her bathroom, and if I could make my way over there, it would help to ease my pain. I pulled myself up into a sitting position and looked about the room. Luckily, I sat pretty close to the lamp we had left on. I reached my hand out to pull the cord from the outlet on the wall. Darkness returned to the room and though it didn't completely knock out my hangover, it did make things better.

I looked around the room to better assess my situation. Tessa's alarm clock shined a red 5:32. Soft, diffused light filtered through the blinds in the room's dog-eyed view. At first I thought it odd, but then I remembered the storm from the night before. It must've meant that the snow had stopped, the skies had cleared up, and the moon illuminated the ground cover. The light that did come through helped me piece together the night. The empty vodka bottle lay sideways on the floor next to open cans of Mountain Dew. I couldn't believe that every soda can was empty because we opened so many of them. Toward the end of the evening, we probably just opened up a new one every time we wanted a refresher and didn't bother looking around for a half-full one. This made the voyage over to the bathroom a little more treacherous, but I thought I could handle it.

A snuffled snore sounded from behind me. I looked back. Tessa was laid out on her stomach with her face smashed into the pillow of her bed. One leg and one arm dangled off the edge. I knew I could gain some company in my misery by waking her up, but I also knew she would consider that a breach of our now-mended friendship. A friend was more important in the next couple of weeks than a person next to me groaning about who had the worst hangover. I could endure the erratic snoring much better than constant whining.

I pushed myself up off the floor. The world spun around in front of my face threatening to put me back down. I closed my eyes until I could make the room slow down. It actually made the world spin faster, and my stomach churned with the juicy goodness I had eaten at the Burger House the night before. Realizing my mistake, I made a mad dash for the bathroom. I tore open the door. Not bothering to turn on the light, I lunged for the toilet. Luckily, I had left the lid up from the night before. The mess I would've made would have been a lot worse than the one I did. The bile burned my throat as it rumbled up, and even though I had turned puking into an art form, it hurt me as I convulsed on my knees in front of the mighty throne. I purged all of the food and drink I had consumed the night before, and after all the painful heaving, I felt better.

I flushed the toilet and laid on the cold bathroom floor until I could regain my strength. When it returned, I got up and turned on the light. The brightness burned through my eyelids, but I could feel my hangover already subsiding. I opened the medicine cabinet and pulled out the bottle of Tylenol. I squeezed the top until it popped off. Two red and white capsules flew out and skidded around the sink until they rested in the bottom of that porcelain bowl. I looked around for a glass to pour some water but couldn't find one, so I turned off the bathroom light and returned to Tessa's room. There had to be something out there to help me get those pills down my throat.

The first Mountain Dew can I shook rattled with nothing but backwash, so I threw it to the side of the room, almost hitting the already overflowing trashcan. The next one I found rewarded me with the weight of a significant amount of flat soda. I popped the pills into my mouth, and washed it down with the warm, sticky drink. The taste reminded me of all the damage I did to myself the night before. It almost made me want to throw up again, but I gagged down the urge.

The clock I had looked at earlier now showed the time at 5:58. I had spent almost a half hour in the bathroom. Tessa hadn't moved an inch, and her snoring became more vocal. I realized that her parents might wake up soon, but there was still some time because they might not have to get up for work due to the snow storm. I wondered if I really wanted to see them when they did get up. My parents would have called looking for me last night. Tessa's parents would have contacted my parents as soon as they got up and saw me there. I needed to get out of that house before they did that, and right then was the best opportunity I would get. I thought about writing Tessa a note to tell her where I was going, but then I realized I didn't know where I should run off to. Plus, if she knew where I was going, she could tell my parents and everything would be over. I needed to get out of there without telling her. It made me feel bad, but it was beyond my control. Still, I couldn't leave without saying good-bye, so I grabbed a pen from her desk and a piece of paper and scribbled on it:

"Thanks for everything. You helped me out a lot last night. As soon as I can I will see you again. Bye, Tristan."

. . .

Sneaking out of the house was a lot easier than I thought it would be. Every job location in the state of Colorado must have instructed their employees to stay home that day, so Tessa's parents took clear advantage of it by not setting their alarm. The house was deathly quiet which made stumbling toward the front door easier to accomplish. At first I feared that everything I bumped into sent alarms that would wake up the whole house, but after making a couple of mistakes, I realized the slumber Tessa enjoyed downstairs would be the same one her parents would be participating in upstairs. As I stepped out of the house into the chilly winter air, I felt like I was in the clear. Now I needed to decide where to go.

I trudged through the two feet of snow down to the edge of their driveway. It made me mad that no one had bothered to shovel their walks yet. When I remembered what time it actually was, I realized I shouldn't have been that mad. The morning felt relaxed without the hustle and bustle of the usual day activities. Even the wildlife must've taken the day off because nothing moved that morning. I looked at the undisturbed blanket of snow covering the earth and felt a sense of calm I hadn't felt for a while. It made me feel all alone in the world. I looked up over the houses across the street and could see the perfect choice for my destination framing them — the Rocky Mountains. The morning sun had not yet risen, but I could still see it because the sun's destination was right around the corner, peeking out from the side of the horizon. Under the cloudless grey sky loomed the magnificent giants. I could hear my most favorite place in the world reverberating to me. I knew I would find the answers I looked for at Red Rocks.

I wasn't dressed for the voyage, but I really didn't care. Ratty old sneakers were on my feet, and the coat I had wouldn't protect me much from the cold. But the skies looked clear and after the sun rose I had a feeling I wouldn't have a problem with the cold. I contemplated whether or not I should go quickly back into Tessa's house and borrow a hat, but I saw my footprints leading away from the front door. I quickly realized that the time I thought I had to escape from the house didn't end when I left. They would be able to easily trace where I was going by the trail I left behind. If I was truly going to escape, I would need to get to a major road where the plow trucks had already cleared the white stuff away. It was there they would lose my trail. I bundled myself up in my coat, praying that the sun would arrive soon as I headed off toward the mountains.

Chapter Thirty-Three

I didn't make it very far before I realized my huge mistake. As I trudged out of Tessa's neighborhood and down to the semi-plowed roads, I enjoyed having the streets all to myself, but it became difficult wading my way through the aftermath of the storm. The only other people using them were the plows, and as long as I got out of the street before they made it to me I stayed relatively dry. It kind of sucked to climb up onto the huge slabs of crusty snow with my choice of footwear, but I preferred it to being scooped up by one of the monstrous blades as it pushed its way down the road, or to have huge amounts of snow bury me. In fact, neither the snow nor the plows made me finally give up my voyage. The cold did.

The temperature chilled me to the core. I couldn't believe it. The wind did not blow, the sun shined, yet as I moved down the street, I could feel my ears go numb. If I hadn't kept my hands in my armpits, I would have lost all my fingers to frostbite. I needed to find some shelter, and once again America's love of convenient food saved me. A Barney's Diner had left its lights on to welcome weary travelers who found themselves out on such a frigid morning. Apparently, the only people forced out on such a terrible day worked at Barney's, or plowed the roads because the restaurant was completely empty. As I entered the building, I could feel the freezing cold clinging to my bones start to warm. My eyes had acclimated to the snow outside, and a yellow hue hung over everything in the restaurant. It made the place look warm and inviting, and after all the cold I had to endure, I ventured further into the lobby.

A waitress sat at the counter of a bar that divided the kitchen from the dining room. A cigarette dangled precariously from her fingers over an ashtray. Her other hand rested near a steaming cup of coffee. She read a tattered copy of some book called *Into the Wild*. The story so enthralled her that she didn't notice I had entered the building. I wondered if I should run away before she looked up from her book, but I didn't want to venture outside again. After I stuck my frozen hand in my pocket, I felt the crumpled fifty-dollar bill Dan had given me for my work the night before. My head still swam from all the vodka sloshing around in my belly, and the smell of coffee and breakfast started to convince me that maybe a full stomach would help make me feel better. I didn't know if I should seat myself or if the waitress did it for me, so I leaned toward her, and said, "Excuse me."

The waitress looked up from her story and smashed her cigarette quickly into the ashtray. "Sorry, but I didn't expect anybody to come in today." When she had snuffed her cigarette out thoroughly, she threw the ashtray behind the counter and waved her hand to clear the air of smoke.

I could picture her boss talking to her about smoking while on the clock, and her nervousness about this gave me a chuckle. "Don't worry about the smoke. Most of my friends share the same habit."

It didn't stop her from cleaning up the area where she had sat. "Still I should show a little more professionalism than this."

"Well, if that makes things better for the next customer, I guess you should always practice perfection. Otherwise, could I get something to eat?"

The waitress looked around the empty room. "Yeah, make yourself comfortable. Grab one of those menus on the counter before finding a seat though. Can I get you something to drink?"

I grabbed one of the menus from the stack and sat at the

counter next to her book which rested on the table like a strained tent. "Yeah, I would love some coffee, water and some orange juice."

She headed behind the counter and reached for a mug to place in front of me. Black, steaming coffee came from a pot that magically appeared in her hands. "Do you need any cream or sugar?"

I didn't know if I did or not but I told her, "I'll take it black."

She finished pouring the coffee and put the pot on the counter. "Do you know what you want to eat?"

"Something that would make me feel a little better."

"Oh, do you have a little of the 'brown bottle flu'?"

"What?"

"Did you drink too much last night?"

"I guess you could say that."

"Then I have the perfect thing for you. Give me five minutes. Enjoy the coffee in the meantime."

She took a step into the kitchen and called back to someone there, "Trucker's special, Earl." In less than a minute, she came back with a glass of water and a cup of orange juice. As I picked up the orange juice, in her hand appeared a bottle of Advil. She shook it like a maraca and looked at me quizzically.

I nodded my head in agreement. "I could use a couple of those."

She poured two pills into her hand and gave them to me. I popped them into my mouth, followed by some orange juice to wash them down with. Even though I knew the effects of the drug hadn't taken yet, having the medicine on its way to my aching head made me feel better.

I put the empty glass back on the counter and the waitress leaned in to offer her hand. "By the way, I'm Annie."

I shook it and smiled. "I'm Tristan."

"Nice to meet you, Tristan." She finished the handshake firmly, and then leaned against the wall behind the counter. "You've tickled my curiosity though."

I took my first sip of coffee and felt its warmth course through my body. "Why?"

"Why would somebody walk through the destructive aftermath of one of Denver's worst blizzards after a night of heavy drinking, wearing the worst clothes ever to survive in those conditions, just to eat at this fine establishment?"

Her directness took me back. I went into my automatic shutdown mode, responding to a question with another question. "What do you mean?"

"Tristan, I worked all night long, with the only customers I saw being the plow truck drivers. Now that I am about to get off work, I have my first real customer, a teenage boy so obviously hungover and underdressed that my curiosity can't help but be piqued. So let me throw this question out to you. What the hell are you doing here?"

This question kept haunting me, but I quickly came to the judgment that I liked Annie, and because of this, I let my guard down a bit. "I've had a rough couple of weeks, and last night it all finally came to a head."

"So you believe making your way through four feet of snow at six o'clock in the morning is the best solution?"

"Better than the alternative."

Annie leaned on the counter. "And what is the alternative?"

I took another sip of my coffee as I contemplated this question. What exactly was the alternative? I crept out of Tessa's house because I feared her parents, or maybe because I really feared the aftermath of our kiss. I walked out of Sister Correggio's Apostolate without any argument because she would have hit me with her ruler, or by creating an argument I would have had to stand up for myself. I let Thomas steal my story and lead me around because I loved him, or maybe I couldn't admit to myself who I really was. I let my parents tell me what to do because they had many years of experience, or maybe because I didn't want to face the alternative. In fact, when given the opportunity to do just that, I'd choose anything but the alternative.

I stared down at the steam rising off my cup of coffee. "It's hard to explain what the alternative is."

"A lot of people have a hard time explaining the alternative, but I guarantee you'll find it more satisfying than the choice you normally make."

Before I could respond, the chef in the kitchen banged on a bell in a window to indicate that Annie should pick up my food.

. . .

Annie went back to reading her book and left me to my breakfast. I almost wished she would come back so we could engage in mindless chatter about the world, or at least talk about the weather. I would even attempt to answer her question. When I finished mopping up the egg yolks with my last piece of toast, her relief came in. This wise woman sat at the end of the counter, and I looked back outside at the cold weather. Clouds had once again covered the sky over Denver, and a couple of snowflakes drifted slowly to the ground. My thoughts drifted back to my destination, and I realized I was going to have difficulty getting to Red Rocks now that I could see the storm starting up again. I needed a ride there and I couldn't call anybody to help me out. I looked back at Annie. Even though she was a complete stranger, I felt a certain bond with her, as if she knew me. Because of this bond, I knew she would be willing to help me achieve my goal.

After Annie greeted her replacement, a girl dressed in the same shabby yellow dress, she looked down at me to see if I had finished my meal. She could tell that I had cleaned my plate, so she put her book down, pulled my check out of her apron, and walked down to me.

"So, Tristan, my long night has come to an end. I was hoping you would pay up so I could get out of here." She placed the check in front of me. Circled in black ink next to scrawled words, "*Thank You,*" was the total — $9.57.

"Here's the thing, Annie," I started off. A scowl came over her face as she squeezed her eyes shut.

"Don't tell me that you came in here, ate our food, and don't have any money."

I could see her mistake and reminded myself to work on my conversation skills after all this was over. "No, that's not it at all. In fact, I have a fifty-dollar bill in my pocket."

I could see the confusion wash over her face. "Then what do you want?"

"I want to get up to Red Rocks."

Annie let out a confused chuckle. "Interesting choice, but what does this have to do with me?"

"Well," I needed to assert myself or I wasn't going to get anywhere. "I'd be willing to give you the whole fifty-dollar bill for the tab in exchange for a ride up to Red Rocks."

I could see her mulling the proposition over in her mind. She had to weigh the fact that she hadn't made much money the night before with the possibility of recouping some of her losses. "What do you need to do up there?"

"Let me worry about that."

"You're not going to rape me or something?"

"Do I look like a deranged serial rapist to you?" I held my arms out in a show of my true innocence.

Tessa looked down at me. "You're right. I do need the money. Give me the fifty and I'll go get my stuff." She walked down to the end of the counter to gather up her book, purse, and coat before she turned back toward me and asked, "You ready to go, gay boy?"

. . .

I instantly regretted my decision to ask this total stranger for a ride to Red Rocks. Yes, the ride offered warmth and speed, but it didn't offer safety. Annie drove a little rattrap, an old Chevy Sprint that somehow survived the past two decades. Dents ran down the side of the car, and she told me not to worry because she always carried a roll of duct tape in case something fell off. I worried about whether the frame or the engine of the car needed the tape. But if I thought the safety of the vehicle worried me, the driver herself added a new perspective to the debate. I had ridden with many friends in cars with the same safety appeal, and I knew they could make it to the destination. But all of this didn't bother me as much as Annie's last statement before we left the restaurant. That concerned me the most. How did she know about my affliction with same-sex attraction? Had she seen the picture as well, or did I let her know some other way? Why could people tell me who I was before I could even tell myself? She didn't seem to have a problem with it, but the fact she knew something about me while I knew nothing about her really bugged me.

I wanted to ask her about it as she started the car and pulled out of the parking lot, but I soon realized that the way she drove added a new risk I hadn't thought about. Twice in two days I had a woman drive me around, and if anybody tells you that all women can't drive, you need to talk to them about Annie and Tessa. In two very distinct ways, the women I rode with drove exceptionally well. Tessa would take her time to make sure everybody was safe. Annie took control of the car and wouldn't let anybody get in her way. She had complete power over the vehicle, and used that power to her advantage as she dominated the road ahead of her. Even through a slush-covered road as a new layer of snow developed, it didn't stop her from speeding along the highway toward our destination. She had rolled down her window and had a cigarette alternately dangling from her mouth, and her fingers as she ashed it out the window. Because of her chaotic control, I worried more about surviving the trip instead of figuring out how she knew I had an affliction with same-sex attraction. I gripped the "oh shit" handle and prayed for an early release from this hell.

Annie, on the other hand, seemed in control of the car enough to start up a conversation. "So, is there some amazing band playing up at Red Rocks today?"

I tried to look over at her but quickly opted to keep my eyes on the road. I don't know why I thought directing my attention there would help, but I worried too much about ending up in a bloody crash to ponder this for long. "Do you think a band would play in weather like this?"

"I don't think so, but I can't think of any other reason why you would want to get to Red Rocks today."

I couldn't tell if she wanted a response to that question or not, so I continued to hang on, and not give her one.

"So, why Red Rocks?"

Apparently, she expected a response. "Because I can think by myself there."

She nodded her head. "Generally, I would agree with you, but I don't know if you have noticed that it's snowing outside. Couldn't you find a warmer place to think by yourself?"

Her response made me mad enough to almost let go of the "oh shit" handle. "No, it has nothing to do with the weather, or warmth."

"What makes Red Rocks the perfect place to think?"

"When you are up there by yourself, and you hear the past reverberating off that natural amphitheater, it whispers to you the answers you need to hear. You can sit in those seats and listen to it while looking down over Denver and forget about all the hustle and bustle of life. You get to leave behind all the noise of society and just *be*. You don't have all the silly distractions trying to tell you how to think, how to act, and how to live. You can learn a lot about yourself. The answers you find really help you. You know you've found the right answers, because they don't come from anybody but yourself."

She pondered what I said. "I get that, but what can be so important to ponder that you paid a complete stranger forty dollars to drive you up there in the middle of a Denver blizzard?"

"I have a lot to think about."

"Oh, I see."

Annie's casual response started to rile me up. "What do you mean by that?"

"I think it means you're struggling with your identity. Society tells you to act one way, but nature tells you something completely different. So, you try to figure out where you fit in all of this. But only one real solution to the whole problem exists."

"And you have this solution?"

She took one eye off the road to look over at me. "Just accept the fact that you are gay."

That fact rose to the forefront again, yet I had no recollection of ever telling her this. "How do you know about my affliction with same-sex attraction?"

She got a chuckle out of that. "Oh, so you've attended Sister Correggio's Apostolate. Tell the old bag 'hi' next time you see her."

"How do you know about Sister Correggio?"

Annie held up her arm. For the first time I saw a tattoo on her wrist. It was a picture of a large eyeball on two skinny legs walking over a large field. She pointed to it like it would explain all the answers. "One-year attendee, five years recovered."

"You have an affliction with same-sex attraction?"

She pointed her lit cigarette in my direction to make her point. "No, I'm gay and proud of that fact, because God made me that way. I don't need some sexually repressed twat dressed like a penguin to tell me otherwise. It took me a long time to struggle with that belief, but when I came to terms with it, I finally felt comfortable in my own skin. So when I see someone else going through the same struggle, I figure I need to help that person out. If that means taking them up to a closed amphitheater in the middle of a blizzard so they can figure it out, then I'll do that."

I looked at this girl driving recklessly toward Denver's foothills and felt an admiration more intense than I've ever had for any other person. I still wasn't ready to go out and tell the world about my homosexuality, but I started to become more comfortable with the concept.

"Of course, the forty bucks helps a little, too," she added as she sped down the highway.

Chapter Thirty-Four

When we arrived at the two massive red rocks protruding from the side of the mountains, the snow had started to fall in blinding waves. It covered the ground and trees in white. We parked in front of two mighty boulders, the only thing immune from the weather's barrage. The park had definitely shut down for the winter months and a sign in the visitor's center proclaimed that operations would resume sometime in March. Annie lit up another cigarette and eased herself comfortably into the driver's seat.

I offered her my hand and said, "Well, thanks for your help."

She ignored my hand. "I hope it doesn't take too long to find what you're looking for."

My outstretched hand went limp trying to interpret what she was saying. "Do you plan on waiting for me?"

She looked around at what was happening outside. "How do you plan on getting back to Denver? You're not going to walk all the way back."

I put my hand back on my lap. "But it's kind of personal. I need to do this by myself."

"Are you crazy? I'm not planning to go out there with you. It's nice and warm in the car, and I plan on staying right here."

There was no amount of persuasion that could change her mind, so I just accepted her offer and exited the car. There was a dramatic shift in the comfort of the environs. Whereas warm air blew from a small vent on the dash of the car, now cold snow blew in my face. Whereas my shoes were dry on the dirty floor of the car, now a powdery snow saturated my socks. Whereas the soothing sounds of the local rock station sung in my ear, now only the howl of the wind banged against my eardrums.

I looked into the car and saw Annie leaning back in her seat sucking on her cigarette, enjoying the warmth and music held within. I turned away from her and trudged up the hill toward my identity.

. . .

I had the whole amphitheater to myself. Not another soul had ventured into the structure since the storm had plopped itself on the Front Range. Not even the woodland creatures dared go into the place. The only hints of humanity's touch in the whole place were the stands and the stage covered in a healthy amount of snow. I shouted out to make sure the place was empty and Red Rocks rewarded me with my own voice echoing back. It comforted me to know nobody could bug me. Nothing out there could influence me. I didn't have society telling me what to think. I didn't have religious leaders trying to mold me into something completely different. I didn't have my parents wondering why they couldn't have the perfect son. I didn't have a friend trying to tell me how to handle my parents. I didn't have a job run by a hypocrite. I didn't have people at school judging me for my clothes or my life style. I didn't have a teacher judging me for my inability to come up with answers she didn't have. I didn't have some relationship that forced me to walk a thin line in order to make sure it didn't implode. No cell phone, radio, Facebook, television, or other form of media could distract me from me. The sound of snow lightly falling to the ground just added to the peace and calm I felt. I could connect with nature and with God if that's what I needed to do.

I looked for a place where I could get out of the weather. A few pine trees offered shelter, but I knew snow would eventually get too heavy on its boughs and tumble down on me. I saw an awning on the stage that offered cover, and I stumbled my way down the stairs to the place where so many famous people tread upon and climbed up. The wind still whipped around the stage bringing a lot of the snow with it, but I noticed a dry spot not affected by the weather in the middle. I trudged through the large drifts until I reached this small circle of concrete. By the time I got there, I wanted to collapse because of all the energy I expended. The only problem was I couldn't find enough space to lie down without falling into a huge drift. I could only sit down Indian-style on the cold concrete and look out on the natural amphitheater. I did this and watched as the snow slowly collected on the ground.

I let my mind go completely blank, and I could feel the tension in my back. Apparently, I had stored up a lot of stress in the past couple of weeks, because I could feel a knot between my shoulder blades. All I could do was close my eyes and put my fists on my knees. I rotated my head around my neck. With each rotation, I could feel the tension slowly escape. A chorus of pops joined the activity, and I could feel myself getting more and more relaxed. Soon the wind didn't bother me anymore. I hardly noticed the snow, and the cold couldn't penetrate my soul. A wave of peace washed over my body, and I eased into the chilly morning air. I no longer had to put on some stupid façade and could free myself from the shackles of society. I just didn't know what that meant.

I opened my eyes and steadied my head. Even though the storm raged on, it couldn't erase the calm I felt on the stage. It created the perfect opportunity to find the answer to the question that bugged me the most. I just needed to know how to go about doing that. Voicing my concern aloud seemed like a good start, so that's what I did, "Who am I?"

The wind took the question and bounced it off the rocks. The weather must have created some weird acoustics, because an echo started to return my question back at me. *"Who am I?"* Then I heard it return from the other side of the amphitheater. "*Who am I?*" Then it started picking up in frequency because I heard it bounce off a couple more times. "*Who am I?*" "*Who am I?*" It built up to an assembly of voices asking the question, "*Who am I?*"

I sat there Indian-style listening to this mantra being asked by a host of ghosts demanding me to answer this question for them. How could they expect me to give them a legitimate answer when I couldn't even find one for myself? Then I started to wonder why I asked the same of them. Didn't I ask them to butt into my life to tell me how I should act and how I should think? If they couldn't figure it out for themselves, why should I expect them to do it for me? Maybe we tried to tell other people how to live their lives so we wouldn't have to decide how to live on our own. On that cold snowy morning, I came to the realization that the only person who could teach me how to live my life was me. So instead of shouting out to the random masses, I, under my breath, said, "So, who am I, really?"

. . .

While pondering that question throughout the morning, I quit worrying about the thousands of things that weighed me down in my life. I focused only on that question. The experience freaked me out a bit. If my parents hadn't raised me Catholic, I would have called it some sort of Zen Buddhist moment. Some spiritual being had taken me from this earthly plain and showed me the truth. I'm sure my teachers had taught me some vocabulary word that would have described the experience perfectly, but I couldn't quite place it. And at that time I could have cared less, because I had discovered an answer to the question that haunted me. As I trudged back through the snow to Annie's car, I felt at peace with myself for the first time in my life. If I could somehow create the same experience for myself at any time, the problems of the world would never bug me again.

By the time I got back to the car, Annie had given up trying to keep it warm. She had pulled a blanket from somewhere in the back and wrapped herself inside of it. I could only see her hands and her face poking out of the blanket. In one hand she held a cigarette and blew the smoke out of where she rolled down the window a crack. In her other hand she held a book which she feverishly read. This one had a bunch of pictures of people standing in front of different American landmarks, and it was called *On the Road*. She evidently didn't hear me come up to the car, because she nearly jumped out of her seat as I knocked on the window.

Annie reached over and unlocked the door for me. As soon as I opened it, she threw the butt of the cigarette out the door. I climbed into the passenger seat, and she started the car up. It coughed and wheezed as I worried about its ability to start, but after taking a couple of gasps the car started up. Annie zipped the car out of the parking lot and down the hill that led back to the highway. Even though the roads required Annie to take more care while driving, she drove with the same reckless abandon she had when coming up. I once again gripped the "oh shit" handle and listened to her as she questioned me about my quest.

"So did you find all the answers up there?"

"I don't think we can ever find *all* the answers."

She pondered this as she took a sharp turn. "You have a point there. People have searched for true enlightenment for ages. But let me ask you this. Did you come closer to finding your answers?"

"I definitely have a better understanding."

She turned off the side road and skidded onto the main road through the small mountain town heading to Red Rocks. "Can you tell me about this better understanding?"

"What?"

"Can you explain what you learned?"

I thought about what she was asking as we drove through the deserted town toward the highway. "Why would I need to explain it?"

"Because the line ends here for you. I'm not going to let you spend the night out in this weather. You need to face up to your problems someday, and what better time than now. This means you have to start telling people what you learned about yourself up at Red Rocks. To be honest with you, this is not going to be easy. They might not accept what you discovered, and they might even try to persuade you to accept another perspective. You need to understand that their problems with your outlook have nothing to do with you. You can't control other people. As much as people think they can influence others, the ultimate decision comes back to the person who holds it. This means that the only person you can control is you. As long as you know yourself and how to live your life, then nobody can take that away from you. In fact, if you don't want people to tell you how to live your life, you need to tell them what you discovered today. When you get home, you have to do this. So practice on me, in order to make sure that what you say will be understood by whomever you say it to. *Capice?*"

What she said made a lot of sense. I had been running away from myself for many years and I had no real idea where I was running to. Oddly enough, they were both the same place. If I wanted happiness in my life, I needed to quit running from it. I needed to accept myself first, and I needed to tell others that they needed to accept it as well. Annie was right — it shouldn't matter if others accepted me or not. The only thing that mattered was my comfort level with myself. With that in mind, I let go of the "oh shit" handle, and turned to face Annie as she merged onto the empty highway. I began to explain what I had come to understand.

Chapter Thirty-Five

I arrived at home and found a group of cars congregated in front of my house. I had no idea they could find that many places to park in our neighborhood. What surprised me even more was that the weather hadn't kept everybody home. It looked like the cars had been there for a while, because a lot of snow was piled on them but very little underneath. They must have arrived at my house before the storm hit, and because of the weather, nobody made an attempt to leave. A gaggle of people probably all huddled together that night in the house waiting for the terrible weather to cease. Some of the women probably cried through the night. Out on the wind, everybody could hear wolves howl. The men would hug their women tightly to reassure them, "*Don't worry honey, only the insane and gay would go out on a night like this.*"

The men would look up from their women and see my mom break down into hysterics. It would remind them why they had come to her home in the first place. They would indiscriminately pass down apologies and the group would once again quiet down as the terrible storm raged on outside.

I could almost believe this scenario if we lived during the time of hobbits, but considering I had spent the night in the warm luxury of Tessa's basement, I knew that most people didn't disguise their purposes with timidity. The anger they would release upon my arrival made me even more nervous. Sadly enough, I didn't recognize many of the cars. One of them was Father Brett's, and another looked like what my principal drove to school. A police car and a fire truck were also parked out front. I couldn't identify the rest of them, which added to my nervousness about entering the house.

I hesitated as Annie lit up another cigarette. "Are you part of some white trash family?"

"What?"

"Well, the last time I saw that many cars parked in front of a house, I was standing in a trailer park. Ironically enough, I saw a cop car there, too. Of course, half of those cars didn't have engines in them, and the other half had so much rust that they probably couldn't make it to the road. It had the same kind of feel, though."

"We are obviously not white trash. They don't let those people live in this neighborhood."

"Hey, white trash doesn't have anything to do with economic reality, but instead a poorly chosen mindset."

I couldn't argue with logic like that, but I still needed her to understand. "We're not white trash. Having this many cars parked in my front yard doesn't happen, ever."

"Oh, then it must be the other thing."

Her casual attitude had me worried. "What other thing?"

Annie put out her hands like a cat ready to pounce and said, "Intervention."

"What? I'm not a drunk!"

"I thought you got drunk last night?"

"Yeah, but I hadn't gotten drunk like that in three weeks."

She waved off what I said, "Well, it's not that kind of intervention anyway."

"Why do I need an intervention?" I turned to look at the house and my heart beat even faster. I knew the answer to that question, but I hoped I would never have to hear it out loud.

"For your affliction with same-sex attraction."

Annie, I had quickly learned, did not let things go unsaid.

"Great. I guess I'll have to find some other place to stay tonight."

Annie smacked me in the back of the head. "Idiot. You can't run away now. You just learned something valuable about yourself, and you need to share it with people so they can start learning to accept you for you. What better opportunity than an intervention? You need to go in there right now and tell those people what they need to hear."

As I rubbed my head, I asked her, "Will you come with me?"

"Hell no! You need to do this on your own. It won't be fun, but it needs to happen. You might hate it, and you might feel terrible afterward, but in the long run, you'll look back at this as one of those defining moments in your life. If you run away from it, you will never define yourself."

Annie's speech didn't give me the courage I needed, but I got out of the car and walked up to the front porch anyway. Behind the door, I could hear a lot of commotion. I knew all the noise was for my benefit. Annie was right. I shouldn't let this moment slip away. I needed to stop running. If I ran away from this right now, I would run away from moments like this for the rest of my life. I had to stand up for myself. With my resolve steeled, I opened the front door to face my intervention.

. . .

I wish I could say I instantly regretted my decision. I wish I could say that all of the people in my house stopped their scheming and looked over in my direction so they could have a good long talk with me. I wish I could say that they made such a big fuss over me that I quickly regretted the words of wisdom I had for them, and changed my mind to become the good little boy they had always hoped I would be. I wish I could say all of this, but I can't. My entrance to home didn't happen anything like this. In fact, it was a bit anticlimactic.

First off, nobody heard me come in. A couple of police officers slept on the couches in the front living room. They apparently had a really rough night and decided that a nap would help them stay alert for the long haul ahead. My mom must have felt sorry for them because they were snuggled up under a couple of Afghans. I walked over to the one closest to me, and tucked him in while removing his wide-brimmed hat from his head. He scrunched up tighter into a ball and mumbled a barely coherent thank you.

Most of the commotion in the house took place in the kitchen. I could hear various voices discussing things. It made me wonder if I could sneak upstairs and curl up in my own bed before anybody realized I had arrived. The words of Annie ringing in my head prevented me from doing this and I searched for the resolve to do the right thing. I looked out the front window to see if Annie was still there. She had driven off, because her part of my story was over. I felt gratitude for having met her, and I made a mental note in my head to someday go back and visit her for breakfast. I could show my gratitude then.

Until then, I had some other business to attend to. I gathered up my courage and entered the kitchen. A flock of people were gathered in there, and it amazed me how many could squeeze into such a tight space.

Sister Correggio stood in one corner next to Sister Denaro. Both of them had rulers that they methodically slapped into the palms of their hands. I could imagine them talking about what they would do to me if they ever caught me alive.

Father Brett sat in another corner talking with the pastor of our church. I could see them talking about what they could do to save my soul. Noticing me would have been a good start.

A couple of kids from my confirmation class ran around the kitchen with sandwiches and coffeepots. They walked around like they belonged in a restaurant, filling up mugs and handing out food. One of them even came up to me and offered me a cup of coffee. I gratefully accepted. It blew my mind that they hadn't noticed they had served me. I figured at least they would have known that the madness going on in my kitchen centered on me.

Mr. Grant, my school's principal, talked with Miss Chompord, my counselor. They apparently talked about my grades at school, and tried to pinpoint the exact moment things started falling apart. I could only assume they believed that my doing drugs was the center of my problems, even though I couldn't recall ever partaking in that habit.

Dan and Tessa came, too. A police officer had them cornered, questioning them about my whereabouts. They must have tracked me down through them, but considering I left Tessa that morning without telling her my destination, the police could find no useful information. They didn't notice me either, because they were busy defending their actions.

A couple of other police officers roamed around my kitchen as well. They all tried to look important and push themselves into conversations. Of course, everybody else constantly shot them down. I chuckled every time it happened, because you could sit there and watch their egos deflate a little more for each denial.

Two firemen seemed less concerned with the proceedings than the police officers were. They found themselves a nice corner so they could lean against the wall. They contented themselves by discussing the Bronco's season while drinking from steaming mugs of coffee. They could care less what was happening in the kitchen.

An EMT officer behaved a little differently. He rummaged through his medical kit. He worried that somebody would hurt themselves and he prepared himself for just such an emergency.

Even Mr. Wood and Emily showed up. They came to console my parents in their time of need, but seemed more concerned with themselves. Mr. Wood tried to convince his daughter that she needed to do the right thing and stay there until somebody found me. Emily tried to convince her father that they needed to leave. Neither of them gained any headway on the other.

My parents made the biggest fuss. They had a map of Denver spread out on the kitchen table. It had red marks all over it, indicating places they had people looking for me. I could see that in between their constant planning, they would take breaks and argue about who was to blame for my absence. They both believed they were winning the argument. In reality, neither of them convinced the other of their guilt in the matter.

The absurdity of the scene made me giggle, and I could feel the joy bubbling up inside of me. All of these people made a huge fuss over me, and none of them took the time to turn their heads and notice that the person they worried about had just strolled into their midst.

The only person missing from the scene was Thomas Edwards, but that didn't bother me. I had come to the realization that Thomas never really cared about me. He just wanted a bit of action, and the last thing I saw him do made that explicitly clear. His parents had probably grounded him for the time being, but as soon as things started to settle down, he would go right back to the lifestyle he enjoyed the most. I could just picture Thomas sitting at home pretending to do what his parents wanted him to do, and as soon as he walked out the door, he'd go back to doing what he wanted. He acted like one of those girls that dressed like "daddy's little girl" when they left the house, but by the time they had made it to school they had changed into a short skirt and revealing shirt.

The image of Thomas wearing a short skirt and tight blouse made my giggle grow into a laugh. The laughter burst out into an uncontrollable roar. I had to put the cup of coffee down before I spilled it all over the floor. It still didn't help me gain control over my laughter. It welled up inside of me. It bent me over. It made me collapse on the floor. It bellowed out of me. Through tear-stained eyes, I could see everybody in the room gather around. They looked at me as I laughed harder while rolling around on the floor. The sight of them and the sudden silence of the room just made me laugh even harder. I had never seen anything more ridiculous, and for the first time in my life, I felt pure joy.

They stood there watching me try to get myself under control.

Silence took over after my invasive display of laughter. My mom finally broke the calm by telling my dad, "I think our son is on drugs."

That just made me laugh even more. Obviously, only one person in the room knew me. My parents obviously thought that person did drugs. I quickly got myself under control again while everybody stared at me, and I got up off the floor.

I looked directly at my mom. My dad hugged her tightly, trying to protect her from the onslaught he thought was sure to come. I suppressed another giggle welling up inside of me and told my mom, "No, I am not on drugs, Mother. I'm gay." A collective gasp sounded in the room. The double entendre I had just created made me laugh even more. I felt I needed to explain my case a little bit more.

"Yes, folks, I'm gay." I looked over at Sister Correggio. "I do not have an affliction with same-sex attraction. I don't need someone to cure me from this awful disease because that awful disease doesn't exist. You need to accept me, though you probably never will. Your business model demands that you don't."

I looked over at Father Brett. "I don't need your religion telling me that I'll end up in Hell, because I won't pay you some attrition based upon some obscure line in some book written thousands of years ago. I learned one thing from your class – Jesus speaks of love, and this anti-gay sentiment you preach does nothing more than promote hate. Quit being a hypocrite, and love me for me."

I turned my attention to Emily as her father hugged her. "Just because an attraction doesn't exist between you and me, does not make me some monster that you need to ostracize. A friendship can still grow here. In fact, if you get over your prejudice, you might find one of the best friends you've ever had. Maybe you should stop looking for love out in the world and find it in your heart instead."

I turned to Mr. Grant and Miss Chompord. "Please forgive my lifestyle. I'm sorry it has made an inconvenience in your lives, but you should care more about your students and help protect them from all the crap this world throws at them. You do your job long enough until the public believes that you've earned your paycheck. You need to do your job *all the time*. If you did your job properly, I would never have felt like an outcast at your school, so instead of doing your job for all the wrong reasons, start doing it for all the right ones."

I turned to Dan. "As far as jobs go, you constantly hide from yours. You walk through life trying to find the path of least resistance in order to get to the end, but we perform at our best when we struggle against the odds. Struggle with life a little bit, and you might actually find joyous enlightenment in it."

I turned to Tessa. "I have never had a better friend. I do realize that all of my bellyaching has put some pressure on our friendship, but that doesn't mean you have to run away from me when that happens. You need to step up and help me out in times of need. I've realized that I need to quit being so narcissistic as well, and help you out, too. For that I apologize, but we both need to work on being there for each other to make our relationship work for each other. If we both did that, I think we would find that we have already saved each other."

I looked at the rest of the crowd. "The rest of you need to just quit with all the drama. Stop worrying about what other people do and just concern yourselves with what you need to do. We all have problems, but until you can take care of your own problems, you shouldn't care so much about other people's problems. Back off."

I saved the most important for last, my parents. I looked them in the eyes, and for the first time in my life I could see fear there. I did not want to frighten them. I just wanted them to understand. "Mom, Dad, I love you very much. You probably don't think so at times, but remember, you frustrate me a lot as well. I know I make you feel the same way from time to time, but I know deep down that you love me, too."

I could see that my opening lines had eased the fear a little, because I had expressed genuine feelings, but I still needed to tell them what I came to tell them. "Even though this love exists between us, I need to make one thing clear in order for us to get along. You need to recognize and accept me as I am. I am gay. Nothing you can say or do will change that. You need to love me without any reservations."

I could see them struggling with this. I could only try to get them to understand me, but they needed to make the ultimate decision for themselves. It wouldn't change the way I felt about them. "The only problem you have with me is that I like boys. Be happy that I don't do drugs and waste my life away. Be happy I don't beat up other people, rape girls, or kill. I will never have a romantic relationship with a girl, but you have a son who loves you very much and always will. Be happy with that."

I went up and grabbed them both in a loving embrace. They hesitated at first, but they eventually hugged me back. We sat there in that kitchen hugging each other, while the rest of society huddled around us to watch.

Chapter Thirty-Six

Tristan Adamson
Literature and Composition
Mrs. Baker

The Reason to Run

Everybody runs. Even people confined to wheelchairs will find that they run, too. They might not engage in a physical act, but it still drains them just as much as running a marathon would. If they would just stop the running, they would discover that they would waste less energy by just facing whatever it is they are running from. They would discover that they don't face as big a problem as they had first believed.

A person also needs to understand what they are running to. Not knowing this can exhaust them just as much. Every person must have a goal in mind because if they do not then they just run around aimlessly. People might think they know where all this running will lead them but if they don't have a specific destination in mind, they could spend countless hours on a path for a place that doesn't bring them to happiness. When they arrive at this place, they will look around and tell themselves, "This was not the destination I had hoped for." Afterward, they will have to start running again, and maybe this time they will find a destination more comfortable with their intentions. In reality, they just need to listen to the words of wisdom by the famous American writer, James Thurber, "All men should strive to learn before they die, what they are running from, and to, and why." Basically, everybody needs to quit running.

I have experienced this in my life. I have exhausted myself running without even knowing it, until I started practicing the ideals of transcendentalism. Essentially, in order to understand transcendentalism, one must first understand one's self, and my journey has allowed me to transcend to this understanding. Society might try to conform me into behaving a certain way that my heart knows is not natural. So I need to stand up for myself and not run away from some regulation handed down by a faceless authoritarian. By doing so, I can achieve true transcendence.

I didn't always believe this. I wouldn't stand up for myself. In fact, I spent most of my time running. I ran away from myself, and sadly, I had no idea where I was running to. I had no idea about my future. I just knew that accepting my self was a difficult thing to do. I wasted a lot of energy while I worked on solving this puzzle. Sadly, though, if I had just accepted myself, I would have found that I was not ashamed.

You have to understand that I am gay. I have struggled with this fact. I worried so much about what other people would think if they found out. My parents would freak out, and disown me. My friends would shun me, and I would spend the rest of my high school career hiding in the corner. My religion would excommunicate me, and I would spend eternity in Hell. I even worried that the school would make a spectacle of me to prevent other people from going down the same path I had apparently chosen. I spent so much time worrying about this that the rest of my life started to fall to pieces. This obsession had gone too far, but how does one get rid of something so obsessive?

One doesn't, because one shouldn't consider the situation to be a problem in the first place. I, like so many other people before me, made the problem bigger than it really was. This exaggeration of one tiny problem causes all the other problems to grow in one's life. Then, things fall apart. I've learned that society should not impose its problems upon me. Society's problems are not my problems, and I need to quit listening to them. If society does not like me, then that is society's problem. I just need to find happiness within myself. In fact, if everybody did that, then everybody would find the world a much happier place. We would no longer try to place people into boxes in which they obviously do not belong.

It took me a long time to realize I needed to stop listening to what other people told me, and to start listening to myself. When I did that, I realized that I found a great person there. It doesn't matter that I struggle with teenage life; it doesn't matter that I have social anxiety; and it really doesn't matter that I am gay.

Yes, that's right. I'm gay.

Have I learned everything about myself? No, but show me a teenager who claims to know himself, and I will show you one of the biggest liars in America. The difference is that I've finally found the right path to find myself. This doesn't mean other people should follow this same path, but it works for me. For the longest time, I ran away from it and I have no idea why. Now that I found the right path, I know where to run. In fact, I don't even run anymore. I'll take a leisurely stroll. I will get to my destination eventually. In the meantime, I will enjoy the peace that I have gained and learn what I can about myself along the way. Even though I have learned a lot about myself in the last couple of days, I know I have a lot more to discover.

Though the path may be different for everyone, we all take the same voyage. Not many people realize this. I can't tell them they need to take this voyage; they need to discover this for themselves. Some people never figure it out. Until they do, they waste a lot of energy running away from something, and they have no idea what it is while still running to the same unknown destination. We must all expend some energy during this thing called life, but we could all make sure that we expend energy in a worthy manner. If we would just listen to the words of wisdom by James Thurber, we just might figure out where we run from, where we run to, and why we expend the energy to get there.

.   .   .

I know I only got a *D* in my English class that semester, and my parents, understandably, were not too happy about it, but with all the stuff I have learned in the process, it was the most valuable grade I'd ever earned. I went into Mrs. Baker's classroom with a cup of Barney's coffee to thank her for helping me find the way, and I once again tipped Annie generously for the service. I have finally learned to ignore all the Facebook drama, teachers' notes, billboard T-shirt fashions, cool car envy, counselor-sponsored interventions, minimum wage wallets, Clearasil lies, home-busy-work assignments, lunchroom indigestion, unsatisfied hormonal dating, and ignorant parents. Instead, I listen to the most important person that I know — *me*.

Purchase other Black Rose Writing titles at
www.blackrosewriting.com/books
and use promo code PRINT to receive a 20% discount.

BLACK ROSE
writing™

CPSIA information can be obtained
at www.ICGtesting.com
Printed in the USA
FSOW02n0503210515
7245FS